THE UNSEEN DROP

Tilly Presland

Uncorked Publishing

Dedication

To the quiet warriors who carry secrets in the shadows, and to the fierce hearts who fight to bring them into the light. This book is for my family—those who stood by me through every twist and turn, believing in the story when the fog was thickest. To my sons, whose unwavering support taught me resilience, and to my readers, who venture into the unseen with me. May you find strength in the truth, no matter how deep it's buried.

"We are all haunted by the things we do not say, and the cliffs we dare not face hold the secrets we cannot bury."
—Shirley Jackson, The Haunting of Hill House

"Truth is a shadow that moves before we see it, a whisper lost in the wind until the ground gives way beneath us."
—Eleanor Grayson, Whispers of the Unseen

FOREWORD

Some stories creep up on you, quiet as fog rolling over a ridge, until they demand to be heard. *The Unseen Drop* is one of those tales—a thriller that began as a whisper in my mind and grew into a storm I couldn't ignore. This isn't just a book about a crime or a chase; it's a dive into the shadows we carry, the secrets we bury, and the truths that surface when we least expect them. I wrote it for anyone who's ever wondered what lies beyond the edge of what we see, and for those who know that the past has a way of clawing its way back.

In these pages, you'll find a village wrapped in mist, a family teetering on the brink, and a mystery that twists tighter with every step. It's a story born from questions I couldn't shake: What happens when a single moment fractures everything? How do we face the guilt we can't confess? And what if the real danger isn't the one we're chasing, but the one we never saw coming? I've poured my love for suspense and the human spirit into this book, hoping to keep you guessing until the final drop falls.

This is my invitation to you: step into the fog, feel the chill of the unknown, and uncover a truth that shifts the ground beneath. *The Unseen Drop* is more than a read—it's a journey into the dark, where the unseen holds the sharpest secrets. I hope it grips you as fiercely as it gripped me while writing it. Welcome aboard, and hold on tight.

INTRODUCTION

Welcome to a story that begins where most end—at the edge of a fall, where the truth slips out of sight. In the pages ahead, you'll step into a village cloaked in fog, a place where the past refuses to stay buried and every shadow hides a secret. This isn't a tale of simple crimes or easy answers. It's about a mother who fights to save her son from a guilt he can't confess, a detective chasing a shadow that moves faster than the law, and a moment on a ridge that broke more than one life.

I've always believed that the most gripping mysteries aren't just about who did it, but why—and what they leave behind. Here, the why is a knot of love, fear, and vengeance, tangled tighter with every step closer to the truth. You'll feel the damp chill of the mist, hear the wind that carries whispers of the past, and sense the weight of something unseen watching from the dark. This is a journey into the cracks of trust, where the ground beneath can give way when you least expect it.

As you turn these pages, ask yourself: What would you do to protect the ones you love? How far would you go to uncover what's hidden? The answers lie ahead, in a drop that reveals more than anyone bargained for. Prepare to question what you see, because in this village, the unseen holds the sharpest edge.

Tilly Presland

PREFACE

Every story begins with a whisper—a fleeting thought that grows louder until it demands to be told. *The Unseen Drop* started with a single image: a boy standing at the edge of a cliff, the fog curling around him, and a shadow moving just beyond sight. I couldn't shake it. What had he done? What had he seen? And what if the truth wasn't his alone to carry? From that spark, this tale unfolded—a journey into the dark corners of guilt, the fragility of trust, and the secrets that bind us tighter than we know.

Writing this book was like walking through that fog myself. I wanted to explore how a single moment—a push, a fall—could ripple through years, fracturing lives in ways no one could predict. I found myself asking: What do we miss when we look away? How do we survive the weight of what we can't confess? Ellie, Noah, and the shadows that haunt them became more than characters; they were companions through sleepless nights, guiding me to an ending that surprised even me.

This isn't just a thriller about who did what—it's a story about the unseen forces that shape us, the lies we tell to protect those we love, and the courage it takes to face what's been buried. I hope you feel the chill of the ridge, the weight of the silence, and the jolt of the truth as it drops. If you find yourself glancing over your shoulder or questioning the shadows in your own life, then I've done my job.

Thank you for stepping into this world with me. Turn the page, and let's uncover the unseen together.

Tilly Presland

PROLOGUE

The ridge rose sharp and jagged against the late afternoon sky of July 23, 2023, its rocky spine cutting through the dense pines that cloaked the hillside above the village. The air was thick with the scent of sap and earth, the sun dipping low, casting long shadows that stretched like fingers across the uneven trail. Twelve teenagers trudged upward, their laughter and shouts bouncing off the stones, a youth group hike meant for bonding and bravado, chaperoned by a man with a gruff voice and steady stride. The wind whispered through the branches, a soft moan that carried a chill despite the summer heat, and the group moved in a loose, careless line, unaware that the day would fracture, leaving a scar that time wouldn't heal.

Near the back, a boy with sharp eyes and a quiet gait lingered, his hands shoved deep into his pockets, his breath steady but his mind restless. Noah Carter, fourteen, watched the others with a guarded stare, his steps deliberate, his silence a shield against the noise. Ahead, another boy—louder, brash, his laughter cutting through the chatter—tossed a small knife between his hands, its blade catching the fading light. Jake Ellis, a spark of defiance in his grin, led the pack, his voice rising over the wind, taunting, teasing, pushing boundaries he didn't know would break. The chaperone, Tom Bennett, called out from the front, his tone firm but distracted, his eyes on the path, not the boys behind him.

The trail narrowed near the summit, the ground sloping steep and treacherous, the pines thinning to expose a sheer drop that plunged into shadow below. Noah's pace slowed, his eyes flicking to Jake, his hands clenching tighter, a tension building he couldn't name. Jake turned, his grin widening, his voice sharp with a challenge that stung, words lost to the wind but heavy with intent. The group pressed on, oblivious, their footsteps crunching gravel, but here, at the edge, something shifted—a spark flared, a shove followed, and a scream pierced the air, raw and jagged, swallowed fast by the trees.

The ridge went still, the wind holding its breath, and the boys ahead froze, their laughter dying, their heads turning slow, uncertain. Tom's shout came late, his boots pounding back, his voice cutting through the haze, but the trail was empty where two had stood. Below, the shadows deepened, the drop a silent witness to a fall that wasn't seen, only felt—a truth splintered in the dark, a lie born in the chaos. One boy ran, his breath ragged, his hands bloodied from a scrape, his eyes wide with a secret he'd carry. Another shape lingered, tall and unseen, a shadow among the pines, watching, waiting, its presence a whisper that would grow louder with time.

The village below stirred, unaware, its lights flickering on as dusk settled, a quiet life that would unravel in years to come. The ridge kept its silence, the wind resuming its moan,

carrying away the echoes of a day that wasn't what it seemed—
a perfect lie etched into the earth, waiting to break free.

PART 1: DR. ELEANOR "ELLIE" CARTER

CHAPTER ONE

Eleanor Carter stood at the front of the lecture hall, her hands resting lightly on the podium, her voice steady as it carried across the room. The space smelled faintly of polished wood and stale coffee, a familiar comfort from her years of guest lectures at universities like this one. Today, though, the audience wasn't students scribbling notes but a mix of local professionals, police officers, and curious townsfolk from the village, all crammed into the community center's largest room. The overhead lights buzzed softly, casting a warm glow on the sea of faces turned toward her. She liked it this way, the intimacy of a small crowd, the way their eyes locked onto hers when she spoke about the minds of killers.

"Thank you all for coming," she said, offering a small, practiced smile. "I know most of you didn't expect a Saturday morning lecture on criminal psychology, but I promise I'll keep it worth your time." A ripple of polite laughter moved through the room, and she relaxed a fraction, her shoulders easing under her tailored blazer. At forty-two, Ellie had perfected this balance: warm enough to charm, sharp enough to command respect. Her dark hair was swept into a neat chignon, and her hazel eyes scanned the crowd with the quiet intensity of someone who spent her life dissecting human behavior.

She clicked the remote in her hand, and the projector hummed to life, splashing an image onto the screen behind her: a grainy mugshot of a man with hollow cheeks and a stare that seemed to pierce through the lens. "This is Martin Hayes," she began. "Convicted of three murders in Leeds, 2018. What made him fascinating wasn't the violence itself but how ordinary he seemed. A postman. A husband. Someone you'd nod to on the street without a second thought." She paused, letting that sink in. "The question I always ask is: what turns a normal person into a killer? Is it impulse? Planning? Or something buried deeper, waiting for the right trigger?"

A hand shot up near the front, a young woman in a navy coat, her pen poised over a notebook. Ellie nodded at her. "Yes?"

"Do you think anyone could kill, given the right circumstances?" the woman asked, her voice clear and eager.

Ellie tilted her head, considering. It was the kind of question she loved, the kind that made her feel alive. "I think most of us have the capacity," she said carefully. "But it's the choice that matters. The moment you cross that line, something shifts. And once it's done, there's no going back." The room grew quiet, the weight of her words settling over them like a fog. She could see it in their faces: intrigue, unease, a flicker of recognition. Good. That was the point.

She moved on, clicking to the next slide, a diagram of the brain with red circles highlighting the amygdala and prefrontal cortex. "Let's talk about control," she said. "The part of us that says 'stop' before we act. In violent offenders, that restraint is often damaged, sometimes by trauma, sometimes by choice." She leaned forward slightly, her voice dropping. "But what happens when the mind lies to itself? When it buries the truth so deep you don't even know it's there?"

Before anyone could respond, a sharp buzz cut through the air. Ellie glanced down at her phone, resting face-up on the podium. A news alert flashed across the screen, bold and insistent: *Woman Found Dead at Ravenswood Estate. Police Investigating.* Her breath caught for a split second, but she forced her expression to stay neutral. Ravenswood. The old manor on the edge of town, abandoned for years, surrounded by gnarled trees and rumors of its own. She knew it well; everyone did. But a death? That was new.

"Sorry, just a notification," she said with a quick laugh, silencing the phone and sliding it into her pocket. "Where was I? Right, repression." She clicked to the next slide, but her rhythm faltered, the words feeling heavier now. The room didn't notice, or if they did, they didn't show it. They were still hooked, nodding along as she wove her way through case studies and theories, her expertise a shield against the unease creeping up her spine.

When the lecture ended forty minutes later, the applause was warm, and a small knot of people gathered around her with questions. She answered them smoothly, shaking hands, accepting compliments. "Dr. Carter, that was brilliant," said an older man with a tweed jacket, his grip firm. "You make it sound almost personal."

"It's what I do," she replied, smiling. "Understanding people is the job." He chuckled and moved off, leaving her to pack up her notes. The room emptied slowly, voices fading into the hall, and she was alone with the hum of the projector cooling down. She pulled her phone out again, hesitating before tapping the news alert.

The article loaded fast. *A woman in her late twenties was discovered early this morning at Ravenswood Estate, dead from apparent stab wounds. Police have not released her identity, but sources say the scene was brutal. Investigations are ongoing.* Ellie's stomach tightened. Stab wounds. Brutal. The words echoed in her head, clinical and cold, the way she'd describe a case study. But this wasn't a case study. This was here, in her village, a place where the worst crime was usually a stolen bicycle.

She closed the app and slipped the phone away, her fingers brushing the edge of her leather satchel. The village wasn't big, maybe a thousand people, all tucked into stone cottages and winding lanes that looked like something from a postcard. Murder didn't belong here. Not in her world, where Daniel would be waiting at home with a glass of wine, where Noah would be hunched over his homework, muttering about calculus. Her life was orderly, predictable, perfect.

As she stepped outside, the March air hit her face, crisp and damp with the promise of rain. The community center sat at the heart of the village, its brick facade glowing under the overcast sky. Beyond it, the forest loomed, a dark fringe that swallowed the horizon where Ravenswood hid. Ellie adjusted her scarf, a soft gray thing Daniel had given her last Christmas, and started toward her car. She told herself it was nothing to worry about. A tragedy, sure, but not her tragedy.

Her phone buzzed again in her pocket. She ignored it this time, climbing into the driver's seat and turning the key. The engine purred to life, and she pulled onto the narrow road, the village slipping past her window in a blur of ivy and chimneys. She didn't need to check the alert to know it would be more of the same: speculation, fear, the kind of chatter that would dominate the town for weeks. She'd deal with it later. For now, she just wanted to get home.

But as she drove, a small, nagging thought took root, sharp and uninvited. What if she knew the woman? What if this wasn't as distant as she wanted it to be? She pushed it down, focusing on the road, the familiar curve toward her house. It was fine. Everything was fine.

CHAPTER TWO

The house came into view as Ellie rounded the final bend, its pale stone walls catching the last of the gray afternoon light. It sat at the edge of the village, where the cottages gave way to open fields, a handsome two-story building with ivy crawling up one side and a slate roof that glistened after the morning's rain. She'd always loved its quiet dignity, the way it stood apart without feeling isolated. Daniel had picked it out ten years ago, back when Noah was still small enough to ride on his shoulders, and she'd agreed without hesitation. It was their sanctuary, a place where the chaos of her work never followed.

She pulled into the gravel drive, the crunch of tires loud against the stillness, and cut the engine. For a moment, she sat there, hands resting on the steering wheel, staring at the front door. It was painted a deep green, chipped in one corner from a storm last spring, and she made a mental note to touch it up soon. Routine thoughts like that kept her grounded. She grabbed her satchel from the passenger seat and stepped out, the air cool against her skin as she crossed the drive.

Inside, the house smelled of rosemary and garlic, a warm thread of comfort drifting from the kitchen. Daniel was cooking again, a habit he'd picked up after long surgeries to unwind. She dropped her keys into the ceramic bowl by the door, its faint clink echoing in the hall, and called out, "I'm home."

"In here," Daniel replied, his voice steady and familiar, pulling her toward the kitchen like a tether. She found him at the stove, stirring something in a cast-iron pot, his sleeves rolled to his elbows. He was tall, broad-shouldered, with dark hair just starting to gray at the temples, and when he turned to look at her, his smile was the same one that had won her over twenty years ago. "Good crowd today?"

"Better than I expected," she said, setting her satchel on the counter. She leaned against the edge, watching him sprinkle salt into the pot. "A few cops showed up, probably hoping I'd solve their cases for them."

He laughed, a low, easy sound. "You probably could, you know. How'd they take the brain stuff?"

"They ate it up. Always do." She reached for a glass from the cupboard, filling it with water from the tap. The kitchen was bright, all white cabinets and butcher-block counters, a window above the sink framing the woods beyond. She took a sip, letting the coolness steady her, then added, "Got interrupted by a news alert, though. That murder at Ravenswood."

Daniel's hand paused over the pot, just for a second,

before he resumed stirring. "Yeah, I saw it on the TV earlier. Nasty business." He didn't look at her, his focus fixed on the simmering stew. "They say who it was yet?"

"Not yet. Just a woman, late twenties. Stabbed." She kept her tone even, the way she would with a client, but the word *stabbed* hung in the air between them. She waited for him to say more, to ask the questions she'd been turning over in her head, but he just nodded and reached for a spoon.

"Poor thing," he said finally, tasting the stew and frowning. "Needs more thyme, I think. You hungry?"

"Starving," she lied, forcing a smile. She wasn't, not really, but the normalcy of it, the rhythm of their evening, felt like something to hold onto. She glanced toward the stairs. "Noah up there?"

"Homework, as usual. Kid's going to burn out before he's seventeen if he keeps this up." Daniel shook his head, but there was pride in his voice, the kind that came with having a son who aced every test without breaking a sweat.

Ellie climbed the stairs, her footsteps muffled by the thick runner that lined them. The house was old, creaky in places, but they'd modernized it over the years: fresh paint, new fixtures, a life built layer by layer. Noah's door was half-open at the end of the hall, light spilling out, and she tapped on it lightly before stepping in.

He was at his desk, hunched over a textbook, his dark hair falling into his eyes. At sixteen, he was all angles, still growing into himself, but there was a quietness to him that had always set him apart. Not shy, exactly, just contained. He looked up as she entered, his expression neutral, almost blank. "Hey, Mom."

"Hey yourself," she said, leaning against the doorframe. "How's calculus treating you?"

"Fine. Just a lot of problems tonight." He tapped his pencil against the page, a steady rhythm, and she noticed the faint shadows under his eyes. He'd been pushing himself lately, more than usual, but she hadn't pressed him on it. Not yet.

"You hear about Ravenswood?" she asked, keeping her voice casual.

He nodded, barely glancing up. "Yeah. Weird, right? Nothing ever happens around here."

"Until it does," she said, studying him. He didn't react, just kept tapping that pencil, and she wondered if he'd seen the same alert she had, if it had stirred anything in him. But his face gave nothing away, and after a moment, she straightened. "Dinner's almost ready. Come down soon, okay?"

"Sure," he said, already turning back to his work. She lingered there, watching him for a beat longer, then headed back downstairs.

In the kitchen, Daniel had set the table, three places with mismatched plates they'd collected over the years. He poured her a glass of red wine without asking, sliding it across to her as she sat. "To surviving another lecture," he said, raising his own glass.

She clinked hers against it, the sound sharp in the quiet. "To that." The wine was smooth, a little tart, and she took a longer sip than she meant to. They ate in companionable silence for a while, the stew rich and hearty, but her mind kept drifting back to that news alert. Stab wounds. Brutal. Ravenswood. It was too close, too real, and she couldn't shake the feeling that it was going to touch them somehow.

"Ellie?" Daniel's voice pulled her back. He was looking at her, his brow creased. "You okay? You've gone quiet."

"Just tired," she said quickly, setting her spoon down. "Long morning."

He reached across the table, his hand covering hers, warm and solid. "Get some rest tonight. You've earned it."

She nodded, squeezing his hand back, but the unease didn't lift. It sat there, coiled in her chest, as Noah's footsteps sounded on the stairs. He joined them at the table, silent as he scooped stew onto his plate, and Ellie watched him, then Daniel, then the empty space beyond the window where the forest loomed. Everything was fine, she told herself again. Everything was fine.

But as the evening stretched on, that coiled feeling tightened, whispering that fine was the last thing they were.

CHAPTER THREE

Ellie woke to the sound of rain tapping against the bedroom window, a soft, insistent rhythm that pulled her from a dream she couldn't quite grasp. Her head felt heavy, like she'd slept too long or not at all, and she lay still for a moment, staring at the ceiling. The room was dim, the curtains drawn tight against the morning, and the clock on her nightstand glowed 7:14 in red digits. Sunday. No lectures, no appointments, just a quiet day at home. She should have felt relieved, but there was a tightness in her chest she couldn't place.

She rolled over, reaching for Daniel, but his side of the bed was empty, the sheets cool under her hand. He was an early riser, always had been, probably downstairs brewing coffee or reading the paper. She sat up slowly, running a hand through her hair, and swung her legs over the edge of the bed. The hardwood floor was cold against her bare feet, sending a shiver up her spine as she padded to the bathroom.

The mirror caught her off guard. Her reflection looked

pale, almost hollow, with faint shadows under her eyes she didn't remember seeing yesterday. She leaned closer, frowning, and noticed a small bruise on her forearm, just below the elbow. It was faint, a purplish smudge no bigger than a coin, but it stopped her cold. She didn't recall bumping into anything, not at the lecture, not in the kitchen last night. She pressed her fingers to it, testing, and a dull ache bloomed under the touch.

"Ellie?" Daniel's voice drifted up the stairs, breaking her focus. "Coffee's on."

"Be right down," she called back, her voice steadier than she felt. She shook off the unease, chalking the bruise up to some clumsy moment she'd forgotten, and splashed water on her face. The cold jolted her awake, and she dressed quickly, pulling on a soft sweater and jeans before heading downstairs.

The kitchen smelled of coffee and toast, a morning ritual that usually settled her. Daniel stood at the counter, pouring steaming liquid into two mugs, his movements precise and unhurried. He glanced over his shoulder as she entered, offering a small smile. "Sleep okay?"

"Like a rock," she said, sliding into a chair at the table. It wasn't true, not quite, but she didn't want to dissect the foggy edges of her night. He set a mug in front of her, black with a hint of steam curling upward, and she wrapped her hands around it, letting the warmth seep into her palms.

"Noah's still out cold," Daniel said, sitting across from her with his own coffee. "Guess calculus finally wore him down."

She nodded, taking a sip. The bitterness grounded her, a sharp contrast to the dull ache in her arm. "He's been at it nonstop. I'll check on him later."

They fell into an easy silence, the kind that came with years of marriage, but her mind wouldn't settle. The rain outside picked up, drumming harder against the windows, and she found herself staring at the glass, at the blurred shapes of the trees beyond. Ravenswood was out there, somewhere in that wet, tangled mess, and the thought of it tugged at her again. The woman. The stab wounds. She hadn't checked her phone since last night, hadn't wanted to, but now the pull was stronger.

"You're thinking about it, aren't you?" Daniel said, his voice cutting through her haze. She looked at him, startled, and saw the faint crease in his brow, the one that meant he'd caught her drifting.

"The murder?" she admitted, setting her mug down. "Yeah. Hard not to."

He leaned back in his chair, studying her. "It's awful, but it's not your case, Ellie. Let the police handle it."

"I know," she said quickly. "I just... it's so close. Feels different, that's all." She forced a smile, but it felt thin, and he didn't push. He never did when she got like this, lost in her own head. It was one of the things she loved about him, his patience, but today it left her feeling exposed.

The morning slipped by in a blur of small tasks: dishes, laundry, a half-hearted attempt to read a journal article on her tablet. By noon, the rain had slowed to a drizzle, and Noah finally shuffled downstairs, his hair a mess, his eyes still heavy with sleep. "Morning," he mumbled, grabbing a banana from the bowl on the counter.

"Afternoon, technically," Ellie teased, glancing up from her spot on the couch. He smirked, a rare flash of lightness, and disappeared back upstairs with his prize. She watched him go, the bruise on her arm itching at the edge of her awareness.

It wasn't until later, when she went to hang her sweater in the closet, that the real crack came. She opened the door, the hinges creaking softly, and reached for a hanger. Something caught her eye, a flash of red tucked between her coats. She froze, her hand hovering, then pushed the fabric aside. There, folded neatly on the shelf, was a scarf she didn't recognize. It was silk, a deep crimson, stark against the muted tones of her wardrobe. She pulled it down, her fingers brushing the smooth surface, and a faint stain caught the light: brown, irregular, crusted into the fibers.

Her stomach dropped. Blood. It looked like blood. She turned the scarf over, her breath shallow, searching for some explanation, but there was nothing. She hadn't worn it, hadn't bought it, hadn't seen it before. The closet smelled faintly of lavender from a sachet she kept there, but now it felt claustrophobic, the walls pressing in.

"Daniel?" Her voice came out sharper than she meant, echoing through the house. He appeared at the foot of the stairs, looking up at her with that same steady calm.

"What's wrong?" he asked, climbing the steps two at a time.

She held up the scarf, her hand trembling slightly. "This. Where did it come from?"

He frowned, taking it from her and examining it. "I don't know. It's not mine. You sure it's not yours?"

"I've never seen it," she said, her pulse thudding in her ears. "And that stain... it looks like blood."

He squinted at it, then shook his head. "Could be anything. Wine, maybe? You were pretty tired last night. Maybe you spilled something and forgot."

"I didn't have wine upstairs," she snapped, then softened her tone. "I didn't. I'd remember."

He handed it back to her, his expression unreadable. "Okay. So it's weird. What do you want to do? Throw it out?"

She stared at the scarf, the red pooling in her vision like a warning. "No. I'll wash it. Figure it out later." She turned away, clutching it tightly, and headed for the laundry room. Her hands moved on autopilot, filling the sink with cold water, adding detergent, watching the suds bloom. But as she submerged the scarf, the stain didn't fade. It darkened, spreading faintly, and she stepped back, her breath catching.

The room tilted, just for a second, and she gripped the counter to steady herself. A memory flickered, sharp and unbidden: darkness, the sound of leaves rustling, a voice she couldn't place. Then it was gone, leaving her staring at the water, her reflection fractured in the ripples. She didn't know how long she stood there, but when she finally looked up, the scarf was still in the sink, and her hands were shaking.

CHAPTER FOUR

Ellie stood at the kitchen window, staring out at the drizzle-soaked garden as the afternoon light faded into a muted gray. The scarf lay folded on the counter behind her, its crimson hue dulled by the failed washing but still glaringly out of place. She'd scrubbed her hands raw after leaving it in the sink, the soap's sharp scent clinging to her skin, but she couldn't shake the image of that stain spreading in the water. It wasn't wine. She knew it in her bones, the way she knew a client was lying before they opened their mouth. Blood had a weight to it, a texture, and this was no spill from a careless night.

The house was quiet now, too quiet. Daniel had gone to the hospital for an emergency consult, his car crunching out of the drive an hour ago, and Noah was upstairs, lost in his books or his thoughts, she couldn't tell which anymore. She'd tried to call Julia, her best friend, to talk through the scarf and the bruise, but the line had gone straight to voicemail. Julia was probably buried in a case, her lawyer brain spinning through depositions. Ellie didn't leave a message. What would she say? *I found a bloody scarf in my closet, and I don't know how it got there*? It sounded unhinged, even to her.

She turned from the window, her reflection catching briefly in the glass: a woman with tight lips and eyes that looked too wide, too searching. She needed air, something to clear the fog in her head. Grabbing her coat from the hall rack, a navy wool thing that hung heavy on her shoulders, she stepped outside. The drizzle had stopped, leaving the air damp and cool, thick with the smell of wet earth. She locked the door behind her and started down the lane toward the village center, her boots scuffing against the uneven pavement.

The village was waking up to the murder now, its pulse quickening in a way she hadn't felt before. As she passed the first row of cottages, their stone walls glistening under the overcast sky, she noticed curtains twitching, faces peering out briefly before ducking away. The news had spread fast, faster than she'd expected for a Sunday. By the time she reached the small square, where the bakery and post office flanked a weathered fountain, a knot of people had gathered near the noticeboard. She recognized a few: Mrs. Hargrove from the library, her white hair tucked under a scarf; Tom Bennett, who ran the hardware store, his hands shoved deep in his pockets.

Ellie slowed her pace, keeping to the edge of the square, but their voices carried on the wind, sharp and urgent. "They're saying it was brutal," Mrs. Hargrove was telling the group, her tone hushed but eager. "Stabbed, left out there like rubbish. Police won't even let anyone near Ravenswood now."

"Some poor girl," Tom muttered, shaking his head. "Heard she was new in town. Not one of ours."

"Lena something," a younger woman piped up, clutching a coffee cup from the bakery. "That's what my cousin said. She worked at the pub for a bit, kept to herself mostly."

Ellie's chest tightened at the name. Lena. It landed like a stone, heavy and cold, though she couldn't say why. She didn't know a Lena, not that she could recall, but the sound of it tugged at something buried, a thread she couldn't pull loose. She kept walking, her head down, but the whispers followed her, weaving through the damp air like smoke.

At the bakery, she stepped inside, the bell above the door jingling softly. The warmth hit her first, then the smell of fresh bread and sugar, a stark contrast to the chill outside. Sarah, the owner, looked up from behind the counter, her round face flushed from the ovens. "Ellie! Didn't expect you today. Usual?"

"Just a coffee, thanks," Ellie said, managing a smile. She liked Sarah, her easy chatter and the way she never pried, but today the woman's eyes lingered a little too long.

"Awful thing, isn't it?" Sarah said as she poured the coffee, steam rising from the pot. "That business at Ravenswood. Makes you wonder who's walking around out there."

"Yeah," Ellie agreed, taking the cup. "Hard to believe it happened here."

Sarah leaned forward, lowering her voice. "They're

saying she might've been mixed up with someone local. A man, maybe. You hear anything like that?"

Ellie shook her head, her grip tightening on the cup. "Not yet. Just the basics." She wanted to ask more, to press for details about this Lena, but the words stuck in her throat. Instead, she paid and slipped back outside, the coffee burning through the paper sleeve into her palm.

She didn't head home right away. The square was still buzzing, more people trickling in, and she veered toward the church instead, its spire cutting through the low clouds. The graveyard stretched out beside it, all mossy stones and crooked crosses, and she found herself wandering among them, the coffee cooling in her hand. She stopped at a bench near the back, sinking onto the damp wood, and let her eyes drift to the forest beyond. Ravenswood was out there, hidden in that dark sprawl, and she could almost feel it watching her back.

Her phone buzzed in her pocket, startling her. She pulled it out, expecting Daniel or Julia, but it was a text from an unknown number. *You were right about the mind lying to itself. Check the news.* No name, no context. Her pulse quickened, and she opened the news app with unsteady fingers. The headline hit her like a slap: *Victim Identified in Ravenswood Murder: Lena Moreau, 28, Recent Resident.*

Lena Moreau. The name burned into her, sharper now, and with it came a flash: a woman's face, dark hair, wide eyes, a voice saying something urgent. Ellie's breath caught, her vision blurring at the edges, and the coffee slipped from her hand, splashing across the gravel. She stood, swaying slightly, and the world tilted again, just like it had in the laundry room. Leaves rustling. A scream cut short. Then nothing, just the graveyard and the rain starting up again, soft and relentless.

She didn't remember walking home, but somehow she was there, standing in the hall, her coat dripping onto the floor. The scarf was still on the kitchen counter, untouched, and she stared at it, her heart pounding. Who was Lena Moreau? And why did Ellie feel like she'd known her all along?

CHAPTER FIVE

Ellie sat at the kitchen table, the red scarf spread out in front of her like an accusation. The house was still, the only sound the faint hum of the refrigerator and the occasional drip of rain from the eaves outside. Her coat hung damp on the rack by the door, a puddle forming beneath it, but she hadn't bothered to clean it up. Her phone rested beside the scarf, the screen dark since that cryptic text an hour ago. You were right about the mind lying to itself. Check the news. She'd read it a dozen times, her thumb hovering over the reply button, but she hadn't typed anything. Who would send that? And why did it feel like they knew her?

The name Lena Moreau circled her thoughts, relentless and sharp, like a splinter she couldn't dig out. She'd seen the news, the bare details: twenty-eight, new to the village, found stabbed at Ravenswood. But that flash of a face, those wide eyes, that voice, it wouldn't let her go. It wasn't just curiosity anymore, the kind that drew her to case files. This was personal, visceral, and it scared her.

She pushed back from the table, the chair scraping against the tile, and grabbed her phone. She needed to talk to someone, someone who wouldn't look at her like she was losing it. Daniel was still at the hospital, and Noah, upstairs, was a wall she couldn't breach right now. Julia was her anchor, always had been. She dialed her number, pacing the kitchen as it rang once, twice, three times before clicking through.

"Ellie, hey," Julia's voice came through, crisp and warm, a lifeline in the static. "Sorry I missed you earlier. Got stuck in a meeting with a client who thinks he's Perry Mason."

Ellie let out a shaky laugh, clutching the phone tighter. "Sounds exhausting. You free now?"

"For you? Always. What's up?" Julia's tone shifted, picking up on something in Ellie's voice. She was good at that, reading people, a skill honed from years in courtrooms.

Ellie hesitated, glancing at the scarf. "I don't know where to start. It's been a weird day."

"Start with the weirdest part," Julia said, a smile in her words. "You know I live for the drama."

"Okay." Ellie took a breath, leaning against the counter. "I found a scarf in my closet this morning. Red silk, not mine. There's a stain on it, looks like blood. And I've got this bruise on my arm I can't explain. Then I got this text, out of nowhere, saying my mind's lying to me. And the murder, Julia, that woman at Ravenswood, Lena Moreau, I feel like I know her somehow, but I don't."

The line went quiet for a moment, long enough that

Ellie checked to see if the call had dropped. "Julia?"

"I'm here," Julia said, her voice steady now, all business. "That's a lot. Let's break it down. The scarf, you're sure it's not Daniel's or Noah's?"

"Daniel didn't recognize it. Noah hasn't seen it, but he wouldn't wear something like that." Ellie rubbed her temple, the ache there growing. "It's not theirs. It's just... there."

"Okay. And the bruise? You didn't knock into something?"

"Not that I remember." Her voice cracked on the last word, and she hated how fragile it sounded. "That's the thing, Julia. I don't remember. I keep getting these flashes, like I'm missing pieces."

Julia exhaled softly. "Ellie, you're scaring me a little. Have you talked to Daniel about this?"

"Not all of it. He thinks I'm just tired." She paced again, her socks silent on the floor. "He's at work now. I didn't want to dump this on him until I figured it out."

"Fair enough. What about the text? Unknown number?"

"Yeah. No clue who sent it." She stopped by the window, staring at the dark woods beyond. "It's like someone's messing with me."

"Or warning you," Julia said, her tone sharp. "Look, you're the psychologist here, but this sounds like stress hitting you hard. That murder's got everyone on edge. Maybe it's triggering something."

"Maybe," Ellie echoed, but it didn't feel right. Stress didn't leave bruises. Stress didn't plant scarves in your closet. "What do I do, Julia? I can't just ignore this."

"You don't ignore it," Julia said firmly. "You investigate it. Start with what you know. Check your phone logs, see if that number's tied to anyone. Look at your calendar, retrace your steps. And for God's sake, tell Daniel when he gets home. He's your husband, not a stranger."

Ellie nodded, though Julia couldn't see it. "Yeah. Okay. I'll try that."

"Good. And Ellie?" Julia's voice softened. "If it gets worse, you call me, day or night. I mean it."

"Thanks," Ellie said, a lump rising in her throat. "I will."

She hung up, setting the phone down carefully, like it might bite. Julia was right. She needed answers, not guesses. She grabbed her laptop from the living room, settling back at the table, and opened her phone logs. The unknown number stared back at her, a string of digits with no name attached. She tried calling it, but it went straight to a generic voicemail, no greeting, just a beep. She hung up without leaving a message.

Next, she pulled up her calendar, scrolling through the past week. Lectures, a grocery run, a dinner with Daniel at the pub. Nothing unusual, nothing that screamed *bloody scarf* or *Lena Moreau*. But as she stared at the screen, her vision blurred, and that flash came again: leaves underfoot, a woman's voice, low and panicked, saying, "You don't understand." Ellie's hands clenched into fists, her nails digging into her palms, and the room spun.

She stumbled to her feet, knocking the chair back, and braced herself against the counter. Her breath came fast, shallow, and she squeezed her eyes shut, willing the dizziness away. When she opened them, the kitchen was steady again, but her heart wouldn't slow. She looked down at her arm, the bruise darker now, or maybe that was the light. Then she saw it: a scratch, faint and red, running parallel to the bruise. Fresh.

Her stomach twisted. She hadn't scratched herself. She hadn't been anywhere to get scratched. The scarf sat there, mocking her, and she grabbed it, shoving it into a drawer, out of sight. But it wasn't out of mind. Nothing was anymore.

Footsteps thudded overhead, Noah moving around upstairs, and she flinched at the sound. She needed to talk to him, to Daniel, to someone, but the words wouldn't come. All she had was a name, a scarf, and a memory that wasn't hers— or was it?

CHAPTER SIX

Ellie stood in the kitchen, her hands pressed against the cool edge of the counter, staring at the drawer where she'd shoved the scarf. The house felt smaller now, the walls leaning in with every creak and sigh of the old beams. The rain had stopped, leaving a heavy silence that pressed against her ears, broken only by the faint thud of Noah's footsteps overhead. She couldn't stay down here, stewing in her own head, not with that scratch on her arm and the name Lena Moreau echoing like a pulse she couldn't silence. She needed to move, to do something, even if it meant facing the quiet wall that was her son.

She climbed the stairs slowly, her hand trailing along the banister, the wood smooth and worn under her fingers. The hallway upstairs was dim, the light from Noah's room spilling out in a narrow wedge across the carpet. She paused outside his door, listening. No music, no tapping pencil, just the soft rustle of pages turning. She knocked lightly, two quick raps, and pushed the door open without waiting for an answer.

Noah sat at his desk, his back to her, hunched over a textbook. His room smelled faintly of cedar from the wardrobe in the corner, mixed with the clean, crisp scent of his laundry. The walls were bare except for a single framed certificate from a math competition last year, its gold foil catching the lamplight. He didn't turn around, just kept reading, his shoulders still as stone.

"Hey," Ellie said, stepping inside. Her voice sounded too loud in the quiet, and she softened it. "Can we talk for a minute?"

He glanced over his shoulder, his dark eyes meeting hers briefly before sliding away. "Sure. What's up?" He closed the book, marking his place with a pencil, and swiveled his chair to face her. There was no warmth in his expression, no curiosity, just that steady, unreadable look he'd worn more and more lately.

Ellie leaned against the doorframe, crossing her arms to hide the scratch and bruise. "I just wanted to check in. You've been quiet since yesterday. Everything okay?"

"Yeah," he said, shrugging. "Just school stuff. Lots to do."

She nodded, searching his face for something, anything, to latch onto. He looked like Daniel in this light, the same sharp jaw and high cheekbones, but there was a distance in him her husband never had. "You heard about the murder, right? Lena Moreau?"

His gaze flicked up, holding hers for a beat longer this time. "Yeah. Everyone's talking about it. Weird she was out at

Ravenswood."

"Did you know her?" The question slipped out before she could stop it, sharper than she'd meant, and she saw his brow crease faintly.

"No," he said, his tone flat. "Why would I?"

"I don't know," she admitted, backtracking. "She was new in town, worked at the pub. I thought maybe you'd seen her around."

He shook his head, leaning back in his chair. "I don't go to the pub. You know that."

"Right," she said, forcing a small smile. "Just curious. It's shaken everyone up, I guess. Me included."

He didn't respond, just watched her, and the silence stretched thin between them. She shifted her weight, the floor creaking under her, and tried again. "Noah, if something's bothering you, you can tell me. You know that, right?"

"I'm fine, Mom," he said, his voice steady, almost too steady. "You don't need to worry about me."

She wanted to believe him, wanted to see the boy who used to climb into her lap with questions about her work, but that boy was gone, replaced by this quiet, closed-off teenager. "Okay," she said finally. "I'll let you get back to it. Dinner's in an hour if Daniel's back by then."

He nodded, turning back to his book without another word, and she stepped out, pulling the door halfway shut behind her. Her chest felt tight, like she'd failed some test she didn't understand. She started down the hall, her socks silent on the carpet, when a sound stopped her: a low thud, like something heavy hitting the floor in Noah's room. She turned back, hesitating, then pushed the door open again.

He was still at his desk, the book open, but a small wooden box sat on the floor beside him, its lid ajar. He looked up, startled, and for a split second, she saw something flicker in his eyes—surprise, maybe, or irritation—before it smoothed away. "Dropped it," he said, bending to pick it up. "It's just some old stuff."

"What kind of stuff?" she asked, stepping closer despite herself. The box was plain, unvarnished, the kind of thing you'd keep trinkets in, but he snapped the lid shut before she could see inside.

"Nothing special," he said, sliding it under his desk. "Coins, junk from school. You don't need to check it."

"I wasn't going to," she lied, though the urge had been there, sharp and sudden. "Just making sure you're okay."

"I'm fine," he repeated, his voice firmer now, and he turned back to his book, dismissing her.

She left the room, her pulse thudding in her ears, and made it halfway down the stairs before stopping again. The box nagged at her, its sudden appearance, the way he'd hidden it. She shook her head, telling herself it was nothing, just a kid's clutter, but the unease wouldn't let go. Neither would the memory of that scarf, or the scratch on her arm, or Lena Moreau's name burning a hole in her mind.

Downstairs, the front door clicked open, and Daniel's

voice called out, "Ellie? You home?" His footsteps echoed in the hall, steady and familiar, and she hurried down to meet him, needing his solidity to anchor her.

"In here," she said, stepping into the kitchen as he shrugged off his coat. He looked tired, lines etched deeper around his eyes, but he smiled when he saw her.

"Rough day at the hospital," he said, dropping his keys into the bowl. "How about you?"

She opened her mouth to tell him—about the scarf, the text, the scratch, Noah—but the words caught, tangled in her throat. "Quiet," she said instead, forcing her lips to curve upward. "Just a quiet day."

He nodded, accepting it, and moved to the fridge, pulling out a beer. She watched him, the normalcy of it almost painful, and wondered how long she could keep pretending everything was fine when the shadows upstairs felt like they were growing longer by the minute.

CHAPTER SEVEN

Ellie watched Daniel sip his beer, the bottle sweating faintly in his hand as he leaned against the kitchen counter. The overhead light cast soft shadows across his face, picking out the fatigue in the lines around his mouth. He'd kicked off his shoes by the door, leaving them in a haphazard pile, and the sight of it, so ordinary, twisted something in her chest. She wanted to tell him everything, to let the words pour out like water breaking a dam, but they stayed locked behind her teeth, heavy and unspoken.

"You sure you're okay?" he asked, setting the bottle down with a quiet clink. His eyes found hers, steady and searching, the way they always did when he sensed her pulling away. "You've got that look."

"What look?" she said, forcing a lightness into her voice. She moved to the sink, rinsing a glass she didn't need to wash, just to keep her hands busy.

"The one where you're overthinking something," he

said, a faint smile tugging at his lips. "Come on, Ellie. I know you."

She turned off the tap, the sudden silence loud in her ears, and dried her hands on a towel. He was right, of course. Twenty years together had made them fluent in each other's silences, but this one felt different, thicker, like it could choke her if she let it. "It's nothing," she said finally, turning to face him. "Just the murder. It's got me rattled, that's all."

He nodded, crossing his arms. "Understandable. Whole town's buzzing about it. I heard some nurses talking at the hospital, saying she was mixed up with someone local. Gossip's already running wild."

"Lena Moreau," Ellie said, the name slipping out before she could stop it. She watched his reaction, searching for a flicker of recognition, but his expression didn't change.

"Yeah, that's her," he said, picking up his beer again. "Poor girl. Sounds like she didn't have much of a chance out there."

Ellie's throat tightened. She wanted to ask if he'd ever met her, if he'd seen her at the pub or passed her on the street, but the question felt absurd, paranoid. Instead, she said, "It's strange, isn't it? Something like that happening here."

"Strange and awful," he agreed. He took a sip, then set the bottle down and stepped closer, resting a hand on her shoulder. "You don't have to carry it, though. It's not your burden."

His touch was warm, grounding, and for a moment

she leaned into it, letting herself believe he was right. But the scarf was still in the drawer, the scratch on her arm still raw, and Noah's cold stare lingered in her mind like a shadow she couldn't shake. "I know," she said, her voice barely above a whisper. "I just can't stop thinking about it."

He squeezed her shoulder gently, then let go, moving to the fridge. "How about I make us something? Take your mind off it. Pasta sound good?"

"Sure," she said, though her stomach churned at the thought of food. She watched him pull out a pot, fill it with water, the routine of it so achingly normal it almost hurt. She should tell him now, while he was here, while the house was still. But the words wouldn't come, and the silence grew heavier, pressing down on her chest.

The doorbell rang, a sharp chime that made her flinch. Daniel glanced at her, eyebrows raised. "Expecting someone?"

"No," she said, frowning. "I'll get it."

She walked to the front door, her socks whispering against the hardwood, and peered through the peephole. It was Tom Bennett from the hardware store, his coat collar turned up against the evening chill. She opened the door, the cold air rushing in. "Tom. Hi."

"Hey, Ellie," he said, his voice gruff but friendly. "Sorry to barge in like this. Just dropping off those screws Daniel asked for last week. Forgot to bring 'em by sooner."

"Oh, right," she said, taking the small paper bag he held out. "Thanks. He'll appreciate it."

Tom nodded, then hesitated, his hands shoved into his pockets. "Heard you were at the square earlier. Everyone's still talking about that girl, Lena. Police were out at Ravenswood all day, cordoning it off. Reckon they'll be knocking on doors soon."

Her grip tightened on the bag, the paper crinkling. "Yeah, I figured they would. Any word on what happened?"

"Not much," he said, shrugging. "Just that it was messy. Some folks are saying it might've been personal, you know? Someone she knew."

Ellie's pulse quickened, but she kept her face neutral. "Makes sense. Small town like this, it's hard to stay a stranger."

"True enough," Tom said. He tipped his head, a half-nod goodbye. "Well, I'll leave you to it. Tell Daniel I said hi."

"Will do," she said, closing the door as he turned away. She stood there for a moment, the bag in her hand, Tom's words circling her head. *Personal. Someone she knew.* She didn't want to think it, didn't want to let it take root, but the idea burrowed in anyway.

Back in the kitchen, Daniel was salting the boiling water, steam curling up around him. "Who was it?" he asked, not looking up.

"Tom," she said, setting the bag on the counter. "Dropping off those screws you wanted."

"Nice of him," Daniel said, stirring the pasta. "He say anything else?"

She hesitated, then shook her head. "Just small talk."

The lie came easily, too easily, and she hated herself for it. She sat at the table, watching him cook, the clatter of the spoon against the pot filling the space where her confession should have been.

Dinner passed in a haze. Noah came down, ate silently, and disappeared back upstairs, leaving his plate in the sink. Daniel talked about the hospital, a patient with a tricky surgery, but Ellie barely heard him. Her eyes kept drifting to the drawer, to the scarf she couldn't unsee, and when they finally cleared the table, she felt like she was moving through water, slow and heavy.

Later, lying in bed beside Daniel, she listened to his breathing deepen into sleep. The room was dark, the curtains swaying faintly with the night breeze, and she stared at the ceiling, the weight of silence pressing harder now. She'd kept it all in—the scarf, the scratch, the text, the flashes of memory— and it was choking her. She turned her head, looking at Daniel's profile in the dim light, and wondered how much longer she could hold it together before the cracks showed through.

Outside, the wind picked up, rattling the window, and she thought she heard something else, a distant rustle, like leaves underfoot. She closed her eyes, willing sleep to come, but all she saw was Lena Moreau's face, and all she felt was the cold certainty that the silence wouldn't last.

CHAPTER EIGHT

Ellie woke to sunlight streaming through the bedroom curtains, a rare break in the March gloom that should have lifted her spirits. Instead, it felt intrusive, too bright against the heaviness that clung to her like damp clothes. She lay still, listening to the house breathe: the faint groan of pipes, the distant clatter of Daniel in the kitchen below. Her head ached, a dull throb at her temples, and she pressed her fingers there, trying to knead it away. She couldn't remember falling asleep last night, only the weight of silence and that rustling sound in her ears, like a memory she couldn't place.

She sat up, the sheets slipping cool against her skin, and glanced at the clock. 8:47. Later than she usually slept, but it was Monday, and she had no appointments until the afternoon. Her arm caught her eye as she swung her legs out of bed, the scratch and bruise still there, sharper now in the morning light. The scratch looked angry, a thin red line that hadn't faded, and she traced it with her fingertip, a shiver running through her. She needed to stop staring at it, stop letting it pull her under, but it was like a thread she couldn't help tugging.

Downstairs, the kitchen smelled of coffee and bacon, a warm haze that greeted her as she stepped in. Daniel stood at the stove, flipping strips in a skillet, his back to her. He was dressed for work, his white shirt crisp and his tie slung over one shoulder, a picture of routine that felt almost staged today. "Morning," he said, glancing back with a smile. "Thought I'd make breakfast before I head out."

"Smells good," she said, sliding into a chair at the table. Her voice sounded hollow, and she cleared her throat, reaching for the coffee pot he'd left out. The mug warmed her hands, a small comfort, but her eyes drifted to the drawer where the scarf hid, its presence a silent scream in the room.

"Noah's already off to school," Daniel said, setting a plate in front of her: bacon, toast, a fried egg. "Left early, said he had a study group."

She nodded, picking up a fork. "He's been pushing himself hard lately."

"Like his mom," Daniel teased, sitting across from her with his own plate. "You two are cut from the same cloth."

She forced a smile, taking a bite of toast, but it tasted like cardboard. The comparison stung, though she couldn't say why. Noah's coldness upstairs last night, that box he'd hidden, lingered in her mind, and she wondered if Daniel saw it too, the distance growing between them all. "Maybe," she said, keeping her tone light. "You heading straight to the hospital?"

"Yeah, busy day," he said, chewing thoughtfully. "Might be late again. You okay on your own?"

"Always am," she said, and he chuckled, accepting it as the truth. She watched him eat, the normalcy of it grating against the chaos in her head, and when he stood to clear his plate, she almost stopped him, almost blurted out everything. But he kissed her forehead, a quick, familiar gesture, and was gone, the front door clicking shut behind him.

The house settled into silence again, and Ellie stayed at the table, staring at her untouched egg. She couldn't eat, couldn't sit still with the scarf and the text and Lena Moreau's name clawing at her. She needed to move, to think. She dumped the food in the bin, rinsed the plate, and grabbed her phone, opening the news app again. The headline was the same, but a new detail caught her eye: *Police seeking witnesses from Friday night near Ravenswood Estate. Anyone with information urged to come forward.*

Friday night. Three days ago. She frowned, scrolling back through her memory. She'd been home, hadn't she? Dinner with Daniel, a glass of wine, then bed. But as she tried to pin it down, the edges blurred, slipping away like water through her fingers. She opened her calendar, checking the date. Blank. No notes, no plans. Just a void where Friday should have been.

Her breath quickened, and she stood, pacing the kitchen. She remembered the lecture on Saturday, the news alert cutting through, but Friday was a blank slate. She grabbed her coat from the rack, needing air, and stepped outside. The sun was higher now, warming the damp pavement, and she walked toward the village, her pace brisk, almost urgent. The square was quieter today, a few people milling about, but the tension lingered, a hum beneath the surface.

She stopped at the bakery, the bell jingling as she pushed the door open. Sarah looked up from wiping the counter, her face brightening. "Ellie, back already? Coffee again?"

"Please," Ellie said, digging out her wallet. "Hey, Sarah, were you working Friday night?"

Sarah nodded, pouring the coffee. "Yeah, till close. Why?"

"Was I in here?" Ellie asked, keeping her voice casual, though her pulse thudded in her ears.

Sarah paused, tilting her head. "Friday? No, don't think so. I'd remember. It was quiet, just a few regulars. Why, you forget where you were?" She laughed, handing over the cup.

Ellie forced a smile, taking it. "Something like that. Thanks." She paid and stepped back outside, the coffee trembling slightly in her hand. If she wasn't at the bakery, where had she been? Home, she told herself. Home with Daniel. But the doubt gnawed at her, sharp and relentless.

She wandered toward the church again, the graveyard stretching out in the sunlight, less ominous now but no less heavy. She sat on the same bench as yesterday, staring at the forest where Ravenswood hid. Friday night. The police wanted witnesses. She closed her eyes, willing the memory to come, but all she got was that rustle of leaves, that panicked voice: *You don't understand.* Her eyes snapped open, and she looked down at her arm. The scratch seemed longer now, or maybe that was her imagination, but it burned under her sleeve.

Her phone buzzed, another text from the unknown number. *Where were you Friday night?* She stared at it, her heart slamming against her ribs, and typed back, *Who is this?* No reply came, just the words glowing on the screen, taunting her.

She stood, the coffee forgotten on the bench, and started home, her steps uneven. The missing hours loomed larger now, a gap she couldn't fill, and with every step, the certainty grew: whatever happened Friday night, it wasn't just in her head. It was real, and it was coming for her.

CHAPTER NINE

Ellie stood in the hallway, her phone still clutched in her hand, the unanswered text glowing like a wound: Where were you Friday night? The house felt too big now, its silence a cavern she couldn't fill, and the sunlight pouring through the windows only sharpened the edges of her unease. She'd walked back from the village in a daze, the coffee left behind on the graveyard bench, her mind spinning with questions she couldn't answer. Friday night. The police appeal. Lena Moreau. It was all closing in, and she couldn't keep it locked inside anymore.

She slipped the phone into her pocket and moved to the living room, sinking onto the couch. The room was tidy, almost too tidy, with its cream cushions and polished oak coffee table, a space that screamed control. She'd built this life with Daniel, layer by careful layer, but now it felt like a stage set, ready to collapse under the weight of what she didn't know. Her eyes drifted to the framed photo on the mantel: her, Daniel, and Noah at the coast last summer, smiling into the wind. She barely recognized herself in it now, that easy grin a stranger's.

The front door opened, and Daniel's voice cut through the quiet. "Ellie? You in here?" His keys clinked into the bowl, a sound she usually found comforting, but today it grated against her nerves.

"Living room," she called, sitting up straighter. He appeared in the doorway, his tie loosened, his face softened by the late afternoon light. He looked tired, but there was a warmth in his eyes that made her chest ache.

"Home early for once," he said, dropping his bag by the armchair. "Thought I'd surprise you. Where's Noah?"

"Still at school, I think," she said, her voice steady despite the storm inside. "Study group."

He nodded, sinking into the chair across from her. "Good. Kid needs a break, but he won't listen to me." He leaned forward, elbows on his knees, and studied her. "You okay? You look pale."

She took a breath, her hands twisting together in her lap. This was it, the moment to crack the silence. "Daniel, I need to ask you something."

His brow creased, but he kept his tone light. "Sounds serious. What's going on?"

"Where were we Friday night?" she asked, watching his face closely. "I can't remember, and it's driving me crazy."

He blinked, leaning back slightly. "Friday? We were here, weren't we? Had that chicken thing I made, watched some TV. You don't remember?"

She shook her head, her pulse quickening. "I don't. It's blank. And the police are asking about Friday night, witnesses near Ravenswood. I keep thinking... what if I was out there?"

"Out where?" His voice sharpened, the warmth fading. "Ravenswood? Ellie, why would you be there?"

"I don't know," she said, her words tumbling out faster now. "I've got this bruise, this scratch, and that scarf in the drawer, the one with the stain. Then these texts, someone asking where I was, telling me my mind's lying. I'm scared, Daniel. I don't know what's happening to me."

He stared at her, his mouth tightening, and for a moment she thought he'd get up, walk away, dismiss it like he had before. But he stood and crossed to her, sitting beside her on the couch, close enough that she could smell the faint antiseptic on his skin from the hospital. "Hey, slow down," he said, his hand resting on her knee. "You're not making sense. What texts? What scarf?"

She pulled the phone from her pocket, showing him the messages: *You were right about the mind lying to itself. Check the news.* And then, *Where were you Friday night?* He read them, his frown deepening, and handed it back. "Unknown number. Could be a prank, Ellie. Kids messing around."

"It's not a prank," she snapped, then softened her tone. "It's too specific. And the scarf, you saw it. That wasn't wine."

He rubbed a hand over his face, exhaling slowly. "Okay. Let's say it's blood. How'd it get in our closet? You think someone planted it?"

"I don't know," she admitted, her voice breaking. "But I keep getting these flashes, leaves, a voice, and I can't place them. What if I was there, Daniel? What if I saw something?"

He took her hand, his grip firm, almost too tight. "You weren't at Ravenswood. You were here, with me. I'd know if you left, Ellie. You're just stressed, that's all. This murder's got you wound up."

She wanted to believe him, wanted his certainty to erase the doubt, but it didn't. "Then why can't I remember?" she whispered, pulling her hand free. "Why do I feel like I'm lying to myself?"

He didn't answer right away, just watched her, his eyes dark with something she couldn't read. "You're not lying," he said finally. "You're tired. You've been working too hard, and this thing's hitting too close to home. Maybe you should see someone, talk it out."

"See someone?" She stood, pacing to the window, the sunlight harsh against her eyes. "You think I'm crazy?"

"No," he said, standing too, his voice firm. "I think you're human. And I think you need help sorting this out before it eats you alive."

She turned to face him, ready to argue, but the doorbell rang again, cutting through the tension like a blade. Daniel sighed, running a hand through his hair. "I'll get it."

He left the room, and she heard muffled voices at the door, then his footsteps returning. He held a small envelope, plain white, with her name scrawled across it in black ink. "Someone dropped this off. No one there when I opened the door."

Her stomach dropped as she took it, her fingers trembling. She tore it open, pulling out a single sheet of paper. A photo, grainy but clear: her, standing in the village square, the bakery in the background. It was from yesterday, her coat unmistakable. Written beneath it in the same black ink: *You were closer than you think.*

She dropped the photo, her breath catching, and Daniel snatched it up, staring at it. "What the hell is this?" he demanded, his voice rising. "Who's sending you this stuff?"

"I don't know," she said, backing away, her knees weak. "But it's real, Daniel. It's not in my head."

He looked from the photo to her, his jaw tight, and for the first time, she saw fear in his eyes. The room spun, the sunlight too bright, and she gripped the couch to steady herself, the missing hours roaring back like a wave she couldn't outrun.

CHAPTER TEN

Ellie stared at the photo trembling in Daniel's hand, her name scrawled beneath it in that jagged black ink: You were closer than you think. The living room felt like it was shrinking, the walls pressing in with every shallow breath she took. The sunlight streaming through the window, once a comfort, now burned her eyes, casting harsh shadows across the floor. Daniel stood frozen, the paper crumpling slightly in his grip, his face a mix of anger and fear she hadn't seen in years.

"Ellie, what is this?" he asked again, his voice rough, almost pleading. "Who's doing this to you?"

"I don't know," she said, her words barely audible. She sank back onto the couch, her legs unsteady, and pressed her hands to her face. The scratch on her arm throbbed under her sleeve, a pulse of heat that matched the pounding in her head. "I don't know, Daniel, but it's not stopping."

He dropped the photo onto the coffee table and sat

beside her, close but not touching, his hands clenched into fists on his knees. "This is insane," he said, more to himself than to her. "First the texts, now this? We need to call the police, Ellie. Someone's targeting you."

She shook her head, the motion sharp and quick. "And tell them what? That I'm getting creepy messages and can't remember Friday night? They'll think I'm unhinged, Daniel. Or worse, they'll start asking questions I can't answer."

He turned to her, his eyes narrowing. "What questions? What aren't you telling me?"

The air between them thickened, heavy with everything she'd held back. She opened her mouth, ready to deflect, but the weight of it all—the scarf, the bruise, the flashes of leaves and that voice—crashed over her. "I think I was there," she whispered, the confession tearing free. "At Ravenswood. Friday night. I don't know how, I don't know why, but I keep seeing it, hearing her."

"Her?" Daniel's voice rose, sharp with disbelief. "Lena? You think you were there when she died?"

"I don't know!" she snapped, standing again, her hands trembling. "I can't remember, but it's there, Daniel, pieces of it. The scarf, the scratch, this photo, it's all connected. And I'm terrified I did something."

He stood too, towering over her, his face flushed. "Did something? Like what, Ellie? You're not making sense. You're a psychologist, not a killer. You were here, with me, I told you that."

"Then why don't I remember?" she shouted, her voice breaking. "Why do I have her blood on a scarf in our closet? Why does someone keep sending me this stuff?"

He stared at her, his jaw tight, and for a moment she thought he'd walk away, leave her to drown in it. But he grabbed her shoulders, his grip firm but not cruel. "Listen to me," he said, his voice low and steady. "You didn't do anything. You're not that person. Someone's messing with you, planting this crap to scare you. We'll figure it out, okay? Together."

She wanted to collapse into him, to let his words rebuild the world she'd known, but the doubt wouldn't let go. She pulled away, wrapping her arms around herself, and paced to the window. The village stretched out below, peaceful in the fading light, but it felt like a lie now, a mask hiding something rotten. "I need to know," she said, more to herself than to him. "I can't keep guessing."

"Then let's call Julia," he said, picking up his phone from the table. "She's a lawyer, she'll know what to do. Or the police, Ellie, someone. You can't carry this alone."

She nodded, numbly, and he dialed Julia's number, putting it on speaker. The line rang twice before her voice came through, crisp and familiar. "Daniel? Everything okay?"

"No," he said, glancing at Ellie. "It's Ellie. She's getting weird messages, photos, stuff about the murder. We need your help."

"Slow down," Julia said, her tone shifting to that calm, courtroom edge. "What kind of messages? What photos?"

Ellie stepped closer, her voice shaky but firm. "Someone's sending me texts about Friday night, asking where I was. Then a photo of me in the square, with a note saying I was closer than I think. And there's a scarf, Julia, with blood on it, in my closet. I don't know how it got there."

The line went quiet, then Julia exhaled. "Okay. That's serious. You need to take this to the police, Ellie. Now."

"I can't," Ellie said, her throat tightening. "I don't remember Friday night. I keep getting these flashes, like I was at Ravenswood, with Lena. What if I was there?"

"Ellie," Julia said, her voice softening but firm. "You're not a murderer. You're stressed, maybe confused, but you didn't kill anyone. Go to the police. I'll meet you there, we'll sort it out."

Daniel ended the call, his hand resting on her arm. "She's right. We'll go together. Get this off your chest."

She nodded, but as she turned to grab her coat, something caught her eye: a glint of metal on the floor, half-hidden under the couch. She bent down, her fingers brushing the carpet, and pulled out a small key, old and tarnished, with a faint engraving: *R.E.* Ravenswood Estate. Her breath stopped, the room tilting, and she clutched it tight, the edges biting into her palm.

"Daniel," she said, her voice barely a whisper as she held it up. "Where did this come from?"

He frowned, taking it from her, turning it over in his hand. "I've never seen it. You think it's...?"

"Ravenswood," she finished, her heart slamming against her ribs. The flashes came faster now: leaves crunching, a door creaking open, Lena's voice, "You don't understand," and then a scream. She stumbled back, her vision blurring, and Daniel caught her, his arms strong around her.

"Ellie, breathe," he said, his voice tight with panic. "What's happening?"

"I was there," she gasped, the memory breaking through like a flood. "I was with her. But I didn't... I didn't kill her. Someone else was there, watching."

He held her tighter, his face pale, and she clung to him, the key still in her fist. The edge of remembering had cut her open, and now there was no going back.

PART 2: DANIEL CARTER

CHAPTER ELEVEN

Daniel sat in the driver's seat, his hands gripping the steering wheel, the leather cool and familiar under his palms. The car idled in their driveway, the engine humming softly, but he hadn't pulled out yet. Ellie sat beside him, her coat pulled tight around her, the tarnished Ravenswood key clutched in her fist like a lifeline. Her breathing was shallow, uneven, and he could feel the weight of her panic radiating across the console. The sun had dipped below the horizon now, painting the village in shades of dusk, and the quiet street outside their house felt too still, too normal for what was happening inside their lives.

"You sure you're up for this?" he asked, glancing at her. His voice was steady, the tone he used with patients before a surgery, but it felt hollow here. "We can wait, Ellie. Take a minute."

She shook her head, her eyes fixed on the dashboard. "No. I need to do this now. Julia's waiting."

He nodded, though every instinct told him to turn back, to lock the doors and keep her safe inside their house where the world couldn't touch her. But the photo, the texts, that damn key, they'd already breached the walls he'd built around their family. He shifted the car into gear and pulled onto the road, the headlights cutting through the gathering dark as they headed toward the police station.

The drive was short, just a few minutes through the village's winding lanes, past cottages with glowing windows and the occasional dog walker braving the evening chill. Ellie didn't speak, and he didn't push her. He kept his eyes on the road, his mind racing back to the living room, to her confession: *I was there. With her. Someone else was watching.* It didn't make sense, not his Ellie, the woman who could dissect a killer's mind without flinching. But the fear in her eyes, the way she'd clung to him, that was real. Too real.

He pulled into the station's small lot, a squat brick building with a single light buzzing over the entrance. Julia's car was already there, parked crookedly, and she stood by the door, her arms crossed, her dark hair pulled back tight. She straightened as they approached, her sharp eyes flicking between them. "You two look like hell," she said, her tone blunt but soft around the edges. "What happened?"

Daniel opened his mouth, but Ellie cut in, her voice trembling but firm. "I found a key. Ravenswood. And I remembered something. I was there, Julia, Friday night. With Lena."

Julia's brow furrowed, and she stepped closer, lowering

her voice. "Okay. Let's take this inside. We'll figure it out, but you need to tell them everything, Ellie. No holding back."

Ellie nodded, and Daniel followed them into the station, his stomach twisting. The lobby smelled of stale coffee and disinfectant, a faint buzz of fluorescent lights overhead. A young officer at the desk looked up, his face blank but curious. "Can I help you?"

"We need to speak to someone about the Ravenswood case," Julia said, her lawyer voice kicking in, smooth and commanding. "It's urgent."

The officer nodded, disappearing through a door, and Daniel guided Ellie to a row of plastic chairs against the wall. She sat, still clutching the key, and he sank down beside her, his hand resting on her arm. "You're doing the right thing," he said, though he wasn't sure who he was convincing.

She didn't respond, just stared at the floor, and he felt the distance between them widen, a crack he couldn't bridge. He'd always been the steady one, the surgeon with hands that never shook, but now he felt useless, his calm unraveling thread by thread. He thought of Noah, home alone, probably buried in his books, oblivious to this. Or was he? That box under his desk, the way he'd shut Ellie down last night, it nagged at Daniel, a splinter he couldn't ignore.

The door opened again, and a man stepped out, tall and lean with a weathered face and eyes that cut through the room. Detective Mark Hollis, Daniel realized, recognizing him from the news clips about Lena's murder. "Dr. Carter?" Hollis said, his gaze settling on Ellie. "I'm told you've got something for me."

Ellie stood, her movements jerky, and held out the key. "This. It's from Ravenswood. And I think I was there, Friday night, when she died."

Hollis took the key, turning it over in his hand, his expression unreadable. "Let's talk in private," he said, nodding toward a side room. Julia followed, then Ellie, and Daniel trailed behind, his heart pounding in a way it hadn't since his first surgery.

The room was small, bare except for a table and a few chairs, the walls a dull gray that swallowed the light. Hollis sat across from them, setting the key down with a faint clink. "Start from the beginning," he said, his voice calm but firm. "What do you remember?"

Ellie took a shaky breath, recounting it all: the scarf, the bruise, the texts, the photo, the flashes of leaves and Lena's voice. Daniel listened, his chest tightening with every word, her story sounding wilder in this sterile room. Hollis scribbled notes, his pen scratching against the pad, and Julia interjected occasionally, keeping Ellie's words measured, legal.

"And you, Mr. Carter?" Hollis said, looking up at Daniel. "Where were you Friday night?"

"Here," Daniel said, too quickly. "At home. With her. We had dinner, watched TV. Normal night."

Hollis's eyes lingered on him, sharp and probing, and Daniel felt a flicker of unease. "Normal," the detective repeated, then turned back to Ellie. "You're sure this key's from

Ravenswood?"

"It's engraved," she said, pointing to the faint *R.E.* "And the memory... it fits. The door, the sound of it."

Hollis nodded, pocketing the key. "We'll look into it. The scarf too, if you've still got it. But I need you to be straight with me, Dr. Carter. If you were there, what happened?"

"I don't know," she said, her voice breaking. "I didn't kill her. Someone else was there, I swear."

The detective leaned back, studying her, and Daniel reached for her hand, squeezing it tight. "She's telling the truth," he said, his voice firm. "She's not a killer."

Hollis didn't respond, just closed his notebook and stood. "Stay available. We'll be in touch."

They left the room in silence, Julia leading the way back to the lobby. Outside, the night air hit Daniel like a slap, cold and biting, and he pulled Ellie close as they walked to the car. "You did it," he said, his breath fogging in the dark. "It's out now."

She nodded, but her eyes were distant, lost somewhere he couldn't follow. He drove them home, the village blurring past, and when they stepped inside, the house felt different, colder. Noah's shoes were by the door, meaning he was back, but the upstairs was quiet.

"Ellie," Daniel said, turning to her as she shed her coat. "We're okay, right? Whatever this is, we'll get through it."

She looked at him, her face pale, and for the first time, he saw doubt in her eyes, not just about herself, but about him.

"I hope so," she said, and slipped upstairs, leaving him alone in the hall, his surgeon's hands trembling in a way they never had before.

CHAPTER TWELVE

Daniel stood in the hallway, staring at the spot where Ellie's coat had fallen from the rack, a dark puddle of wool against the hardwood. Her footsteps had faded upstairs, leaving him alone with the echo of her words: I hope so. The house was quiet now, save for the faint hum of the heating kicking on, but it didn't feel like home anymore. It felt like a stranger's place, full of corners he didn't trust. He rubbed his hands together, trying to shake the tremble that lingered from the police station, but it wouldn't leave. His surgeon's hands, the ones that cut and stitched with precision, felt foreign to him tonight.

He moved to the kitchen, needing something to do, and poured a glass of water from the tap. The cold bit his throat as he drank, grounding him, but his eyes kept drifting to the drawer where Ellie had hidden that scarf. She'd told Hollis about it, promised to bring it in tomorrow, and the thought of it sitting there, stained and silent, made his skin crawl. He set the glass down with a clink and leaned against the counter, replaying her confession in his head. *I was there. With her. Someone else was watching.* It didn't fit, not with the Ellie he knew, the woman who'd built her life on understanding chaos, not creating it.

But her fear, that was real. And the key, the photo, the texts, they weren't figments of her imagination. Someone was pulling strings, and he hated how helpless it made him feel. He'd told Hollis they were home Friday night, dinner and TV, a normal evening, but now, standing here, he tried to picture it. Chicken, he'd said. He remembered cooking, the sizzle of it in the pan, Ellie at the table with a glass of wine. Or was it Thursday? The days blurred, a smear of routine, and a small, sharp doubt pricked at him. What if he was wrong?

The stairs creaked behind him, and he turned, expecting Ellie, but it was Noah, his lanky frame slouched in a hoodie, his hair falling into his eyes. "Hey, Dad," he said, his voice low, almost cautious. "You guys just get back?"

"Yeah," Daniel said, forcing a casual tone. "Had to run an errand. You eat yet?"

Noah nodded, moving to the fridge. "Grabbed something after school. Study group ran late." He pulled out a carton of juice, pouring it into a glass, and Daniel watched him, the boy's movements slow, deliberate.

"Everything okay with you?" Daniel asked, leaning against the counter again. "You've been quiet lately."

Noah shrugged, taking a sip. "Just school. Lots of tests coming up."

Daniel nodded, but the silence stretched, and he couldn't shake the memory of that box under Noah's desk, the way he'd snapped it shut when Ellie asked. "Your mom's not feeling great," he said, testing the waters. "This murder's got her rattled. You hear much about it?"

"Some," Noah said, his eyes flicking up briefly. "Kids at school are talking. Say it was messy, out at Ravenswood. Creepy place."

"Yeah," Daniel agreed, studying him. "Creepy's right. You ever go out there?"

Noah's hand paused on the glass, just for a second, then he shook his head. "No. Why would I? It's falling apart."

"Just wondering," Daniel said, keeping his voice light. "Thought maybe you and your friends might've explored it sometime."

"Nope," Noah said, finishing his juice and rinsing the glass. "Not my thing." He turned to head back upstairs, but Daniel stopped him.

"Noah," he said, stepping closer. "If you know anything about this, about your mom or that night, you'd tell me, right?"

Noah looked back, his expression blank, almost too blank. "Yeah, Dad. I'd tell you. Night."

He disappeared up the stairs, leaving Daniel alone again, the doubt in his gut growing sharper. Noah was a good kid, smart, focused, but that pause, that look, it stuck with him. He shook it off, telling himself he was reading too much into it, but the unease wouldn't let go.

He wandered back to the living room, the photo still on the coffee table where he'd dropped it. Ellie in the square, her coat stark against the gray day, the note beneath it: *You were closer than you think.* He picked it up, turning it over, and noticed something he'd missed before: a faint smudge on the corner, dark and irregular, like a fingerprint in ink. Or blood. His stomach turned, and he set it down, wiping his hand on his pants as if it could erase the feel of it.

The clock on the mantel ticked past nine, and he knew he should check on Ellie, but his feet took him to the hall closet instead. He opened it, the hinges creaking, and rummaged through the coats until he found her gray scarf, the one he'd given her last Christmas. It was tangled with a jacket, and as he pulled it free, something fell to the floor with a soft thud: a single leaf, dry and curled, the kind that littered the woods around Ravenswood.

He stared at it, his breath catching, and picked it up, the brittle edges crumbling between his fingers. It could've come from anywhere, he told himself. A walk, a breeze, anything. But the lie felt thin, and when he looked up, the mirror on the wall caught his reflection: a man with shadowed eyes and a crack running through the glass, splitting his face in two. He hadn't noticed that crack before, and the sight of it sent a chill down his spine.

"Daniel?" Ellie's voice drifted down from the stairs, soft and tentative. He shoved the leaf into his pocket, closing the closet door, and turned to face her.

"Coming," he called, his voice steady despite the tremor

in his hands. He climbed the stairs, the leaf burning a hole in his pocket, and wondered how much longer he could hold the mirror together before it shattered completely.

CHAPTER THIRTEEN

Daniel climbed the stairs, the leaf in his pocket a quiet weight against his thigh, its brittle edges pressing through the fabric. The hallway was dark, the single bulb overhead casting a faint glow that barely reached the corners. Ellie stood at the top, her silhouette framed by the bedroom doorway, her hair loose around her shoulders. She looked fragile in the dim light, her arms wrapped around herself, and for a moment he saw the woman he'd married, not the one unraveling before him.

"You okay?" he asked, pausing a few steps below her. His voice sounded too loud in the stillness, and he softened it. "You've been up here a while."

"I couldn't sleep," she said, her tone flat, almost hollow. "Just needed some quiet after... everything."

He nodded, climbing the last steps to join her. "Yeah. It's been a hell of a day." He reached out, brushing her arm, and she flinched slightly, a reflex she tried to cover with a small smile.

It didn't reach her eyes, and that stung more than he expected.

"Let's get some rest," he said, guiding her into the bedroom. The room smelled faintly of her lavender lotion, a scent that usually calmed him, but tonight it felt cloying, out of place. He kicked off his shoes, the thud of them hitting the floor too sharp, and climbed into bed beside her. She lay still, her back to him, and he listened to her breathing, waiting for it to deepen, to tell him she'd slipped away from the chaos in her head. It didn't come.

He stared at the ceiling, the shadows shifting with the wind outside, and tried to piece together Friday night again. Chicken, wine, the TV flickering with some show he couldn't name. It was there, solid in his mind, but the leaf, the scarf, Ellie's flashes, they gnawed at it, eroding the edges. He rolled onto his side, facing her, and whispered, "Ellie?"

She didn't move, but her voice came soft and low. "Yeah?"

"You're sure you don't remember anything else? About that night?"

She tensed, the mattress creaking faintly under her. "I told you what I saw. The leaves, her voice, someone else. That's all I've got."

He nodded, though she couldn't see it, and let the silence settle again. But it wasn't enough, not with the leaf burning a hole in his pocket, not with Noah's blank stare replaying in his head. He waited until her breathing finally slowed, a shallow rhythm that told him she'd drifted off, then slipped out of bed, careful not to wake her.

The hallway was colder now, the air biting at his bare feet as he padded to Noah's room. The door was cracked open, a sliver of lamplight spilling out, and he pushed it wider, peering in. Noah was asleep, sprawled across his bed, one arm flung over the edge, his textbook open on the floor. Daniel stepped inside, the cedar scent stronger here, and scanned the room. The wooden box was still under the desk, its lid shut tight, and he hesitated, his hand hovering over it. He shouldn't. Noah deserved his privacy. But the doubt won, and he lifted the lid.

Inside were coins, a few old pens, a keychain from a school trip, just junk like Noah had said. Daniel exhaled, a mix of relief and guilt washing over him, and started to close it when something caught his eye: a folded piece of paper, tucked into the corner. He pulled it out, unfolding it carefully, and froze. It was a receipt, dated Friday night, from the pub in the village. 9:47 p.m. A pint of lager and a glass of wine. His stomach dropped, the paper trembling in his hand. Noah didn't drink, not that he knew, and he'd said he was home, studying.

He shoved the receipt back, closing the box, and stood, his mind racing. Noah had lied. Or had he? Maybe it was old, misdated, but the ink was crisp, the paper uncreased. He left the room, shutting the door softly, and leaned against the wall, his breath shallow. If Noah was out Friday night, where was he? And where was Ellie?

Downstairs, he moved to the kitchen, needing water, needing something to steady him. The drawer with the scarf loomed in the corner of his vision, and he couldn't ignore it anymore. He opened it, pulling the red silk out, its weight heavier than it should have been. The stain was still there, dark and crusted, and he held it under the light, his surgeon's eyes narrowing. Blood, he was sure of it now, the way it clung to the fibers, the faint metallic tang he hadn't noticed before. But there was something else, a faint mark near the edge: a partial fingerprint, smudged but distinct.

His hands shook as he set it down, the leaf still in his pocket, the receipt burning in his memory. He thought of Ellie upstairs, her flinch, her hollow voice, and Noah, asleep with a lie hidden under his desk. The village outside was quiet, the night pressing against the windows, but inside, the cracks were spreading, staining everything he'd trusted.

He poured the water, drank it fast, and sat at the table, the scarf in front of him. He couldn't go to the police yet, not without knowing more, but he couldn't stay here, pretending it was fine. Tomorrow, he'd confront Noah, check Ellie's story again, find a way to stitch this back together. But as he sat there, the doubt grew, a dark stain he couldn't wash out, and he wondered if the hands that saved lives could hold his family together when the truth finally cut through.

CHAPTER FOURTEEN

Daniel woke to the sound of rain pattering against the bedroom window, a soft, relentless rhythm that matched the ache in his head. He'd barely slept, the scarf and the pub receipt haunting him through the night, their images flickering behind his eyes like a bad dream. Ellie lay beside him, her breathing deep and even now, her face smoothed out in sleep. He watched her for a moment, the curve of her cheek pale in the gray morning light, and wondered how much she was hiding, how much she even knew herself.

He slipped out of bed, the floor cold against his feet, and dressed quietly, pulling on a sweater and jeans. The house was still, the kind of quiet that felt heavy, expectant, and he moved downstairs, his steps careful on the creaky stairs. The kitchen greeted him with the faint smell of last night's coffee, the scarf still on the table where he'd left it. He stared at it, the red silk stark against the wood, and his stomach twisted. He needed answers, not just for Ellie, but for himself.

The clock on the wall read 6:32, early enough that Noah might still be asleep. Daniel poured a glass of water, the tap gurgling briefly, and drank it standing, his eyes drifting to the stairs. He couldn't wait any longer. The receipt, that damn timestamp, 9:47 p.m., it didn't fit with Noah's story, and the lie—if it was a lie—gnawed at him. He set the glass down and climbed back upstairs, his resolve hardening with every step.

Noah's door was closed this time, no light seeping out, and Daniel knocked once, a sharp rap that echoed in the hall. No answer. He turned the knob and pushed it open, the hinges creaking softly. Noah was in bed, the covers pulled up to his chin, but his eyes flicked open as Daniel stepped in, alert in a way that didn't match someone just waking.

"Dad?" Noah said, sitting up, his voice thick with sleep —or pretending to be. "What's wrong?"

"We need to talk," Daniel said, keeping his tone even, though his pulse thudded in his ears. He closed the door behind him, the room dim with the curtains drawn, the air thick with that cedar scent. "Now."

Noah rubbed his eyes, pushing his hair back, and swung his legs over the edge of the bed. "Okay. What's going on?"

Daniel pulled the receipt from his pocket, where he'd stashed it last night, and held it out. "This. Found it in your box. Friday night, 9:47, at the pub. You said you were home, studying. What's the truth, Noah?"

Noah's face didn't change, not at first. He took the receipt, glancing at it, then set it on the bed beside him. "It's old," he said, shrugging. "Must've got mixed up in there. I don't remember."

"Don't lie to me," Daniel said, his voice rising despite his effort to stay calm. "The ink's fresh, the paper's clean. You were out Friday night. Where?"

Noah looked up at him, his dark eyes steady, almost too steady. "I was here, Dad. Like I said. Maybe it's from another night, I don't know. Why's it matter?"

"It matters because your mom's losing her mind over this murder," Daniel snapped, stepping closer. "She thinks she was at Ravenswood, and now I've got a receipt saying you were out when you shouldn't have been. So tell me the truth, Noah. Were you there? Did you see something?"

Noah stood, his height matching Daniel's now, and the room felt smaller, the air tighter. "I wasn't at Ravenswood," he said, his voice low, firm. "I don't know what Mom's going through, but I wasn't there. I swear."

Daniel searched his son's face, looking for the crack, the tell he'd seen in patients who lied about their symptoms, but Noah didn't flinch. "Then explain the receipt," he said, his hands clenching at his sides. "Because it's not adding up."

"I can't," Noah said, his tone flat. "Maybe someone else used my stuff, I don't know. I was here."

Daniel wanted to believe him, wanted to see the boy he'd raised, not this cold, closed-off teenager staring back at him. But the doubt was a thread pulling loose, unraveling everything. "If I find out you're hiding something," he said, his voice dropping, "it's going to break us, Noah. All of us."

Noah didn't respond, just held his gaze, and Daniel turned away, leaving the room before he said something he couldn't take back. The hallway felt longer now, the walls pressing in, and he stopped at the top of the stairs, his breath ragged. He needed air, space, something to clear the fog in his head.

Back downstairs, he grabbed his coat from the rack and stepped outside, the rain a fine mist against his face. The village was waking up, lights flickering on in the cottages, a car rumbling past on its way to the main road. He walked toward the garage, needing to move, and opened the side door, the musty smell of oil and wood hitting him. His tools lined the walls, a sanctuary of order, but today it offered no peace.

He rummaged through a shelf, looking for nothing in particular, when his hand brushed something soft, tucked behind a box of nails. He pulled it out, frowning: a glove, black leather, worn at the fingertips. It wasn't his, didn't fit the rough work he did here, and as he turned it over, a dark stain caught the light, crusted into the leather. Blood, his surgeon's eye told him, unmistakable now after years of seeing it on his hands.

His chest tightened, the glove heavy in his grip, and he thought of Ellie's scarf, the leaf, Noah's receipt. This wasn't coincidence. He stuffed the glove into his pocket, the rain tapping harder against the roof, and stood there, the thread of his life unraveling faster now, pulling him toward a truth he wasn't sure he could face.

CHAPTER FIFTEEN

Daniel stood in the garage, the rain drumming a steady beat against the tin roof, the blood-stained glove a heavy weight in his pocket. The dim light from a single bulb overhead flickered, casting jagged shadows across the cluttered shelves, and the air smelled of damp wood and motor oil. He turned the glove over in his hands again, its leather cool and worn, the dark crust along the fingertips unmistakable. He'd seen blood too many times—on his scalpel, on his gloves, on the sterile drapes of an operating room—but this was different. This wasn't controlled, wasn't clean. This was chaos, and it was in his house.

He shoved the glove back into his pocket, his breath fogging in the chilly space, and stepped outside, locking the garage behind him. The rain had thickened, soaking his sweater as he crossed the drive, but he barely felt it. His mind churned, piecing together the fragments: Ellie's scarf, Noah's receipt, the leaf, and now this. Each one a cut, small and precise, slicing through the life he'd built. He needed to talk to

Ellie, to lay it all out and see what she knew, but the thought of her flinch last night, the doubt in her eyes, stopped him cold. What if she didn't have answers? What if she had too many?

Inside, the house was warmer, the heat humming through the vents, but it didn't touch the chill in his bones. He kicked off his wet shoes by the door, the thud echoing in the hall, and climbed the stairs, the glove pressing against his thigh with every step. Ellie was in the bedroom, sitting on the edge of the bed, her phone in her lap, her face pale against the gray light filtering through the curtains. She looked up as he entered, her eyes tired but sharp, and set the phone down.

"You're soaked," she said, her voice soft, almost tentative. "Where'd you go?"

"Garage," he said, peeling off his sweater and tossing it over a chair. "Needed to think." He hesitated, then sat beside her, the mattress dipping under his weight. "Ellie, we need to talk. Really talk."

She nodded, pulling her knees up, wrapping her arms around them. "I know. After last night, the police, I thought... maybe we'd get a break. But it's not stopping, is it?"

"No," he said, his throat tight. He reached into his pocket, pulling out the glove, and held it out to her. "Found this in the garage, behind some stuff. It's not mine. And that's blood."

Her eyes widened, and she took it, her fingers trembling as she turned it over. "Blood?" she whispered, her voice breaking. "Daniel, where did this come from?"

"I don't know," he said, watching her closely. "But it's not the first thing that doesn't fit. The scarf, the leaf in your coat, Noah's receipt from Friday night. It's piling up, Ellie, and I can't keep pretending it's nothing."

She set the glove down between them, her hands retreating to her lap. "Noah's receipt? What are you talking about?"

"He's got one from the pub, Friday, 9:47," Daniel said, his voice steady but edged with strain. "He said he was home, studying, but he lied. I asked him this morning, and he swore he wasn't at Ravenswood, but I don't know if I believe him."

Ellie's face tightened, her lips pressing into a thin line. "You think Noah's involved? Our son?"

"I don't know what to think," he said, standing, pacing to the window. The rain streaked the glass, blurring the village beyond, and he rubbed a hand over his face. "But you said you were there, with Lena. And now this glove, the scarf, it's all pointing somewhere, Ellie. Were you with him? Did he see you?"

"No," she said, her voice rising. "I don't remember Noah there. It was just her, Lena, and someone else, watching. I told you that. I'd know if Noah was there."

"Would you?" he snapped, turning to face her. "You can't even remember the whole night. How do you know what you saw?"

She flinched, harder this time, and stood, her hands clenched at her sides. "Don't do that, Daniel. Don't turn this on me. I'm trying to figure it out, same as you."

He took a breath, forcing his voice to soften. "I'm not turning it on you. I'm scared, Ellie. For you, for him, for us. This isn't just some random mess. Someone's leaving these things, and it's tearing us apart."

She sank back onto the bed, her shoulders slumping. "I know," she said, quieter now. "I feel it too. But I don't have the answers. I wish I did."

He sat beside her again, the glove a dark stain between them, and took her hand, her skin cold against his. "Then let's find them," he said. "Together. No more hiding stuff. You tell me everything you remember, and I'll do the same."

She nodded, squeezing his hand back, but her eyes drifted to the glove, and he saw the doubt flicker there again. "Okay," she said. "But what about Noah? If he's lying..."

"We'll talk to him," Daniel said, his resolve firming. "Tonight, when he's home. All three of us. No secrets."

She didn't respond, just stared at the glove, and the silence stretched, heavy and sharp. He wanted to pull her close, to stitch this back together, but the cuts were too deep now, and he wasn't sure his hands were steady enough anymore.

The doorbell rang, a sudden chime that made them both jump. Daniel stood, his heart thudding, and moved to the window, peering out. A police car sat in the drive, its lights off, rain beading on the hood. "It's Hollis," he said, his voice tight. "He's back."

Ellie's face paled, and she grabbed the glove, shoving it

under a pillow. "What does he want now?"

"I don't know," Daniel said, heading for the stairs. "But we're about to find out."

He descended, the rain louder now, a steady roar that matched the pulse in his ears, and opened the door to Hollis's stern face, the detective's coat dripping onto the mat. The unseen cut had widened, and Daniel felt the thread of his life slipping through his fingers, faster than he could grasp.

CHAPTER SIXTEEN

Daniel opened the door wider, the rain a steady roar behind Detective Hollis as the man stepped inside, his coat dripping onto the hardwood. The hall smelled of wet wool and tension, the air thick with the unspoken weight of why he was here. Hollis's face was grim, his jaw set, and his eyes flicked past Daniel to the stairs where Ellie stood, halfway down, her hand gripping the banister. She'd pulled a sweater over her shoulders, but it didn't hide the pallor of her skin or the way her gaze darted to Daniel, searching for something he couldn't give her.

"Evening," Hollis said, his voice low, steady, the kind of calm that carried an edge. "Mind if we sit? This won't take long."

"Sure," Daniel said, his throat tight. He gestured toward the living room, his wet socks leaving faint prints on the floor as he led the way. Ellie followed, her steps silent, and the three of them settled into an awkward triangle: Hollis in the armchair, Daniel and Ellie on the couch, the coffee table between them like a barrier. The photo from yesterday still lay there, its edges curling slightly, and Daniel resisted the urge to sweep it away.

Hollis pulled a notebook from his pocket, flipping it open with a practiced motion. "We've been looking into that key you brought in," he said, his eyes on Ellie. "Matches the lock on a side door at Ravenswood. Old, but functional. We're testing it for prints now."

Ellie nodded, her hands clasped tight in her lap. "Okay. That's good, right?"

"Depends," Hollis said, leaning forward slightly. "We also pulled some evidence from the scene. Blood, mostly. Matches Lena Moreau's type, but there's something else." He paused, his gaze shifting to Daniel, and the room seemed to shrink, the rain outside fading to a dull hum. "We found a partial print on a knife handle. Not hers. And it's a match to one we lifted from your kitchen yesterday."

Daniel's stomach dropped, a cold, sharp plunge that left him breathless. "My kitchen?" he said, his voice rougher than he meant. "You took prints from our house?"

"Standard procedure," Hollis said, his tone even. "You gave us the scarf, we checked the area. Knife block on the counter had your prints, Ellie's, and a third set. The third matches the knife at Ravenswood."

Ellie's hand flew to her mouth, a small, choked sound escaping, and Daniel felt the couch shift as she leaned away from him. "That's impossible," she said, her voice trembling. "I didn't... I told you, I didn't kill her."

"I'm not saying you did," Hollis said, raising a hand. "Prints don't mean you held the knife that night. Could've been moved, used before. But it ties your house to the scene, and that's a problem."

Daniel's mind raced, his surgeon's precision scrambling to stitch this together. The knife block in the kitchen, a sleek set he'd bought years ago, always there, unremarkable. He pictured it now, the handles worn from use, and tried to remember the last time he'd noticed one missing. "Wait," he said, leaning forward, his hands gripping his knees. "You're saying someone took a knife from our house and used it on her?"

"Possible," Hollis said, his eyes narrowing slightly. "Or it was already there, and someone brought it back. We're still piecing it together. Where's your son tonight?"

"Noah?" Daniel's voice sharpened, the name a jolt through him. "He's at school, study group. Why?"

Hollis scribbled something in his notebook, then looked up. "We need to talk to him too. Those prints, the third set, they're smaller. Could be a teenager's. We'll need his to rule him out."

Ellie's breath hitched, and she grabbed Daniel's arm, her fingers digging in. "No. Not Noah. He's got nothing to do with this."

"We don't know that," Hollis said, his tone firm but not unkind. "We're not accusing him, just covering bases. You said you were there, Ellie, and now we've got a link from your home. We can't ignore it."

Daniel felt her grip tighten, her nails pressing through his sleeve, and he turned to her, his heart pounding. "Ellie, tell him. Noah was here, right? Friday night, with us?"

She hesitated, her eyes wide, searching his face, and that pause cut deeper than anything Hollis had said. "I don't know," she whispered, her voice breaking. "I can't remember, Daniel. I thought he was, but..."

"But what?" he pressed, pulling his arm free, his voice rising. "You're saying he might've been out there too?"

"I don't know!" she shouted, standing, her hands trembling. "I'm trying, okay? I don't know what's real anymore!"

Hollis stood too, pocketing his notebook. "Let's keep this calm," he said, his voice cutting through the room. "We'll need Noah's prints, voluntary for now. And that scarf, if you've still got it. I'll be back tomorrow. Sit tight, and don't go anywhere."

He left, the door clicking shut behind him, and Daniel sat there, the rain filling the silence Hollis left behind. Ellie sank back onto the couch, her face in her hands, and he stared at her, the blade of doubt turning sharper now. The knife, Noah's prints, her blank memory—it was all slicing through him, and he couldn't stop the bleed.

"You need to tell me," he said, his voice low, steady despite the storm inside. "Everything. Right now. No more gaps."

She looked up, tears streaking her face, and nodded.

"Okay. But you won't like it."

He braced himself, the surgeon's hands steadying for the cut, but nothing could prepare him for the wound she was about to open.

CHAPTER SEVENTEEN

D aniel sat on the couch, the living room shadowed by the rain-streaked windows, the air thick with the echo of Hollis's departure. Ellie was beside him, her hands twisted together in her lap, tears drying into faint tracks on her cheeks. The silence stretched, heavy and taut, until he couldn't stand it anymore. He leaned forward, resting his elbows on his knees, and fixed his eyes on her. "Ellie," he said, his voice low but firm. "You said I won't like it. Tell me anyway. All of it."

She took a shaky breath, her gaze dropping to the floor, and for a moment he thought she'd pull back, retreat into that hollow space she'd been living in. But she nodded, a small, jerky motion, and started talking, her words slow at first, like she was pulling them from somewhere deep and buried.

"I've been trying to piece it together," she said, her voice trembling but steadying as she went. "Friday night, I thought we were here, like you said. Dinner, TV, normal. But it's not there, Daniel. Not all of it. I keep seeing flashes, and they're not just dreams. They're real."

He stayed quiet, his hands clenching slightly, letting her find her way. The rain tapped against the glass, a soft counterpoint to the storm building inside him.

"I remember leaving," she said, her eyes flicking up to meet his, wide and haunted. "Late, after you went to bed. I don't know why, not exactly, but I had this feeling, this pull, like I had to go somewhere. I took the car, drove out toward Ravenswood. I didn't plan it, I just... went."

Daniel's chest tightened, his breath catching. "You left? After I was asleep?"

She nodded, swallowing hard. "I think so. It's blurry, but I see the road, the trees, the estate looming up in the dark. I parked, got out, and then I saw her. Lena. She was there, outside, near that side door. She looked scared, Daniel, like she was waiting for someone. She saw me, and she said, 'You don't understand.' Then it's all pieces—leaves crunching, her voice rising, and this shadow, someone else, moving behind her."

He leaned back, his mind racing, trying to stitch this into what he knew. "A shadow? You mean the someone else you keep talking about?"

"Yes," she said, her hands trembling now. "I didn't see their face, just a shape, tall, moving fast. Then she screamed, and I... I don't know what happened next. It's black, like I shut down. The next thing I remember is waking up here, Saturday morning, thinking it was a nightmare. But the scarf, the key, the glove, it's all real."

Daniel's throat burned, his surgeon's hands itching to fix something, anything, but this was a wound he couldn't touch. "You're saying you saw her die," he said, his voice rough. "And you don't know if you... if you did something?"

"No," she said quickly, her eyes locking onto his. "I didn't kill her, Daniel. I couldn't. But I was there, and I didn't stop it. I don't know why I went, or how I got back, but I was there."

He stood, pacing to the window, the rain blurring the world outside into a gray smear. His mind spun, replaying her words, the image of her driving out alone, standing in the dark with Lena Moreau. "Why didn't you tell me?" he asked, turning back to her. "Saturday, when you woke up, why didn't you say something?"

"I didn't know it was real," she said, standing too, her voice rising. "I thought it was stress, a breakdown, something my mind cooked up. I deal with killers, Daniel, I know how they think, and I couldn't believe I'd be part of that. But then the scarf showed up, the texts, and I couldn't deny it anymore."

He stared at her, the woman he'd loved for two decades, and saw a stranger in her place, someone with secrets he couldn't fathom. "And Noah?" he asked, his voice dropping. "Hollis said those prints could be his. You think he was there too?"

Her face crumpled, and she shook her head, tears spilling again. "I don't know. I didn't see him, I swear. But that receipt... if he was out, if he followed me, or... God, Daniel, what if he saw me there?"

The room tilted, and Daniel gripped the windowsill, the cold glass grounding him. Noah, his son, out in the night, maybe at the pub, maybe at Ravenswood. The glove in the garage, the knife from their kitchen, it was all weaving together, a thread he couldn't untangle. "We need to ask him," he said, his voice steady despite the chaos inside. "When he gets home, we sit him down. No more lies."

Ellie nodded, wiping her face with her sleeve, but her eyes were distant, lost in the memory she'd just carved open. "What if he doesn't know?" she whispered. "What if he's innocent, and I've pulled him into this?"

"Then we'll deal with it," Daniel said, crossing back to her, his hands on her shoulders. "But we can't keep guessing. Hollis is coming back tomorrow, and if those prints are Noah's, we need to know before he does."

She leaned into him, her forehead against his chest, and he held her, the rain a steady drum outside. But as he stood there, the glove in his pocket, the receipt in Noah's room, and Ellie's confession ringing in his ears, he felt the wound open wider, a cut he couldn't close. The blade had turned, and it was slicing through everything he'd thought was true.

The sound of the front door opening jolted them apart, and Noah's voice called out, "I'm home." Daniel met Ellie's gaze, her eyes wide with fear, and he knew the next cut was coming, whether they were ready or not.

CHAPTER EIGHTEEN

Daniel pulled away from Ellie as Noah's voice echoed through the hall, "I'm home," the words casual, oblivious to the storm waiting for him. The rain had softened to a drizzle outside, but inside, the air crackled with tension, thick and unyielding. Ellie's eyes met his, wide and wet with fear, and he gave her a small nod, a silent promise to hold it together. His hands felt unsteady, the surgeon's calm slipping, but he clenched them into fists and stepped toward the kitchen, where Noah's footsteps thudded against the tile.

"Hey," Noah said, glancing up as Daniel and Ellie entered. He stood by the counter, peeling off his damp jacket, his school bag slung over one shoulder. His dark hair was slick with rain, falling into his eyes, and he brushed it back with a quick, careless motion. "You guys look weird. What's up?"

"Sit down," Daniel said, his voice low, steady, though his pulse hammered in his ears. He pulled out a chair at the table, the scrape of it loud in the quiet, and gestured for Noah to take it. Ellie hovered behind him, her arms crossed tight, her breathing shallow.

Noah frowned, dropping his bag by the fridge, and sat, his lanky frame slouching slightly. "Okay. What's this about?"

Daniel sat across from him, Ellie sinking into the chair beside him, and he pulled the receipt from his pocket, sliding it across the table. "This," he said, tapping it with his finger. "Friday night, 9:47, the pub. You said you were here, studying. You lied, Noah. Why?"

Noah's eyes flicked to the receipt, then back to Daniel, his expression blank for a moment too long. "I told you," he said, his voice even. "It's old. Must've got mixed up in my stuff."

"Don't," Daniel said, leaning forward, his hands flat on the table. "Don't do that. The ink's fresh, the paper's clean. You were out that night, and we need to know where."

Noah's jaw tightened, a small, almost imperceptible shift, and he glanced at Ellie, then back to Daniel. "What's this really about? Mom's thing with the murder?"

Ellie's breath caught, and she leaned in, her voice trembling but firm. "Noah, the police found a knife at Ravenswood, with prints from our house. They think it could be yours. Were you there? Did you see me?"

Noah's eyes widened slightly, the first crack in his calm, but he recovered fast, leaning back in his chair. "Ravenswood? No way. I wasn't there. Why would I be?"

"Because I was," Ellie said, her words spilling out, raw and desperate. "Friday night, I went out, to Ravenswood. I saw Lena, and someone killed her. I don't remember everything, but I was there, Noah. And if you were too..."

"Hold on," Noah said, sitting up straighter, his voice rising. "You think I was there? Killing someone? That's crazy, Mom."

"Then explain the receipt," Daniel cut in, his tone sharp now. "Explain why you're lying about where you were. Because the police are coming tomorrow, and if those prints are yours, we're out of time."

Noah's gaze darted between them, his hands gripping the edge of the table, and for a moment, Daniel thought he'd break, spill whatever he was holding back. But then he leaned back, crossing his arms, his face settling into that cold, unreadable mask Daniel had seen too often lately. "I went to the pub," he said, his voice flat. "Met a friend, had a drink. That's it. I wasn't at Ravenswood, and I didn't see you, Mom."

"Who?" Daniel pressed, his hands clenching again. "What friend?"

"Just a guy from school," Noah said, shrugging. "Doesn't matter. I was back by eleven, you were asleep. That's the truth."

Ellie shook her head, tears welling up again. "Noah, please. If you know something, anything, tell us. We're trying to protect you."

"Protect me?" Noah said, a bitter edge creeping into his voice. "You're the one freaking out over some scarf and a key. I'm fine. I didn't do anything."

Daniel stared at him, searching for the lie, the tell he'd missed all these years. Noah's eyes were steady, too steady, and the cold beneath them chilled him more than the rain ever could. "The glove," he said, pulling it from his pocket and setting it on the table. "Found this in the garage. Blood on it. Yours?"

Noah's gaze dropped to the glove, and this time the crack was bigger, a flicker of something—fear, maybe—crossing his face before he smoothed it away. "No," he said, his voice quieter now. "Not mine. I don't know where it came from."

"Then whose?" Daniel asked, leaning closer, his voice dropping to a near whisper. "Because it's here, Noah, in our house, with blood on it. Same as the scarf, same as the knife. Tell me something that makes sense."

Noah stood, the chair scraping back, and grabbed his bag. "I don't know," he said, his tone sharp, final. "I'm done with this. I didn't do anything, and you're both losing it." He turned and headed for the stairs, his footsteps heavy, leaving the glove and receipt on the table like accusations.

Ellie reached for Daniel's hand, her fingers cold against his. "He's lying," she whispered, her voice breaking. "He knows something."

Daniel nodded, his eyes still on the stairs where Noah had disappeared. "Yeah," he said, his throat tight. "But what?" He pulled the glove back into his pocket, the weight of it heavier now, and stood, moving to the window. The village lights glowed faintly through the drizzle, a world that felt miles away from this kitchen, this family tearing itself apart.

He thought of Hollis coming tomorrow, the prints, the

knife, and Noah's cold, steady gaze. The wound was open, bleeding out, and beneath it all, he felt the chill of something deeper, something his son wasn't saying. The blade had turned, and now it was cutting through the last threads of trust he had left.

CHAPTER NINETEEN

Daniel stood at the kitchen window, the drizzle outside blurring the village lights into soft, watery smudges. The house was silent again, Noah's footsteps long faded upstairs, but the tension lingered, a tight coil in his chest that wouldn't unwind. Ellie sat at the table behind him, her hands wrapped around a mug of tea she hadn't touched, the steam curling up in thin wisps. The glove and receipt lay between them, silent witnesses to the fracture splitting their family, and Daniel felt the weight of Hollis's return tomorrow pressing down like a stone.

"He's hiding something," Ellie said, her voice low, barely above a whisper. "I saw it in his eyes, Daniel. He knows more than he's saying."

Daniel turned, leaning against the counter, his arms crossed. "I know," he said, his throat tight. "But he's not going to tell us, not tonight. He's shut us out."

She nodded, her gaze dropping to the table, and he saw

the exhaustion in her, the way her shoulders slumped under the sweater. "What do we do?" she asked, looking up at him, her eyes pleading for a plan, for the steady hand he'd always been.

He took a breath, his mind racing, and made a decision he hadn't voiced until now. "I'm going to look," he said, his voice firm despite the tremor in his hands. "His room. If he's got something, it's there."

Ellie's eyes widened, a flicker of fear crossing her face. "Daniel, that's... he'll hate us for it."

"He already does," he said, sharper than he meant, then softened his tone. "He's lying, Ellie. The receipt, the glove, the knife prints, it's too much. I need to know what he's keeping from us before Hollis does."

She didn't argue, just nodded again, and he felt a pang of guilt for dragging her into this, for making her complicit. But he couldn't stop now. He pushed off the counter and climbed the stairs, the wood creaking under his weight, each step heavier than the last. Noah's door was closed, no light seeping out, and he hesitated, his hand on the knob, listening. The faint sound of breathing came through, steady and deep, and he turned it slowly, easing the door open.

The room was dark, the curtains drawn tight, and the cedar scent hit him again, mixed with the faint musk of teenage clutter. Noah lay on his bed, one arm flung across his chest, his face slack in sleep. Daniel stepped inside, closing the door halfway behind him, and moved to the desk, his socks silent on the carpet. The wooden box was still there, tucked under the edge, and he lifted the lid, his heart thudding in his ears. The coins and pens stared back at him, the receipt gone —Noah must have taken it—but nothing new jumped out. He closed it, his hands shaking slightly, and scanned the room.

The bookshelf caught his eye, a narrow unit against the wall, its shelves sagging under textbooks and old comics. He ran his fingers along the edges, feeling for anything out of place, and paused at a thick calculus book near the bottom. It was angled wrong, jutting out just enough to notice, and he pulled it free, the weight heavier than it should have been. He opened it, flipping past equations, and found a hollowed-out section, a crude pocket carved into the pages. Inside was a small notebook, black and worn, its cover unmarked.

Daniel's breath caught, and he glanced at Noah, still asleep, before flipping it open. The pages were filled with tight, neat handwriting, dates and notes in Noah's precise script. He scanned the first few, his pulse racing: *March 2—Met J at pub, 8 p.m. Said she's close to figuring it out. March 4—Saw her again, woods near R.E. Too risky.* Then, Friday's entry, March 6: *9:47 pub, then followed her. She met someone. Argument. Knife out. Messy. Back by 11.*

His stomach lurched, the words blurring on the page, and he flipped forward, finding a later note: *March 8—Mom's asking questions. Scarf was a mistake. Need to clean up.* Daniel's hands trembled, the notebook slipping slightly, and he forced himself to keep reading, each line a cut deeper into his chest. The last entry, from yesterday: *They're onto me. Glove's gone. Have to stay calm.*

He closed the notebook, his breath shallow, and tucked it back into the book, sliding it onto the shelf with unsteady hands. Noah hadn't moved, his chest rising and falling, but the room felt colder now, the air sharp with what Daniel had found. He stepped back, his mind spinning, and left the room, closing the door behind him, the click loud in the silence.

Downstairs, Ellie looked up as he entered the kitchen, her eyes searching his face. "What?" she asked, standing, her voice tight. "Did you find something?"

He nodded, sinking into a chair, his hands flat on the table to stop the shaking. "A notebook," he said, his voice hoarse. "In his calculus book. He was out Friday night, followed Lena to Ravenswood. Saw her argue with someone, saw the knife. He's been covering it up, Ellie. The scarf, the glove, he knows."

Her face drained of color, and she sat hard, her hands gripping the mug. "He saw it?" she whispered. "He was there?"

"Yeah," Daniel said, his throat burning. "And he's not telling us. He's playing it cool, but he's scared. He wrote that we're onto him."

Ellie's eyes filled with tears, and she shook her head, her voice breaking. "Why wouldn't he tell us? If he saw who did it, why hide it?"

"I don't know," Daniel said, leaning forward, his hands clenching again. "But he's not just a witness, Ellie. The glove, the prints, he's in this deeper than he's letting on. We need to get him to talk, now, before Hollis comes back."

She nodded, wiping her face, but the fear in her eyes mirrored his own. The hidden edge had sliced through, and the cold beneath Noah's calm was a truth Daniel couldn't unsee, a wound he couldn't stitch shut.

CHAPTER TWENTY

Daniel sat at the kitchen table, the notebook's words burning behind his eyes, each line a scar etched into his mind. The rain had stopped, leaving the night outside still and heavy, the village lights faint through the fogged window. Ellie was beside him, her untouched tea cold now, her hands trembling as she stared at the glove he'd set back on the table. The receipt lay beside it, crumpled from his grip, and the air between them felt like a held breath, waiting to shatter.

"We can't wait," he said, his voice low, rough with the strain of holding it together. "Hollis will be here tomorrow, and if those prints are Noah's, we're done. We need him to tell us everything, now."

Ellie nodded, her eyes red-rimmed but sharp with a desperate resolve. "I know," she said, her voice barely above a whisper. "But what if he won't? What if he just keeps lying?"

"Then we make him," Daniel said, standing, his chair

scraping against the tile. His hands clenched at his sides, the surgeon's steadiness gone, replaced by a raw, unsteady need to cut through the fog of secrets choking his family. "He's our son, Ellie, but he's in this, and we can't protect him if we don't know what he's done."

She stood too, her sweater slipping off one shoulder, and followed him to the stairs. The house creaked around them, the old wood groaning under their weight as they climbed, the silence heavier with every step. Noah's door was still closed, no sound leaking out, and Daniel didn't knock this time. He pushed it open, the hinges squeaking faintly, and stepped inside, Ellie close behind.

Noah was awake, sitting on his bed, his back against the headboard, a book open in his lap. The lamp cast a soft glow over his face, his dark eyes flicking up to meet theirs, steady and unreadable. "What now?" he said, his voice flat, almost bored, and Daniel felt a surge of anger flare in his chest.

"We found your notebook," Daniel said, stepping closer, his hands in his pockets to hide the trembling. "Hidden in your calculus book. Friday night, you followed Lena to Ravenswood, saw her argue, saw the knife. You wrote it down, Noah. Stop lying."

Noah's face didn't change, but his fingers tightened on the book, the pages crinkling slightly. "You went through my stuff?" he said, his tone cold, a quiet edge beneath it. "That's messed up, Dad."

"What's messed up is you keeping this from us," Daniel snapped, his voice rising. "The police have a knife with prints from our house, maybe yours. They're coming tomorrow, and if you don't tell us the truth, they'll take you apart. What happened out there?"

Noah set the book down, slow and deliberate, and stood, his height matching Daniel's now, his presence filling the room. "I told you," he said, his voice steady, too steady. "I went to the pub, met a friend, came home. That's it."

"And the notebook?" Ellie cut in, stepping forward, her voice shaking but fierce. "You wrote about following her, Noah. You saw her die. Why won't you tell us?"

Noah's gaze shifted to her, and for a moment, something flickered in his eyes—anger, maybe, or fear—before it vanished, smoothed over by that icy calm. "It's just stuff I made up," he said, shrugging. "Notes, ideas. I write things down sometimes, doesn't mean they're real."

"Bullshit," Daniel said, his hands pulling free, clenching again. "The scarf, the glove, the receipt, it's all real, Noah. You were there, and you're covering it up. Who was it? Who killed her?"

Noah's jaw tightened, and he took a step back, his back hitting the wall. "I wasn't there," he said, his voice dropping, a hard edge cutting through. "You're both freaking out over nothing. I don't know anything."

Ellie moved closer, reaching for him, her hand trembling. "Noah, please," she said, tears spilling now. "If you saw something, if you're scared, we can help you. But you have to tell us."

He pulled away, his arm brushing hers aside, and the rejection hit her like a slap, her face crumpling. "I don't need help," he said, his tone cold, final. "I didn't see anything, I didn't do anything. Leave me alone."

Daniel's anger broke, a flood he couldn't hold back, and he grabbed Noah's arm, his grip tight. "You're not walking away from this," he said, his voice a growl. "A woman's dead, and you're tied to it. Tell me the truth, or I swear I'll drag you to Hollis myself."

Noah yanked free, his eyes flashing, and for the first time, Daniel saw something raw beneath the calm, a crack wide enough to glimpse the cold beneath. "You'd turn me in?" Noah said, his voice low, bitter. "Your own son? Nice, Dad."

"If you're lying, yeah," Daniel said, his chest heaving. "Because I can't let this destroy us. Tell me who was there."

Noah stared at him, the room silent except for Ellie's quiet sobs, and then he turned away, grabbing his jacket from the chair. "I'm done," he said, his voice flat again. "I'm going to bed. Wake me when the cops get here."

He brushed past them, heading for the door, but Daniel caught the faint tremble in his hand, the way his shoulders tensed. Noah paused at the threshold, glancing back, and said, "You should've trusted me." Then he was gone, his footsteps fading down the hall to the guest room, the door slamming shut behind him.

Ellie sank onto the bed, her face in her hands, and Daniel stood there, his breath ragged, the notebook's words looping in his head: *Knife out. Messy. Back by 11.* He moved to the desk, pulling the calculus book free again, and opened it to the hollowed-out section. The notebook was still there, but something else caught his eye—a small, folded piece of cloth, tucked into the corner. He pulled it out, unfolding it, and his stomach dropped. A strip of red silk, identical to the scarf, stained with the same dark crust.

He turned to Ellie, holding it up, his voice barely a whisper. "He kept this. A piece of it. Why?"

She looked up, her eyes wide with horror, and shook her head, no words left. The breaking point had come, and the cold beneath Noah's lies was a blade Daniel couldn't pull out, cutting deeper than he'd ever imagined.

PART 3: NOAH CARTER

CHAPTER TWENTY-ONE

Noah lay on the guest room bed, the mattress stiff beneath him, the faint smell of dust and old linen filling his nose. The house was silent now, the kind of quiet that pressed against his ears, heavy with the fight that had just torn through the kitchen and his room. He stared at the ceiling, the dim glow of a streetlight seeping through the blinds, casting thin stripes across the plaster. His parents thought they'd cornered him, thought they could crack him open with their questions and that damn notebook, but he wasn't going to break. Not yet.

He rolled onto his side, his hand brushing the edge of his jacket, still damp from the drizzle he'd walked through coming home. The confrontation replayed in his head, his dad's grip on his arm, his mom's tears, the way they'd looked at him like he was a stranger. He'd seen it coming, the moment they found the receipt, but the notebook, that was sloppy. He should've burned it, should've kept it somewhere they'd never look, but he hadn't, and now they knew more than he wanted. Not everything, though. Not the part that mattered.

Friday night flickered in his memory, sharp and jagged, like a film he could pause and rewind. He'd told them the pub story, the friend, the drink, and it was half-true, enough to hold them off. But the rest, the part he'd written down, that was real too. He'd followed her, Lena Moreau, out to Ravenswood, not because he'd planned it, but because he had to know. She'd been digging, asking questions, getting too close to something he'd buried deep, and he couldn't let her keep going.

He sat up, running a hand through his hair, the strands still wet against his fingers. The guest room was sparse, just a bed, a nightstand, a lamp with a cracked shade, but it felt safer than his own room now, less exposed. He'd grabbed his jacket and stormed out after they'd thrown the glove at him, his dad's voice ringing in his ears: *Tell me the truth, or I'll drag you to Hollis myself.* The threat had landed, harder than he'd expected, but he'd kept his face still, his voice cold, the way he'd learned to play it.

The notebook had been a mistake, but it wasn't a confession, not really. He wrote things down to think, to sort out the mess in his head, not to get caught. *9:47 pub, then followed her. She met someone. Argument. Knife out. Messy.* That was the truth, or most of it. He'd watched from the trees, the shadows thick around Ravenswood, the old estate looming like a ghost in the dark. Lena had been there, her voice sharp, panicked, arguing with someone he couldn't see, not clearly.

Then the knife flashed, quick and brutal, and she'd gone down, a crumpled shape in the leaves.

He hadn't stayed long, hadn't wanted to, but he'd seen enough. The scarf was an accident, snagged on a branch as he'd slipped away, and he'd torn off a piece later, keeping it like a reminder, a stupid move he couldn't explain even to himself. The glove, though, that wasn't his. He'd found it in the garage days ago, tucked behind some junk, and left it there, figuring it was his dad's. But now, with the police sniffing around, it was another thread they could pull.

Noah stood, pacing the small room, his socks silent on the worn rug. His parents were downstairs, probably plotting, deciding whether to turn him in or cover for him. He didn't trust them anymore, not after tonight, not with the way his dad had looked at him, like he was a problem to solve, not a son. His mom was worse, all tears and guilt, like she thought she'd failed him. Maybe she had, but not the way she thought.

He stopped by the window, peering through the blinds. The village was asleep, the street empty except for a stray cat slinking under a car. Tomorrow, Hollis would come, asking for prints, digging deeper, and Noah knew he couldn't run. Not yet. He had to play it quiet, keep the game going, let them think they had him figured out until he could decide what to do. The knife prints, that was the wildcard. If they were his, he'd have to explain it, twist it somehow, but he wasn't sure they were. He hadn't touched a knife that night, hadn't gotten close enough.

His phone buzzed in his pocket, a low hum that made

him flinch. He pulled it out, the screen glowing in the dark: a text from an unknown number. *You can't hide it forever. They'll find out.* His stomach twisted, the same cold knot he'd felt when the first messages came, the ones his mom had gotten too. Someone knew, someone who'd been there, and they were tightening the noose.

He deleted the text, his thumb steady despite the shake in his chest, and slipped the phone back into his pocket. He didn't know who it was, not yet, but he'd find out. He'd watched Lena die, seen the shadow move, and he'd kept it locked inside, a secret he'd planned to bury. But now, with his parents closing in and the police at the door, the quiet game was getting harder to play, and the cold beneath his calm was starting to crack.

CHAPTER TWENTY-TWO

Noah woke to the gray light of dawn creeping through the guest room blinds, the air cool and still against his skin. He hadn't slept much, maybe an hour or two, his mind looping through Friday night, the notebook, and that text: You can't hide it forever. They'll find out. The words sat heavy in his chest, a weight he couldn't shake, and he lay there, staring at the ceiling, the stripes of light shifting as the morning stirred outside. The house was quiet, his parents probably downstairs, plotting their next move, and he knew he'd have to face them soon, Hollis too, with his questions and that damn knife.

He rolled out of bed, his bare feet hitting the rug, and pulled on his jeans, the denim cold from the night air. The guest room felt like a cage now, too small to hold the thoughts spinning in his head, and he grabbed his jacket, slipping it over his hoodie. He needed to move, to think, to figure out how to keep the pieces from falling apart. His phone stayed in his pocket, silent since the text, but he could feel its presence, a ticking clock he couldn't stop.

The stairs creaked under his weight as he descended, slow and quiet, listening for his parents. The kitchen was empty, the table cleared of the glove and receipt, but the tension lingered, a faint hum in the air. He saw a note taped to the fridge in his mom's neat handwriting: *Gone to see Julia. Back soon. Please stay home.* He snorted softly, crumpling it in his hand and tossing it into the bin. Stay home. Like that was an option with the police coming and his secrets spilling out.

He stepped outside, the morning air sharp with the scent of wet grass and woodsmoke, the village waking up in slow, sleepy blinks. The drizzle had left puddles on the pavement, reflecting the overcast sky, and he shoved his hands into his pockets, heading toward the edge of town. He didn't have a plan, not really, just a need to breathe, to get away from the house and the weight of his parents' eyes. Ravenswood loomed in his mind, the memory of that night sharper now, cutting through the fog he'd tried to wrap it in.

He'd followed Lena because she'd been asking about him, not directly, but through whispers he'd caught at school, at the pub. She'd moved to the village a few months ago, quiet at first, but then she'd started talking, digging into things she shouldn't have. He didn't know how she'd found it, the thing he'd buried two years ago, but she had, and she'd been close to pulling it free. That night, he'd seen her at the pub, her dark hair catching the light as she leaned over the bar, her voice low, urgent, talking to someone he couldn't place. He'd waited outside, then followed her car, the taillights red blurs in the dark, until she'd stopped at Ravenswood.

He'd stayed back, hidden in the trees, the leaves damp under his shoes, watching as she paced near the side door, her phone pressed to her ear. Then the shadow came, tall and quick, and the argument flared fast, words he couldn't catch, just the tone—angry, scared. The knife had been a flash, a glint in the moonlight, and she'd fallen, her scream cut short. He hadn't moved, hadn't breathed, just watched, the weight of it pinning him there until the shadow slipped away, leaving her still in the dirt.

Noah stopped walking, his breath fogging in the cold, and realized he'd reached the forest's edge, the trees dark and tangled ahead. Ravenswood was out there, a mile or so, and he felt its pull, a sick tug in his gut. He hadn't gone back since, hadn't wanted to, but now, with the police closing in, he wondered if he'd missed something, a clue to who that shadow was.

A voice broke the silence behind him. "Early for a walk, isn't it?" He turned, his heart jumping, and saw Tom Bennett from the hardware store, his coat collar up, a cigarette glowing between his fingers. The man's face was weathered, his eyes sharp despite the early hour, and Noah forced his own to stay steady.

"Yeah," Noah said, shrugging. "Couldn't sleep. Too much going on."

Tom nodded, taking a drag, the smoke curling up into the gray sky. "Heard about your mom and that murder. Police been around, huh?"

"They're asking questions," Noah said, keeping his voice casual, though his pulse thudded in his ears. "Nothing big."

Tom's eyes narrowed slightly, studying him. "Small town, big mess. That Lena girl, she was trouble, you know? Always poking where she shouldn't."

Noah's stomach tightened, but he kept his face blank. "Didn't know her," he said, shoving his hands deeper into his pockets. "Just heard the talk."

"Right," Tom said, flicking ash onto the ground. "Well, watch yourself, kid. Cops don't let go once they start digging." He turned, walking off toward the square, and Noah watched him go, the weight of watching settling heavier now.

He stood there, the forest whispering behind him, and pulled out his phone, checking it again. No new texts, but the quiet felt wrong, like a pause before something worse. He'd seen the shadow, hadn't stopped it, and now it was coming for him, one way or another. The game wasn't quiet anymore, and the cold beneath his calm was cracking wider, letting the truth bleed through.

CHAPTER TWENTY-THREE

Noah lingered at the forest's edge, the damp air clinging to his skin, the trees ahead whispering with the faint rustle of leaves stirred by a morning breeze. Tom Bennett's figure had disappeared into the village square, his warning echoing in Noah's ears: Cops don't let go once they start digging. The words felt like a thread tightening around his chest, pulling harder with every step he took back toward the house. He didn't want to go, didn't want to face his parents' eyes or the questions he couldn't answer, but staying out here, so close to Ravenswood, was worse.

He turned, his sneakers scuffing against the wet pavement, and started home, his hands shoved deep into his jacket pockets. The village was waking up now, curtains twitching in cottage windows, a delivery van rumbling down the lane. He kept his head down, avoiding the occasional glance from a neighbor shoveling their walk or a dog walker tugging a leash. They didn't know, not yet, but he felt their stares anyway, like they could see the weight he carried, the shadow he'd watched slip away that night.

The house came into view, its stone walls pale in the gray light, and he slowed, his stomach knotting at the sight of his mom's car still gone. Good. He needed space, time to think before Hollis showed up with his notebook and that steady, cutting gaze. He let himself in, the door clicking shut behind him, and stood in the hall, listening. The quiet was different now, sharper, like the house itself was holding its breath, waiting for him to slip.

He climbed the stairs to his room, the guest bed left unmade, and shut the door behind him, leaning against it. His desk loomed in the corner, the calculus book still on the shelf where his dad had found it, the notebook inside a trap he couldn't unmake. He crossed to it, pulling the book free, and flipped it open, the hollowed-out section staring back at him. The notebook was there, the strip of red silk beside it, its stain dark and accusing. He picked it up, running his thumb over the crust, and felt a shiver crawl up his spine. He should've gotten rid of it, burned it with the rest, but he hadn't, and now it was another thread they could pull.

The memory of Friday night sharpened again, unbidden, the way it did when he let his guard down. Lena's voice, high and frantic, cutting through the dark: *You don't know what you're doing.* The shadow's quick, fluid motion, the knife glinting once before it struck. He'd stayed still, hidden in the trees, his breath fogging in the cold, watching as she fell, her body crumpling into the leaves. He hadn't moved, hadn't screamed, just watched, the weight of it settling into him like a stone he couldn't shift.

A knock on the door jolted him, the silk slipping from his fingers back into the book. He slammed it shut, shoving it onto the shelf, and turned as the door creaked open. His dad stood there, his face drawn, his eyes shadowed with something heavier than exhaustion. "Noah," he said, his voice low, careful. "We need to talk."

"I said I'm done talking," Noah said, crossing his arms, his tone flat but firm. "You've got your answers."

"No, we don't," his dad said, stepping inside, closing the door behind him. The room felt smaller now, the air tighter, and Noah's pulse quickened, though he kept his face still. "Your mom's with Julia, trying to figure this out, but I'm here, and I'm not letting this go. That notebook, the silk, it's not just ideas, Noah. You were there, and you saw something. Tell me who."

Noah's jaw tightened, and he looked away, his eyes landing on the window, the gray sky beyond. "I told you," he said, his voice steady despite the knot in his chest. "I went to the pub, came home. The rest is just stuff I wrote."

His dad moved closer, his hands clenching at his sides. "Stop it," he said, his voice rising, sharp with frustration. "The police have a knife with prints, maybe yours. They're coming today, and if you don't tell me the truth, I can't help you. Who was it, Noah? Who killed her?"

Noah met his gaze, holding it, the cold he'd cultivated locking into place. "I don't know," he said, each word deliberate. "I wasn't there. You're seeing what you want to see."

His dad's face flushed, and he stepped forward, close enough that Noah could smell the coffee on his breath. "I'm seeing a son who's lying to me," he said, his voice dropping, a growl of anger and fear. "That silk, the glove, you're tied to this, and I'm not letting you throw your life away over it. Tell me, or I'll take it all to Hollis right now."

Noah's hands twitched, the thread tightening, but he kept his voice calm, his eyes steady. "Go ahead," he said, shrugging. "They won't find anything that sticks. I didn't do it."

His dad stared at him, searching, and Noah held the look, the quiet game stretching thin between them. Then his dad turned, his shoulders slumping, and pulled the door open. "You're making a mistake," he said, his voice quiet now, heavy with something Noah couldn't name. "I hope you know what you're doing."

The door clicked shut, and Noah let out a breath he hadn't realized he'd been holding, his hands unclenching. He moved to the window, peering out, and saw his dad's car pull out of the drive, heading toward the village. Alone again, but not for long. Hollis would come, and the thread would tighten more, pulling at the edges of what he'd buried.

He thought of Lena, her questions, the thing she'd almost uncovered, and the shadow that had silenced her. He hadn't lied, not completely. He didn't know who it was, not yet, but he'd seen enough to guess, and that guess was a weight he couldn't shake, a thread he couldn't cut loose.

CHAPTER TWENTY-FOUR

N oah stood at his bedroom window, the gray morning light filtering through the blinds, casting faint bars across his face. The village stretched out below, quiet except for the occasional car rumbling past, its tires hissing on the wet pavement. His dad's car was gone, off to wherever he'd stormed after their fight, and his mom was still with Julia, leaving the house empty, a hollow shell that echoed with the weight of what they'd found. He pressed his forehead against the cool glass, his breath fogging it briefly, and tried to steady the churn in his gut. Hollis would be here soon, and the quiet game he'd been playing was fraying at the edges.

He turned away, his room feeling smaller now, the walls too close, the cedar scent from the wardrobe sharp in his nose. The calculus book sat on his desk, its spine creased from his dad's hands, and he resisted the urge to open it again, to touch the notebook and that strip of silk. He'd messed up keeping them, letting them sit there like evidence waiting to be found, but burning them now wouldn't erase what his parents knew. They'd seen too much, and the police were closing in, their questions a thread he couldn't snap.

Friday night played in his head again, a loop he couldn't stop. Lena at Ravenswood, her voice cutting through the dark, the shadow moving fast, the knife flashing once before she fell. He'd watched it happen, hidden in the trees, his heart pounding but his body still, like he'd been carved from the cold. He hadn't run to her, hadn't called out, just watched, the weight of it settling into him like a stone he'd carried ever since. He didn't know why he'd stayed silent, not then, not now, but it was tied to the thing she'd been digging for, the secret he'd buried two years ago, a truth he'd thought was dead until she'd started asking.

He moved to his bed, sitting hard, the springs creaking under him. His hands rested on his knees, steady despite the shake he felt inside, and he thought about that secret, the one Lena had almost pulled free. It wasn't murder, not like hers, but it was close enough—something he'd done, something he couldn't undo, and she'd found a thread, a whisper from someone who'd seen too much. He'd followed her to stop her, to scare her off, but he hadn't planned on the shadow, hadn't expected the knife. Now she was gone, and he was left holding the pieces, trying to keep them from cutting him open.

The doorbell rang, a sharp chime that sliced through the quiet, and Noah's head snapped up, his pulse jumping. He stood, smoothing his hoodie, and took a slow breath, forcing the mask back into place. Hollis. It had to be. He checked his phone—9:17, earlier than he'd expected—and headed downstairs, his steps deliberate, his face blank. He opened the door, the cold air rushing in, and there stood the detective, his coat damp, his eyes steady and unreadable.

"Noah," Hollis said, his voice calm but firm, the kind that didn't leave room for games. "Your parents around?"

"No," Noah said, leaning against the frame, his tone casual. "Mom's with a friend, Dad's out. Just me."

Hollis nodded, pulling a small kit from his pocket, the kind they used for prints. "Good enough. We need to talk, and I need your fingerprints. Voluntary, for now. You okay with that?"

Noah's stomach twisted, but he shrugged, keeping his eyes steady. "Sure. Whatever gets this over with."

Hollis stepped inside, setting the kit on the hall table, and gestured for Noah to sit. "Let's make it quick," he said, opening it, pulling out an ink pad and card. "You know why I'm here. The knife at Ravenswood, prints from your house. We're ruling people out, starting with you."

Noah sat, rolling up his sleeve, and pressed his fingers into the ink, then onto the card, the black smudges stark against the white. "I didn't touch any knife," he said, his voice flat, practiced. "I was here Friday night, like I told them."

Hollis watched him, his pen hovering over his notebook. "Your parents say different. Found a receipt, a notebook, some silk. You've been out, Noah, and they think you saw something. What's your story?"

"My story's the same," Noah said, wiping his hands on his jeans, leaving faint streaks. "Pub with a friend, home by eleven. They're freaking out over nothing."

Hollis's eyes narrowed, just a fraction, and he leaned forward, his voice dropping. "Nothing's a dead woman at Ravenswood, and your family's tangled in it. You're smart, Noah. I can see that. If you saw something, now's the time to say it, before we find out another way."

Noah met his gaze, the mask fraying but holding, the cold beneath it locking tight. "I didn't see anything," he said, each word measured. "You're wasting your time."

Hollis sat back, scribbling something, then closed the kit with a snap. "We'll see," he said, standing. "Prints'll tell us more. Stay put, Noah. We're not done."

He left, the door clicking shut, and Noah stayed in the chair, his hands clenched, the ink still tacky on his skin. The thread was tightening, the mask slipping, and he felt the weight of watching shift, the shadow from that night looming closer, its face still hidden but its presence sharp enough to cut.

CHAPTER TWENTY-FIVE

Noah sat at the kitchen table, his fingers still tacky with ink from Hollis's kit, the faint smears darkening the creases of his skin. The house was quiet again, the detective's car long gone down the lane, but the silence felt louder now, an echo that pressed against his ears. He stared at the spot where the glove and receipt had been, cleared away by his parents, and felt the thread of his control fraying thinner, the mask he'd worn for days slipping under the weight of what they knew. Hollis had his prints now, and soon they'd match them to the knife, or they wouldn't, and either way, the game was shifting.

He stood, the chair creaking beneath him, and moved to the sink, running his hands under cold water. The ink faded, swirling down the drain, but the feeling didn't, a tight knot in his chest that wouldn't loosen. He'd kept his voice steady with Hollis, his face blank, but the detective's eyes had cut through him, sharp and steady, like he could see the shadow Noah carried from that night. He dried his hands on a towel, the rough fabric scraping his skin, and tried to push it down, the memory of Lena's scream, the glint of the knife, the stillness that followed.

The front door opened, a soft thud against the quiet, and his mom's voice called out, "Noah? You here?" He turned, his pulse jumping, and saw her step into the kitchen, her coat damp, her face pale with worry. Julia followed, her dark hair pulled tight, her eyes flicking to him with that lawyer's sharpness he'd always hated.

"Yeah," he said, leaning against the counter, his tone flat. "Where else would I be?"

His mom set her bag down, her hands trembling slightly as she brushed wet strands from her face. "Hollis was here," she said, not a question, her voice tight with something he couldn't place. "What did he want?"

"Prints," Noah said, shrugging, keeping his eyes on her. "Said it's routine. Took them and left."

Julia stepped forward, her arms crossed, her voice calm but edged. "Routine doesn't mean nothing, Noah. They've got a knife from your house, and now your prints. What'd you tell him?"

"What I told you," he said, meeting her gaze, his mask locking back into place. "I was at the pub, home by eleven. Didn't see anything, didn't do anything."

His mom moved closer, her eyes searching his face,

pleading. "Noah, please," she said, her voice breaking. "If you know something, tell us. Hollis isn't stopping, and we can't help you if you keep shutting us out."

He looked away, his jaw tightening, the echo of silence ringing louder now. "There's nothing to tell," he said, his words clipped, practiced. "You're making it bigger than it is."

"It's not bigger than a murder," Julia said, her tone sharp, cutting through the room. "Your mom was there, Noah, at Ravenswood. She saw Lena die, and you're tied to it—receipt, notebook, silk. You think Hollis won't put that together?"

Noah's stomach twisted, but he kept his face still, his hands steady in his pockets. "She was there, not me," he said, his voice low, firm. "I don't know what she saw, but I wasn't part of it."

His mom's breath hitched, and she reached for him, her hand hovering before dropping. "Noah," she whispered, tears welling up. "I don't remember everything, but if you were there, if you saw... we can fix this. Please."

He stepped back, the counter hard against his spine, and shook his head. "I wasn't," he said, the lie smooth now, a reflex. "You're the one freaking out, not me."

Julia's eyes narrowed, and she opened her mouth, but the doorbell rang again, a sharp chime that made them all freeze. Noah's heart thudded, the thread tightening, and he watched his mom move to the door, her steps unsteady. She opened it, and Daniel stood there, his face drawn, rain beading on his coat, a small plastic bag in his hand.

"Ellie," he said, his voice rough, stepping inside. "I went to the station, talked to Hollis. They found something else at Ravenswood." He held up the bag, and Noah saw it—a phone, cracked but intact, its screen dark. "It's Lena's. They're pulling data, calls, texts. Hollis says there's a number on it, one that's been texting you, Ellie. And Noah."

The room went still, the air sucked out, and Noah felt the mask fray, a crack running through it he couldn't hide. His mom's eyes widened, turning to him, and Julia's sharpened, pinning him where he stood. "Noah," his dad said, his voice low, heavy. "What's on your phone?"

"Nothing," Noah said, too fast, his hands clenching in his pockets. "I don't know what he's talking about."

But the echo of silence broke, the text from last night flashing in his mind: *You can't hide it forever. They'll find out.* His pulse roared, the thread snapping, and he knew the weight of watching was about to bury him, the shadow's voice reaching through the dark to pull him under.

CHAPTER TWENTY-SIX

Noah stood frozen in the kitchen, his hands buried in his pockets, the air thick with the weight of his dad's words. The plastic bag in Daniel's hand gleamed under the overhead light, Lena's cracked phone a dark shape inside, its presence a silent scream that filled the room. His mom's eyes were wide, locked on him, tears hovering at the edges, while Julia's gaze cut through him, sharp and steady, waiting for him to crack. He felt the thread snap, the mask he'd worn for days splintering under their stares, but he clenched his jaw, forcing the cold back into place.

"What's on your phone, Noah?" his dad repeated, stepping closer, the bag still in his grip. His voice was low, rough with a mix of anger and fear, and Noah hated how it made his chest tighten, how it pulled at something he'd buried deep.

"Nothing," Noah said again, slower this time, his tone flat, his eyes flicking to the floor. "I don't know what they found. I didn't text her."

"Then why's your number on it?" Julia said, her voice calm but unrelenting, stepping forward to stand beside Daniel. "Hollis said it's been texting you and Ellie. Same pattern, same timing. You're lying, Noah, and it's not helping."

"I'm not lying," he snapped, his head jerking up, meeting her gaze. "I don't know whose number that is. Maybe someone's messing with us, I don't know."

His mom moved then, her hand reaching for his arm, her touch light but trembling. "Noah, please," she said, her voice breaking. "If you've been getting texts, show us. We can figure this out together. Don't shut us out."

He pulled away, the motion sharp, and stepped back, the counter digging into his spine. "There's nothing to show," he said, his voice steady despite the shake in his hands. "You're all freaking out over some phone. It's not mine."

Daniel set the bag on the table, the plastic crinkling softly, and ran a hand through his hair, his face tight with strain. "Hollis is pulling the data now," he said, his eyes on Noah. "Calls, texts, everything. If you're on there, Noah, they'll know. And if you're hiding something, it's going to come out."

Noah's pulse roared in his ears, the text from last night flashing in his mind: *You can't hide it forever. They'll find out.* He'd deleted it, wiped it clean, but if it was on Lena's phone, if it traced back to him, the quiet game was over. He thought of Friday night, the shadow moving fast, the knife cutting through the dark, and the weight of watching settled heavier, a stone he couldn't shift. He hadn't texted her, not that night, not ever, but someone had, and they were using his number, or hers, to pull him in.

"Let them pull it," he said, shrugging, his voice cold now, a shield he couldn't drop. "They won't find anything, because I didn't do anything."

His mom's face crumpled, and she turned away, her hands pressing to her mouth, a quiet sob escaping. Julia stepped closer, her voice dropping, soft but firm. "You're digging a hole, Noah," she said. "I'm trying to help you, but if you keep this up, I can't. Show us your phone, right now, or this gets worse."

He stared at her, the room shrinking, the air too thick to breathe, and felt the fraying mask crack wider. "No," he said, his tone final, and pushed past her, heading for the stairs. His dad called after him, "Noah, don't walk away," but he didn't stop, his footsteps heavy on the wood, his chest tight with the echo of silence he couldn't escape.

He reached his room, slamming the door shut, and leaned against it, his breath shallow, his hands shaking now that no one could see. The calculus book stared at him from the desk, the notebook inside a trap he couldn't unmake, and he crossed to it, pulling it free. He flipped it open, the strip of silk falling onto the desk, its stain dark and accusing, and he stared at it, his mind spinning back to Ravenswood. Lena's voice, *You don't know what you're doing,* the shadow's quick strike, the way he'd stood there, watching, letting it happen.

His phone buzzed in his pocket, a low hum that made his heart stop. He pulled it out, the screen glowing in the dim room, and saw another text from the unknown number: *They're close now. You should've talked.* His stomach dropped, the words a knife twisting in his gut, and he deleted it, his thumb steady despite the tremor running through him. Someone knew, someone who'd been there, and they were tightening the thread, pulling him toward the edge.

He sank onto the bed, the silk in his hand, and pressed it to his forehead, the fabric cool against his skin. The shadow's voice was in those texts, he was sure of it, a whisper from the dark he couldn't silence. He'd watched Lena die, kept it locked inside, but now it was spilling out, and the weight of his secret —the thing she'd almost uncovered two years ago—was rising, a shadow of its own he couldn't outrun.

CHAPTER TWENTY-SEVEN

Noah sat on his bed, the strip of red silk crumpled in his fist, its stain a dark smear against his palm. The room was dim, the blinds still drawn, the gray morning light seeping through in thin, weak lines. His phone lay beside him, silent now, but the last text burned in his mind: They're close now. You should've talked. The words felt like a hand closing around his throat, steady and cold, and he couldn't shake the certainty that whoever sent it had been there, at Ravenswood, watching him watch Lena die. The shadow's voice, reaching out from the dark, and he was running out of ways to keep it quiet.

He stood, shoving the silk into his pocket, and paced the small space, his socks silent on the carpet. The house creaked around him, the faint hum of the heating kicking on, but it didn't touch the chill in his bones. His parents were downstairs, or gone again, he didn't know, didn't care. They'd seen the phone, heard about the texts, and now Hollis had his prints, the knife, the data—pieces of a puzzle he'd tried to scatter, pulling together faster than he could stop. The secret he'd buried two years ago, the one Lena had sniffed out, was rising, and he felt its weight like a stone dragging him under.

Friday night replayed in his head, sharper now, the edges cutting deeper. He'd followed her to Ravenswood, hidden in the trees, the damp leaves sticking to his shoes. She'd been pacing, her phone pressed to her ear, her voice sharp with panic: *You don't know what you're doing.* Then the shadow, tall and quick, the argument flaring, the knife flashing once before she fell. He'd stayed still, his breath shallow, watching as the shadow slipped away, leaving her crumpled in the dirt. He hadn't moved, hadn't screamed, just turned and walked back to his car, the scarf snagging on a branch, a mistake he'd tried to bury with the rest.

A knock on his door jolted him, quick and sharp, and he froze, his heart thudding in his chest. "Noah?" It wasn't his mom or dad, but a voice he knew, softer, older—Mrs. Hargrove, the librarian, her white hair always tucked under a scarf when she walked her dog past their house. He opened the door, his face smoothing into the mask, and saw her standing there, her coat damp, her eyes bright with something he couldn't read.

"Hey," he said, leaning against the frame, his tone casual despite the knot in his gut. "What's up?"

She smiled, small and tight, and stepped inside without waiting for an invite. "I saw your parents leave," she said, her voice low, careful. "Thought I'd check on you. Heard about the police, that poor girl at Ravenswood. Terrible thing."

"Yeah," Noah said, closing the door, his hands in his pockets, the silk pressing against his thigh. "They're asking everyone, I guess."

She nodded, her eyes flicking around the room, lingering on the desk, the calculus book. "Small town," she said, her tone shifting, softer now, almost knowing. "Hard to keep secrets here. Lena, she came to the library sometimes, you know. Asked about old records, things from years back. Said she was writing something, but I think she was looking for someone."

Noah's stomach tightened, but he kept his face still, his voice steady. "Didn't know her," he said, shrugging. "Just heard the talk."

Mrs. Hargrove's smile faded, and she stepped closer, her voice dropping to a whisper. "You're a good boy, Noah," she said, her eyes locking onto his. "But I saw you, that night. Coming back late, your jacket all wet. You didn't see me, out with Daisy, but I saw you."

His breath stopped, the mask cracking, and he felt the thread snap, the unseen hand tightening its grip. "I was at the pub," he said, too fast, his voice rougher than he meant. "Got caught in the rain, that's all."

She tilted her head, studying him, and reached into her coat pocket, pulling out a small, folded paper. "Found this in the library," she said, holding it out. "Dropped from her bag, I think. Your name's on it."

He took it, his hand steady despite the shake inside, and unfolded it. A note, scribbled in Lena's tight script: *Noah Carter —check 2023, summer. He knows.* His heart slammed against his ribs, the secret he'd buried two years ago staring back at him, and he crumpled it, shoving it into his pocket with the silk.

"Don't know what that means," he said, his voice cold now, a shield snapping back into place. "Maybe she got me mixed up with someone else."

Mrs. Hargrove nodded, but her eyes didn't leave his, sharp and quiet. "Maybe," she said, stepping back. "But secrets don't stay buried, Noah. Not here." She turned, leaving as quietly as she'd come, the door clicking shut behind her.

He sank onto the bed, the paper and silk burning in his pocket, the shadow's voice louder now, echoing through the note, the texts, the night he'd watched Lena die. The unseen hand was pulling, and he felt the mask fray, the silence he'd kept shattering under a truth he couldn't outrun.

CHAPTER TWENTY-EIGHT

Noah sat on the edge of his bed, the crumpled note and silk strip clenched in his hand, their weight heavier than the paper and fabric should have been. The room was still, the gray light from the window fading as the morning thickened into a dull, overcast haze. Mrs. Hargrove's words echoed in his head, soft and sharp: I saw you, that night. The note burned against his palm, Lena's handwriting a jagged scar: Noah Carter—check 2023, summer. He knows. His secret, the one he'd buried two years ago, was clawing its way up, and the shadow from Ravenswood was pulling the strings, tightening the thread around his silence.

He stood, shoving the note and silk back into his pocket, and paced to the window, his breath fogging the glass. The village below was quiet, the cottages huddled under the heavy sky, but he felt exposed, like every window hid eyes watching him unravel. Mrs. Hargrove had seen him coming back, wet and late, and now she had Lena's note, a piece of the puzzle he'd thought was lost. He didn't know how much she understood, how much Lena had told her, but it was too much, and the crack in his mask was widening, letting the cold beneath seep through.

Friday night flashed again, unbidden, the memory sharper now, cutting deeper. Lena pacing at Ravenswood, her voice tight with fear, the shadow striking fast, the knife glinting once before she fell. He'd watched from the trees, his hands clenched, his heart pounding but his feet rooted, the weight of it settling into him like a stone he couldn't shift. He hadn't run, hadn't called out, just turned away, the scarf snagging as he fled, a mistake he couldn't undo. He'd kept it quiet, locked it inside, but now it was spilling out, the shadow's voice in those texts, Mrs. Hargrove's knowing look, his parents' desperation—all of it widening the fracture he couldn't hold together.

The stairs creaked outside his door, and he turned, his pulse jumping, the mask snapping back into place. His dad's voice came through, low and strained. "Noah, come down. Now."

He took a breath, steadying himself, and opened the door, stepping into the hall. His dad stood at the bottom of the stairs, his face tight, his hands clenched at his sides. His mom was behind him, her eyes red, Julia beside her, her sharp gaze fixed on Noah as he descended. The kitchen smelled of coffee and damp coats, the air thick with the tension they'd left behind.

"Sit," his dad said, pointing to the table, his voice rough but steady. Noah sat, his hands in his lap, the silk and note pressing against his thigh, and waited, his face blank, his heart thudding.

"We talked to Hollis again," his dad said, sitting across from him, his mom and Julia taking the chairs beside him. "They're running your prints against the knife. Results'll be back soon. And that phone, Lena's, they've got texts from a number we don't know, sent to you and your mom. You need to tell us what's going on, Noah, before this buries us."

"There's nothing to tell," Noah said, his voice flat, his eyes on the table. "I don't know the number. I didn't text her."

His mom leaned forward, her hands trembling as she reached for him, stopping short. "Noah, please," she said, her voice breaking. "Mrs. Hargrove was just here, after you went upstairs. She said she saw you that night, coming back late, wet. She gave us this." She slid a folded paper across the table, a photocopy of the note, Lena's script stark against the white: *Noah Carter—check 2023, summer. He knows.*

Noah's stomach dropped, but he kept his face still, his hands steady. "She's old," he said, shrugging. "Probably mixed me up with someone else. I was at the pub, got wet walking home. That's it."

"Don't," his dad snapped, his hand slamming the table, the sound sharp in the quiet. "Don't lie to us anymore. She saw you, Noah, and this note, it's Lena's. What happened in 2023? What does she mean, 'he knows'?"

Noah's jaw tightened, the crack widening, and he felt

the shadow's hand close tighter, the unseen force pulling at the edges of his secret. "I don't know," he said, his voice cold, a shield he couldn't drop. "She's dead, ask her."

His mom's breath hitched, a sob escaping, and Julia leaned in, her voice low, firm. "You're not helping yourself, Noah," she said, her eyes piercing his. "Hollis is coming back with those results, and if your prints are on that knife, this isn't just about lying. It's about murder. Tell us what you saw, who was there."

He stared at her, the room shrinking, the air too thick to breathe, and felt the mask splinter, the cold beneath it seeping out. "I didn't see anything," he said, each word deliberate, a lie he'd honed to perfection. "I wasn't there."

His dad stood, pacing to the window, his hands in his hair. "You're killing us, Noah," he said, his voice rough with despair. "We're trying to save you, and you're throwing it away."

Noah didn't respond, his eyes on the table, the photocopy staring back at him, the echo of 2023 ringing in his ears. The summer he'd crossed a line, the thing he'd buried, the secret Lena had sniffed out. He hadn't killed her, he knew that, but he'd watched, and the shadow knew, and now the crack was too wide to hold, the unseen hand pulling him toward a truth he couldn't face.

CHAPTER TWENTY-NINE

Noah sat at the kitchen table, the photocopy of Lena's note staring up at him, its words a quiet hammer in his chest: Noah Carter—check 2023, summer. He knows. The room smelled of cold coffee and damp air, the overcast light filtering through the window in a dull, heavy glow. His mom's sobs had faded to a shaky silence, her hands pressed to her face, while his dad stood by the sink, his back rigid, his breathing loud in the stillness. Julia watched him from across the table, her eyes sharp and steady, a lawyer's gaze that cut through the mask he'd worn too long. The crack had widened, and he felt the cold beneath it spilling out, the noose tightening around his silence.

He kept his hands in his pockets, the silk strip and crumpled note pressing against his thigh, a secret he couldn't bury deep enough. His dad turned, his face drawn, his voice rough with strain. "Noah," he said, stepping closer, "this isn't a game anymore. Hollis has your prints, Lena's phone, and now this note. Mrs. Hargrove saw you that night. You're out of excuses. Tell us what happened in 2023, what she knew."

Noah's jaw clenched, his eyes flicking to the table, the words he'd rehearsed locking in his throat. "I don't know what she meant," he said, his voice flat, a lie he'd polished to a shine. "It's nothing. She got it wrong."

"Stop it," his mom said, her voice breaking as she looked up, tears streaking her face. "Just stop. We're trying to help you, Noah, but you're pushing us away. What happened that summer? What does 'he knows' mean?"

He felt the thread snap, the weight of 2023 rising like a tide he couldn't hold back. Two years ago, the summer he'd crossed a line, a mistake he'd buried under the village's quiet streets. It wasn't murder, not like Lena's, but it was close— a moment of anger, a shove, a fall, and a secret he'd kept from everyone, even himself, until Lena started digging. She'd found something, a whisper, a record, and he'd followed her to stop her, to keep it dead. But he hadn't expected the shadow, the knife, the scream that cut the night in two.

"I don't know," he said again, his tone cold, steady, though his hands shook in his pockets. "She's making stuff up. I wasn't there."

Julia leaned forward, her voice low, firm. "You're not listening, Noah," she said, her eyes pinning him. "Hollis isn't guessing. He's got evidence—your prints, texts, witnesses. You're in this, and if you don't talk, he'll bury you. What did Lena know? Who's 'he'?"

The doorbell rang, a sharp chime that sliced through the room, and Noah's heart slammed against his ribs, the noose tightening. His dad moved to the door, his steps heavy, and Noah heard Hollis's voice, calm but edged, filtering in from the hall. "Daniel, I need to see Noah. Now."

His dad stepped back, letting Hollis in, the detective's coat damp, his notebook already in hand. He stood in the doorway, his eyes locking onto Noah, steady and unreadable. "Got the print results," he said, his voice cutting through the tension. "Partial match on the knife handle, Noah. Not enough for a full ID yet, but it's close. Care to explain?"

Noah's stomach dropped, but he kept his face blank, his hands still, the mask fraying but holding. "I didn't touch a knife," he said, his tone flat, rehearsed. "I was here, like I said."

Hollis stepped closer, setting the notebook on the table, its pages open to a list of numbers and times. "Lena's phone says different," he said, tapping the page. "Texts to you, from you, Friday night. One at 9:52, right after your pub receipt. 'Meet me at R.E.' Ring any bells?"

Noah's breath caught, the shadow's voice roaring in his ears, but he shook his head, slow and deliberate. "I didn't send that," he said, his voice steady despite the crack widening inside. "Someone's got my number wrong."

His mom's sob broke the quiet, and his dad slammed a hand on the counter, his voice raw. "Noah, for God's sake, stop lying! They've got you on this, and you're digging a hole we can't pull you out of!"

Hollis raised a hand, his gaze never leaving Noah. "Let's

keep this simple," he said, his tone calm, cutting. "You're coming with me, Noah. Station. We'll sort it there. Voluntary, for now, but I've got enough to hold you if I need to."

Noah stood, his legs steady though his chest burned, the noose tight now, pulling him under. "Fine," he said, his voice cold, a shield he couldn't drop. "I've got nothing to say."

His mom reached for him, her hands trembling, but he stepped back, avoiding her touch, and followed Hollis to the door, the silk and note a weight he couldn't shed. The shadow's voice was in those texts, he knew it, a hand reaching from the dark, and as he walked out into the gray morning, the crack widened, the silence he'd kept shattering under a truth he couldn't outrun.

CHAPTER THIRTY

Noah sat in the police station's interrogation room, the chair hard beneath him, the air cold and stale with the scent of disinfectant and old coffee. The walls were a dull gray, scratched and scuffed, and a single bulb buzzed overhead, casting harsh light across the table where his hands rested, still smudged with faint traces of ink. Hollis sat across from him, his notebook open, his pen poised, his eyes steady and unyielding, cutting through the mask Noah had worn for days. The noose had tightened, and the silence he'd kept was breaking, splintering under the weight of what they'd found.

His parents were outside, somewhere in the lobby with Julia, their voices muted through the closed door, but he could feel their desperation, their fear, pressing against him like a second skin. The silk strip and crumpled note burned in his pocket, a secret he couldn't shed, and the memory of Lena's note—*Noah Carter—check 2023, summer. He knows*—rang in his ears, a hammer striking the crack that had widened too far to hold.

Hollis tapped his pen against the table, a soft, rhythmic sound that filled the quiet. "Let's go over it again," he said, his voice calm but firm, a blade wrapped in velvet. "Friday night, 9:47, you're at the pub. Receipt proves it. Then a text from your number to Lena's, 9:52, says 'Meet me at R.E.' She's dead an hour later, stabbed with a knife that's got a partial print matching yours. You're saying you didn't send it, didn't meet her, didn't see her die. That right?"

Noah kept his eyes on the table, his hands still, his voice cold and steady. "Yeah," he said, the lie a reflex now, honed to a sharp edge. "I didn't send anything. I was home by eleven, like I told you."

Hollis leaned forward, his pen stopping, his gaze locking onto Noah's. "Here's the problem," he said, his tone dropping, cutting deeper. "Your mom was there, at Ravenswood, saw Lena die, saw someone else—a shadow, she says. Mrs. Hargrove saw you coming back late, wet, shaken. And this note, Lena's, ties you to something from 2023. You're in this, Noah, and the prints, the texts, they're piling up. Tell me what happened, or I'll fill in the blanks myself."

Noah's chest tightened, the shadow's voice echoing through the texts, the note, the night he'd watched Lena fall. He'd followed her to Ravenswood, hidden in the trees, the damp leaves clinging to his shoes, her voice sharp with panic: *You don't know what you're doing.* The shadow had moved fast, the knife flashing once, and she'd crumpled, her scream cut short. He'd stayed still, his breath shallow, watching as the shadow slipped away, leaving her in the dirt. He hadn't killed her, he knew that, but he'd watched, and the secret she'd been digging for—the thing from 2023—was why he'd been there, why he'd kept silent.

"I didn't see anything," he said, his voice flat, his eyes lifting to meet Hollis's. "I don't know what she was talking about. 2023's nothing."

Hollis sat back, his pen tapping again, his eyes narrowing. "Nothing's a dead girl and a knife from your house," he said, his tone steady, unrelenting. "You're sixteen, Noah, smart, good grades, no record. But you're lying, and I can see it. That text, 'Meet me at R.E.,' it's your number. Someone sent it, and if it wasn't you, who was it?"

Noah's hands clenched, the silk pressing harder against his thigh, and he felt the crack widen, the cold beneath his mask spilling out. "I don't know," he said, his voice rougher now, the lie fraying at the edges. "Maybe someone took my phone, messed with it. I didn't send it."

Hollis flipped a page in his notebook, pulling out a printout, and slid it across the table. A text log, stark and black: *9:52 p.m., Friday—Meet me at R.E.* Sent from his number, received on Lena's. "This says you did," Hollis said, tapping the paper. "And your mom got one too, same night, from the same number: 'You were right.' Explain that."

Noah's stomach dropped, the shadow's voice roaring in his head, and he stared at the log, the crack breaking wide open. He hadn't sent those texts, he was sure of it, but they'd come from his phone, and the weight of 2023—the summer he'd crossed a line, the secret he'd buried—was pulling him under. "I didn't," he said, his voice trembling now, the mask shattering. "I swear, I didn't send them."

Hollis leaned in, his voice low, cutting. "Then who did, Noah? Who was there? Your mom saw someone, you've got this note, and you're tied to it. Tell me, or you're not walking out of here."

The room shrank, the air too thick to breathe, and Noah felt the silence break, the noose tightening until he couldn't hold it anymore. "I saw her die," he said, the words spilling out, raw and jagged, his hands shaking on the table. "At Ravenswood, Friday night. I followed her, but I didn't kill her. Someone else did, a shadow, tall, fast. I watched, that's all. I didn't send those texts."

Hollis's pen stopped, his eyes narrowing, and the quiet stretched, heavy and sharp. "You watched," he said, his voice steady, probing. "Who was it, Noah? Give me a name."

Noah's breath hitched, the shadow's face a blur in his mind, and he shook his head, his voice breaking. "I don't know," he said, the truth cutting through him. "I didn't see. But they know me, and they're coming."

The door opened, Julia stepping in, her face tight, and Hollis stood, his notebook closing with a snap. "We're done for now," he said, his eyes still on Noah. "But you're staying here till we sort this out."

Noah sank back, the silence broken, the shadow's voice louder now, and he felt the noose tighten, the crack wide open, the truth he'd buried rising to pull him under.

PART 4: LENA MOREAU

CHAPTER THIRTY-ONE

Lena Moreau sat at a small table in the village library, the air thick with the musty scent of old books and polished wood. The late September light streamed through the high windows, casting golden patches across the worn carpet, and she shifted in her chair, her pen tapping a quiet rhythm against the notebook in front of her. The library was nearly empty, just Mrs. Hargrove at the desk sorting returns and a teenage girl flipping pages in the corner, her headphones a faint buzz in the stillness. Lena liked it here, the quiet, the way it let her think, untangle the threads she'd been pulling since she'd moved to this sleepy little place three months ago.

She'd come for a fresh start, or that's what she'd told herself—new job at the pub, a cheap flat above the bakery, a chance to leave the city's noise behind. But it wasn't long before she'd noticed the cracks, the whispers beneath the village's postcard charm. People talked, not to her, but around her, their voices dropping when she passed, their eyes lingering a beat too long. It wasn't just small-town curiosity, she'd decided. It was something heavier, something buried, and she'd always had a knack for finding what others wanted hidden.

Her notebook was open to a fresh page, her handwriting tight and slanted: *September 23, 2024—Heard it again at the pub. 'That Carter kid, something off about him.' No details, just looks. Check records?* She'd caught the snippet last night, two regulars hunched over their pints, their voices low but not low enough. Noah Carter, sixteen, quiet, smart, the kind of kid who didn't stand out until you looked closer. She'd seen him around, slouched in a hoodie, his eyes sharp but guarded, and something about him stuck with her, a thread she couldn't let go.

She flipped back a page, her notes from last week catching her eye: *Summer 2023—accident on the ridge. Teen missing, never found. Rumors, no proof.* She'd overheard it from Sarah at the bakery, a casual mention of a kid who'd vanished two years ago, a hiking trip gone wrong, the kind of story that faded into village lore. But the way Sarah's voice had dipped, the quick glance over her shoulder, it didn't feel faded. It felt alive, and when she'd tied it to those pub whispers about Noah, the thread tightened, pulling her in.

Lena leaned back, stretching her arms, the chair creaking under her. She'd always been like this, restless, chasing questions no one else asked. Her sister used to tease her, call her a bloodhound with a pen, but it had landed her stories back in the city—small ones, sure, but enough to keep her going. This, though, felt different, bigger, a shadow beneath the village's quiet streets she couldn't ignore.

Mrs. Hargrove shuffled over, her white hair tucked under a scarf, her smile small but warm. "Finding what you need, dear?" she asked, her voice soft, a librarian's whisper honed over years.

"Not yet," Lena said, returning the smile, her pen stilling. "You got old newspapers here? Like, back a couple years?"

Mrs. Hargrove nodded, her eyes flicking to the notebook, curious but not prying. "In the back, on microfiche. Not much gets digitized around here. What're you after?"

"Just poking around," Lena said, keeping her tone light, casual. "Heard some old stories, thought I'd check them out."

The older woman hesitated, her smile tightening, then pointed toward a corner room. "Over there," she said, her voice a touch quieter. "Let me know if you need help." She shuffled off, leaving Lena with the faint rustle of her skirt and a feeling she couldn't shake, like Mrs. Hargrove knew more than she'd let on.

Lena stood, grabbing her notebook, and headed to the microfiche room, a cramped space with a single machine humming softly in the dark. She flicked it on, the screen glowing blue, and started with summer 2023, her fingers steady as she loaded the film. The headlines flickered past— village fetes, a new shop opening, nothing big—until she hit July. A small article, buried on page three: *Teen Missing After*

Ridge Fall. Search Called Off. No name, just a vague mention of a group hike, a slip, a body never found. The police had ruled it an accident, case closed, but the words stuck with her, sharp and cold.

She scribbled in her notebook: *July 2023—ridge accident, teen gone. Noah Carter there?* She didn't know yet, didn't have proof, but the thread was there, tugging her deeper. She thought of his face, that guarded look, and wondered what he'd been like two years ago, what he'd seen, what he'd done. The search had begun, and she felt the shadow beneath the village shift, a mystery she couldn't let go, not knowing it would pull her toward a night she wouldn't survive.

CHAPTER THIRTY-TWO

L ena leaned against the bar at the village pub, the wood smooth under her elbows, the air thick with the scent of spilled beer and frying chips. It was late October 2024, a slow Tuesday night, the hum of conversation low and steady around her. A handful of regulars nursed their pints, their voices a soft murmur beneath the crackle of the jukebox in the corner, playing some old folk tune she didn't recognize. She wiped a glass dry with a rag, her movements automatic, her mind elsewhere, spinning through the threads she'd been pulling since that day in the library a month ago.

The microfiche article still haunted her, the sparse details of the 2023 ridge accident looping in her head: a teen missing, a fall, a search called off. She'd dug deeper since then, spending her off hours hunched over the machine, her notebook filling with scraps—dates, weather reports, a vague mention of a youth group outing gone wrong. No name, no clear link to Noah Carter, but the whispers she'd caught at the pub kept tying back to him, a quiet buzz that grew louder the more she listened. *That Carter kid, something off about him.* She'd seen him again last week, slouched in a corner booth with a friend, his eyes flicking to her once, sharp and guarded, before looking away.

She set the glass down, her fingers lingering on its rim, and glanced at the clock above the bar—9:15, still an hour till close. The pub was her best source, the place where tongues loosened after a few drinks, and she'd learned to linger, to listen without asking too much. Last night, Tom Bennett from the hardware store had let something slip, his voice slurred over his third pint: *That summer, up on the ridge, kid never came back. Carter boy was there, saw it all.* He'd clammed up when he'd noticed her nearby, but it was enough, a thread she couldn't let go.

The door swung open, a gust of cool air cutting through the warmth, and Sarah from the bakery stepped in, her coat dusted with early frost. She waved at Lena, sliding onto a stool with a tired smile. "Rough day," she said, her voice soft, worn. "Give me a cider, will you?"

"Sure," Lena said, grabbing a bottle from the cooler, popping the cap with a quick twist. She slid it across, her tone casual as she leaned in. "Long shifts at the bakery, huh? Bet you hear all the gossip there."

Sarah laughed, a small, dry sound, and took a sip. "More than I want sometimes. People talk when they're waiting for bread."

"Like what?" Lena asked, wiping the counter, keeping her eyes on the rag. "Heard anything about that ridge thing, couple years back?"

Sarah's hand paused, the bottle halfway to her mouth, and she glanced at Lena, her smile fading. "You're still on about that?" she said, her voice quieter now, cautious. "It's old news, Lena. Kid fell, they never found him. Sad, but done."

"Yeah, but people keep mentioning it," Lena said, her tone light, probing. "Heard Tom say something about the Carter boy being there. Noah, right? You know him?"

Sarah set the bottle down, her fingers tapping the glass, and looked away, her eyes flicking to the door. "He's just a kid," she said, her voice tight. "Comes in sometimes, quiet, keeps to himself. Don't know what Tom's on about."

Lena nodded, filing it away, the thread pulling tighter. Sarah knew something, or suspected it, and the way her voice had dropped, the quick glance, it was more than idle talk. She'd seen Noah's family too—Ellie Carter, the psychologist, all poise and smiles, and Daniel, the surgeon, steady and warm. They didn't fit the picture of a kid with secrets, but the village did, its quiet streets hiding shadows she could feel.

"Fair enough," Lena said, smiling, letting it drop for now. "Just curious. Small towns, you know, always something under the surface."

Sarah nodded, her shoulders relaxing, and took another sip. "You're not wrong," she said, her tone softening. "But some things are better left alone."

Lena turned away, grabbing another glass to dry, her mind racing. She didn't believe in leaving things alone, not when they tugged at her like this. The ridge accident, Noah's name, the whispers—it was all weaving together, a pattern she couldn't see yet but could feel, sharp and cold beneath the village's calm. She'd started asking at the library too, nudging Mrs. Hargrove for more, and the old woman's hesitations, her quick glances, only fueled her. Tomorrow, she'd go back, dig into school records, anything tying Noah to that summer.

The pub door opened again, and she glanced up, her breath catching as Noah stepped in, his hoodie pulled low, his hands in his pockets. He didn't look at her, just headed for a booth in the back, but she felt his presence like a jolt, the thread pulling hard now. She watched him sit, his eyes flicking once to the bar, meeting hers for a split second before sliding away, and she knew, deep in her gut, that he was the key, the shadow she'd been chasing all along.

CHAPTER THIRTY-THREE

Lena sat at her small kitchen table, the flat above the bakery quiet except for the faint hum of the fridge and the occasional creak of the old building settling. It was early November 2024, the sky outside her window a deep, bruised purple, the village sinking into dusk. A single lamp glowed beside her, casting a warm circle over the notebook open on the table, its pages crowded with her tight, slanted handwriting. She sipped a mug of tea, the steam curling up in thin wisps, and traced a finger over her latest entry: November 2—school records, summer 2023. Noah Carter, youth group trip, ridge. No mention of missing kid, but he was there.

She'd spent the morning at the library again, charming Mrs. Hargrove into letting her peek at old school files under the guise of a vague "local history project." The woman had hesitated, her eyes sharp behind her glasses, but she'd relented, handing over a box of dusty records from the village school. Lena had found it buried in the attendance logs—a youth group outing, July 2023, a hike up the ridge led by a teacher named Mr. Ellis. Noah's name was there, scrawled in faded ink, one of twelve kids listed. The missing teen wasn't mentioned, no asterisk, no note, but the date matched the newspaper article, and the thread she'd been pulling sharpened into something solid, something she could feel.

She leaned back, the chair creaking under her, and rubbed her eyes, the ache of hours bent over microfiche and files settling into her bones. Noah Carter had been on that ridge, the summer a kid vanished, and the whispers she'd caught—Tom at the pub, Sarah's quick glances—kept circling back to him. She'd seen him again last night at the pub, his hoodie low, his eyes flicking to her with that guarded sharpness before he'd slipped out, leaving his drink half-full. He knew she was watching, she was sure of it, and the thought sent a shiver through her, not fear exactly, but a thrill, the kind that came with chasing a story too big to let go.

Her phone buzzed beside the notebook, a text from her sister, Claire: *Still alive out there? Call me sometime.* Lena smiled faintly, setting it aside, but the normalcy of it felt distant, drowned out by the shadow sharpening in her mind. She flipped back a page, her notes from last week catching her eye: *Tom—'Carter boy saw it all.' Sarah—'Better left alone.'* She'd pressed Sarah again yesterday, casual over a coffee run, but the woman had shut down, her smile tight, her words clipped: *"Don't stir up old ghosts, Lena."* It only made her dig harder.

She stood, stretching, and moved to the window, peering down at the quiet street below. The bakery's sign swayed faintly in the breeze, its lights off, the village settling into night. She thought of Noah's family—Ellie Carter, all poise and quiet strength, pouring drinks at a charity event last month; Daniel, steady and warm, chatting with regulars at the pub. They didn't fit the picture of a kid with a secret, but Noah did, his silence a wall she couldn't breach, his eyes a window to something dark.

The door downstairs thudded, a soft knock echoing up, and Lena frowned, crossing to the stairwell. She opened it, the cold air rushing in, and saw Tom Bennett standing there, his coat collar up, his face shadowed under the streetlight. "Hey," he said, his voice gruff, hesitant. "Got a minute?"

"Sure," she said, stepping back, her pulse quickening as he climbed the stairs. He smelled of tobacco and sawdust, his hands shoved deep in his pockets, and she gestured to the table, her notebook still open. "What's up?"

He sat, glancing at the pages, his brow creasing. "Heard you've been asking about the ridge," he said, his voice low, rough. "That summer, '23. People talk, Lena. You're stirring stuff up."

She sat across from him, keeping her tone light, curious. "Just chasing a story," she said, smiling faintly. "Heard you mention Noah Carter was there. What happened?"

Tom's eyes flicked to hers, sharp and wary, and he rubbed a hand over his jaw. "Was a bad day," he said, his voice dropping. "Kid fell, they said. Never found him. Noah was with the group, yeah, but it's done. Let it be."

"Who fell?" she pressed, leaning in, her pen hovering

over the notebook. "No name in the papers, but you know, don't you?"

He shifted, his chair scraping, and looked away, his voice tightening. "Don't matter," he said, standing abruptly. "Just stop asking, Lena. For your own good."

He turned, heading down the stairs, the door thudding shut behind him, and Lena sat back, her heart pounding, the thread pulling tighter. Tom knew, and his warning only sharpened the shadow in her mind, the shape of Noah Carter growing clearer, darker. She scribbled a new entry: *November 3 —Tom confirms Noah on ridge. Knows more, won't say. Danger?* The search was narrowing, the mystery deepening, and she felt the pull, the shadow sharpening into a truth she couldn't turn away from, not knowing it would lead her to Ravenswood and a night she wouldn't survive.

CHAPTER THIRTY-FOUR

L ena stood in the library's microfiche room, the air cool and still, the hum of the machine a low pulse beneath her fingers. It was mid-November 2024, the village outside cloaked in a damp fog that pressed against the windows, blurring the world into shades of gray. The screen glowed blue in front of her, casting sharp shadows across her face as she scrolled through another reel, her notebook open beside her, its pages dense with notes. She'd been here for hours, the ache in her neck a dull reminder of time slipping away, but she couldn't stop, not now, not after Tom's warning last night had sharpened the thread she'd been pulling for weeks.

Her latest entry stared up at her, scribbled in the dim light: *November 13—Tom says stop asking. Knows more about ridge, scared. Noah key.* She'd replayed his words all night, his gruff *"For your own good"* ringing in her ears, a warning that only fueled her. He'd confirmed Noah Carter was on that ridge in July 2023, the summer a kid vanished, and the fear in his eyes, the way he'd bolted from her flat, told her there was more, something the village had buried deep. She'd seen Noah at the pub again two nights ago, his hoodie low, his gaze flicking to her with that same guarded sharpness, and she knew he felt her watching, felt the thread tightening between them.

She scrolled past grainy headlines—weather updates, a lost dog notice—until a small article caught her eye, dated July 28, 2023, a week after the ridge accident. *Local Youth Group Mourns Loss.* Her breath caught, and she leaned closer, the text flickering on the screen. It was brief, a single paragraph: *The village youth group held a memorial for a member lost in a hiking accident on the ridge earlier this month. No body recovered, police say, due to treacherous terrain. Survivors shaken but unharmed.* No names, no details, but the date lined up, and the word *survivors* stuck with her, sharp and cold.

She flipped to her notebook, her pen scratching fast: *July 28—memorial, no body. Noah survivor?* She'd found the attendance log last week—Noah Carter, part of that group, up on the ridge when it happened. Tom had said he'd *seen it all*, and now this, a quiet confirmation that something had gone wrong, something more than a slip on a trail. She thought of his face, that teenage stillness hiding something dark, and felt the edge of truth sharpening, a shadow she was closing in on.

The door creaked behind her, and she turned, her pulse jumping as Mrs. Hargrove stepped in, her scarf slipping slightly, her eyes bright with that quiet curiosity Lena had come to recognize. "Still at it?" the older woman asked, her voice soft, a librarian's hush laced with something heavier.

"Yeah," Lena said, forcing a smile, her pen stilling. "Found a bit more on that ridge thing. You remember it?"

Mrs. Hargrove's smile tightened, and she adjusted her scarf, her hands slow, deliberate. "Hard to forget," she said, her tone careful. "Sad day. Those kids, they were shaken up, coming back without one of their own."

"Noah Carter was there, right?" Lena asked, keeping her voice light, watching her closely. "Heard he was part of the group."

The woman's eyes flickered, a quick dart to the side, and she nodded, her voice dropping. "He was," she said, almost a whisper. "Quiet boy, even then. Didn't say much after, just… kept to himself."

Lena's stomach tightened, the thread pulling harder, and she leaned in, her tone casual but probing. "What happened up there? Papers don't say much, but people talk."

Mrs. Hargrove hesitated, her hands clasping together, and looked away, her voice barely audible. "They said he fell," she said, her words measured. "A boy, Jake, I think. Slipped off the edge, too steep to climb down. But some thought… well, it's just talk. Kids arguing, maybe a push. No proof, though."

Lena's pen froze, the name *Jake* cutting through her, and she scribbled it down, her heart pounding. "A push?" she asked, her voice steady despite the jolt. "You mean someone did it?"

Mrs. Hargrove shook her head, stepping back, her eyes wide now, wary. "No, no," she said, too fast. "Just rumors, Lena.

Don't go stirring that up. It's done."

She turned, slipping out before Lena could press further, the door clicking shut behind her. Lena sat back, her breath shallow, the edge of truth razor-sharp now. Jake. A name, a boy lost, and Noah there, a survivor who'd seen it— or done it. She thought of Tom's fear, Sarah's silence, the way Noah's eyes met hers at the pub, and felt the shadow sharpen, a truth she was brushing against, too close to turn back.

She packed her notebook, her hands trembling slightly, and left the library, stepping into the fog, the village quiet around her. The thread was pulling her toward Noah, toward Ravenswood, toward a night she didn't know would end her, and she felt the mystery deepen, the psychological weight of it pulling her to the edge of a truth she couldn't yet see.

CHAPTER THIRTY-FIVE

L ena stood behind the bar at the village pub, the dim light casting long shadows across the worn wood, the air thick with the murmur of voices and the faint clink of glasses. It was late November 2024, a crisp Friday evening, the room half-full with regulars hunched over their drinks, their laughter a low hum beneath the jukebox's soft croon. She wiped a spill from the counter, her movements steady, but her eyes kept drifting to the corner booth where Noah Carter sat, his hoodie pulled low, his hands wrapped around a soda he hadn't touched. He'd been coming in more lately, always alone now, his presence a quiet weight she couldn't ignore.

She'd been watching him for weeks, ever since the library, ever since Mrs. Hargrove had whispered *Jake* and the rumor of a push on the ridge in 2023. Her notebook was upstairs in her flat, its pages dense with threads—Tom's fear, Sarah's silence, the youth group records, that memorial article

—all pulling her toward Noah, the face in the dark she'd been chasing. She'd seen the way he moved, the guarded sharpness in his eyes, the way he'd glance at her and look away, quick and deliberate, like he knew she was closing in. Tonight, she'd decided, was the night to pull the thread harder, to see what broke loose.

She finished pouring a pint for a regular, sliding it across with a nod, and waited until the bar slowed, the clock ticking past ten. Noah hadn't moved, his soda still full, his fingers tapping a slow rhythm against the glass, and she felt the pull, the edge of truth she'd been brushing against since July sharpening into something she couldn't let go. She grabbed a rag, untied her apron, and stepped out from behind the bar, her heart thudding in her chest as she crossed the room.

"Hey," she said, stopping at his booth, her voice casual, a smile tugging at her lips. "Mind if I sit? Bar's quiet for a sec."

Noah's eyes flicked up, dark and steady, and he shrugged, his voice low, flat. "Sure. Whatever."

She slid into the seat across from him, the vinyl creaking under her, and set the rag on the table, her hands resting lightly beside it. Up close, he looked younger, his face smooth but shadowed, his jaw tight with something she couldn't name. "You come in a lot lately," she said, keeping her tone easy, conversational. "Not much for the crowd, huh?"

"Not really," he said, his eyes dropping to the soda, his fingers stilling. "Just killing time."

She nodded, leaning in slightly, her voice softening.

"Heard you're into hiking," she said, testing the waters. "Ever go up the ridge? Sounds like a tough spot."

His hand twitched, a small, sharp motion, and his eyes snapped back to hers, sharper now, a crack in the stillness. "Not much," he said, his tone steady but edged. "Why?"

She shrugged, her smile widening, disarming. "Just talk," she said, watching him closely. "Heard about an accident up there, couple years back. Kid fell, they say. You ever hear that story?"

Noah's face didn't change, but she saw it, the flicker in his eyes, the way his shoulders tensed, a shadow passing through him she could feel. "Yeah," he said, his voice colder now, deliberate. "Old news. Happens sometimes."

"Jake, right?" she pressed, her heart pounding, the name a blade she couldn't resist wielding. "That's what they called him. Must've been rough, being up there when it happened."

His hand clenched around the glass, the soda sloshing slightly, and he leaned back, his eyes narrowing, the mask slipping just enough for her to see the dark beneath. "Don't know what you're talking about," he said, his voice low, a warning threaded through it. "I wasn't there."

She tilted her head, her smile fading, her voice dropping to match his. "People say you were," she said, steady, unyielding. "Tom, Sarah, they remember. Said you saw it all. What'd you see, Noah?"

He stood, abrupt and silent, the glass thudding against the table, and grabbed his jacket, his eyes locked on hers, cold and sharp. "You're digging where you shouldn't," he said, his voice a quiet blade, cutting through the hum of the pub. "Leave it alone."

He turned, heading for the door, his steps quick, deliberate, and Lena watched him go, her breath shallow, the thrill of the chase mixing with a chill she couldn't shake. She'd seen it, the crack in his calm, the shadow in his eyes, and it was enough, a glimpse of the face in the dark she'd been chasing. He'd been there, on the ridge, with Jake, and whatever happened, he carried it, a secret she was closer to than ever.

She stood, her legs unsteady, and moved back to the bar, her mind racing. She'd write it down tonight—*November 22— Noah reacts to Jake. Knows more, scared.* The thread was pulling her toward Ravenswood, toward a truth she could feel, sharp and cold, and she didn't know it was pulling her toward a night she wouldn't survive, a shadow waiting in the dark with a knife she couldn't see.

CHAPTER THIRTY-SIX

L ena stood outside the pub, the night air biting at her skin, the fog thick and damp against her face. It was late November 2024, the village quiet except for the distant hum of a car fading down the lane, the pub's neon sign buzzing faintly behind her. She pulled her coat tighter, her breath fogging in the cold, and watched Noah Carter's figure disappear into the mist, his hoodie a dark blur moving fast down the street. Her heart still pounded from their confrontation, his warning—You're digging where you shouldn't—ringing in her ears, a blade that cut through her but didn't stop her. She'd seen the crack in him, the shadow in his eyes when she'd said Jake, and it was enough to pull her deeper.

She hesitated, her boots scuffing the wet pavement, then followed, her steps quick and silent, the thrill of the chase outweighing the chill she'd felt in his voice. She'd left the pub early, telling the manager she wasn't feeling well, her notebook tucked into her bag upstairs, but she didn't need it now. The thread was sharp in her mind, Noah's reaction a beacon she couldn't ignore—his clenched hand, his cold stare, the way he'd bolted when she'd pressed about the ridge. He was hiding something, something tied to Jake, to 2023, and she was too close to let it go.

The fog swallowed the village, the streetlights glowing like faint halos, and she kept her distance, tracking his shape as he turned off the main road, heading toward the edge of town. The houses thinned, their windows dark, and the trees loomed closer, their branches skeletal against the sky. She knew where he was going—Ravenswood, the old estate, its ruins a shadow in the woods she'd heard about but never seen. Her pulse quickened, the connection snapping into place: if Noah was tied to the ridge, to Jake, Ravenswood might be where he went to think, to hide, to face whatever he carried.

She slowed as he veered into the forest, his figure slipping between the trees, and she followed, the ground soft and damp under her boots, the air heavy with the scent of pine and wet earth. The fog thickened, muffling sound, and she moved carefully, her hands brushing branches, her eyes locked on his fading shape. He stopped near a clearing, the outline of Ravenswood's crumbling walls just visible through the mist, and she crouched behind a tree, her breath shallow, watching as he stood still, his head bowed, his hands in his pockets.

He didn't move for a long moment, and she felt the weight of it, the silence between them stretching tight, a thread she could almost touch. Then he reached down, pulling something from his pocket—a small, dark object she couldn't make out—and knelt, digging into the dirt with his hands. Her stomach tightened, the scene eerie in the fog, and she shifted, straining to see. He buried it, quick and deliberate, then stood, brushing his hands on his jeans, his head turning slightly, like he sensed her.

She ducked lower, her heart slamming against her ribs, and waited, the cold seeping into her knees. He lingered, his gaze sweeping the trees, and she held her breath, the fog a thin shield between them. Then he turned, heading back toward the village, his steps faster now, and she waited until he was gone, the crunch of leaves fading into the night.

She crept forward, her hands trembling as she reached the spot, the earth freshly turned, a small mound under the shadow of Ravenswood's walls. She knelt, digging with her fingers, the dirt cold and gritty, until she hit something hard—a metal box, rusted and small, its lid scratched but intact. She pried it open, her breath catching as she saw a folded paper inside, yellowed and worn. She unfolded it, the fog curling around her, and read the faded ink: *Jake—July 23, 2023. I didn't mean it. I'm sorry.*

Her chest tightened, the words a punch she hadn't expected, and she stared at them, Noah's handwriting unmistakable from the school records she'd seen. *I didn't mean it.* The ridge, Jake's fall, a push—rumors turned real, a confession buried here, under Ravenswood's shadow. She thought of his face in the pub, the crack in his calm, and felt the trail deepen, the mystery sharpening into a truth she couldn't unsee.

She tucked the note into her coat, replacing the box, and stood, her legs shaky, the fog pressing closer. Noah had been there, had done something to Jake, and he'd kept it hidden, a secret she'd pulled free. She didn't know what it meant yet, not fully, but she knew it was big, dark, and she was on the edge of it, too close to stop. She turned back toward the village, the note burning in her pocket, unaware that the shadow she chased was watching, its knife waiting for a night she couldn't escape.

CHAPTER THIRTY-SEVEN

L ena sat at her kitchen table, the flat above the bakery cloaked in the stillness of late November 2024, the fog outside her window a thick, gray curtain that muffled the village below. A single lamp glowed beside her, its light pooling over the rusted metal box she'd dug up at Ravenswood last night, the folded note inside now spread flat on the table. Noah's handwriting stared up at her, faded but stark: Jake—July 23, 2023. I didn't mean it. I'm sorry. The words looped in her mind, a quiet hammer striking the edges of her thoughts, and she traced them with her finger, the paper cool and brittle under her touch.

She hadn't slept, not really, just drifted in and out of a restless haze, the note's weight anchoring her to the table. Her notebook lay open beside it, her latest entry scrawled in a shaky hand: *November 23—Found Noah's note at Ravenswood. Jake's death, not an accident? He did it.* She'd felt the pull of the past sharpen when she'd unearthed it, the confession a crack in the shadow she'd been chasing, and now it was pulling her deeper, a thread she couldn't cut loose. Noah Carter had been on that ridge, had done something to Jake—a push, a shove, something he hadn't meant—and the guilt had driven him to bury this, a secret she'd pulled free.

She stood, her chair scraping the floor, and paced to the window, the fog pressing against the glass like a living thing. Her reflection stared back, pale and hollow-eyed, the thrill of the chase mixing with a chill she couldn't shake. She'd seen Noah's face in the pub, the crack in his calm when she'd said *Jake*, and now this note, his own words tying him to a death the village had buried. She thought of Tom's warning, Mrs. Hargrove's whispers, Sarah's tight-lipped silence—they all knew, or suspected, and Noah's family, Ellie and Daniel, they carried it too, a shadow beneath their perfect lives she could feel.

Her phone buzzed on the table, a sharp jolt in the quiet, and she crossed back, picking it up. A text from Claire: *You're obsessed, sis. Call me, I'm worried.* Lena's lips twitched, a faint smile, but she set it down, the normalcy of it too distant now. She didn't have time for worry, not when she was this close. She grabbed her notebook, flipping to an earlier page: *July 28, 2023—memorial, no body. Noah survivor?* Then Tom's words: *Carter boy saw it all.* And now this note, a confession that turned rumors into truth. *I didn't mean it.* She needed more, needed to know what happened, who Jake was, why Noah had kept it buried.

The pub wouldn't open for hours, but she couldn't wait.

She pulled on her coat, the note slipping into her pocket beside her keys, and headed downstairs, the bakery's stale sweetness lingering in the air as she stepped into the fog. The village was silent, the streets empty, and she walked toward the square, her boots clicking softly, her mind racing. She'd seen Sarah at the bakery yesterday, her hands busy with dough, her eyes avoiding Lena's when she'd asked about Noah again. *"Leave it alone,"* she'd said, her voice tight, but Lena couldn't, not now, not with this.

The bakery's lights were off, but a flicker caught her eye —a figure moving inside, too early for opening. She knocked, the glass rattling, and Sarah appeared, her apron dusted with flour, her face creasing with surprise. "Lena?" she said, opening the door a crack, her voice low, wary. "What're you doing here?"

"Couldn't sleep," Lena said, forcing a smile, her tone light despite the weight in her pocket. "Thought I'd grab a coffee, chat a bit. You got a minute?"

Sarah hesitated, her eyes flicking past Lena into the fog, then nodded, stepping back. "Sure," she said, her voice tight. "Come in, but make it quick."

Lena followed her inside, the warmth of the ovens cutting through the chill, the scent of yeast and sugar thick in the air. Sarah moved to the counter, pouring coffee from a pot, her hands steady but her shoulders tense. "What's on your mind?" she asked, sliding the mug across, her eyes avoiding Lena's.

Lena took it, sipping to buy time, then leaned in, her

voice soft, probing. "Noah Carter," she said, watching her closely. "You know about the ridge, Jake, what happened in '23. I found something, Sarah. He was there, and it wasn't an accident."

Sarah's hand froze on the counter, her breath catching, and she looked up, her eyes wide, sharp with fear. "You don't know what you're doing," she said, her voice low, urgent. "I told you, let it be. It's not your story."

"But it's his," Lena said, her tone firm, unyielding. "He wrote it down, Sarah. 'I didn't mean it.' Jake's dead, and Noah's carrying it. What happened up there?"

Sarah stepped back, her hands clenching, and shook her head, her voice trembling. "You're gonna get hurt, Lena," she said, almost a whisper. "Leave it alone, please. I don't know everything, but I know enough. He's not right, that boy."

Lena's stomach tightened, the pull of the past a force she couldn't resist, and she stood, the coffee untouched. "I can't," she said, her voice steady, resolute. "Thanks, Sarah." She turned, stepping back into the fog, the note burning in her pocket, the trail deepening toward Ravenswood, toward a truth she couldn't turn away from, a shadow she didn't see waiting.

CHAPTER THIRTY-EIGHT

L ena sat on the edge of her bed, the flat above the bakery shrouded in the gray light of late November 2024, the fog outside her window a thick veil that dulled the village's edges. The rusted metal box from Ravenswood sat on her nightstand, its lid open, Noah's confession note—Jake —July 23, 2023. I didn't mean it. I'm sorry—crumpled beside it, its words a quiet roar in her mind. She hadn't gone back to sleep after leaving Sarah at the bakery hours ago, her body wired with the pull of the past, her notebook open on her lap, its pages a tangled map of the mystery she'd been chasing for months.

Her latest entry stared up at her, scrawled in the dim glow of her lamp: *November 23—Sarah knows, scared. Noah not right, she says. Jake's death his fault?* She'd felt the pieces aligning since she'd found the note last night, the thread sharpening with every step—Tom's fear, Mrs. Hargrove's whispers, Sarah's trembling warning—and now it was coming together, a shadow taking shape around Noah Carter. She'd seen his crack at the pub, felt his guilt in the note, and Sarah's words had sealed it: *He's not right, that boy.* Something had happened on the ridge, something Noah had done, and the village had buried it, but she was pulling it free.

She stood, her legs stiff from sitting too long, and moved to the window, the fog pressing against the glass, her reflection a ghost in the haze. Her hands shook slightly, the thrill of the chase mixing with a cold unease she couldn't name, and she thought of Noah's eyes, sharp and guarded, the way he'd warned her to stop. She'd pushed too hard, she knew it, but she couldn't turn back, not now, not when the pieces were aligning into a truth she could almost touch. Jake, a boy lost on the ridge, a push, a fall, and Noah's *I didn't mean it*—it wasn't just guilt, it was a confession, and she needed to know why, how, who he was hiding it from.

The pub was closed today, a rare Sunday off, and she'd planned to dig more at the library, but her phone buzzed on the bed, a sharp interruption in the quiet. She grabbed it, expecting Claire again, but it was Tom Bennett, his name a jolt on the screen: *Meet me at the shop. Noon. Got something.* Her stomach tightened, the pieces shifting again, and she typed back a quick *Okay*, her heart pounding as she checked the time—11:37. She pulled on her coat, the note slipping into her pocket beside her keys, and headed downstairs, the bakery's warmth fading as she stepped into the fog.

The village was hushed, the streets empty, the fog swallowing sound as she walked toward Tom's hardware store, its sign a faint blur in the mist. She pushed the door open at noon sharp, the bell jingling, the air inside sharp with the scent of metal and wood. Tom stood behind the counter, his coat still on, his face drawn, his hands fidgeting with a screwdriver. "Lena," he said, his voice gruff, low, his eyes flicking to the door. "Lock it."

She did, the click loud in the quiet, and turned, her tone steady despite the knot in her chest. "What's this about, Tom? You said you've got something."

He nodded, stepping out from the counter, his hands shoving into his pockets. "Couldn't sleep after last night," he said, his voice rough, strained. "You're digging too deep, but you're not wrong. About Noah, the ridge."

Her pulse quickened, the pieces aligning tighter, and she leaned in, her voice soft, urgent. "What happened up there? Jake, the fall—tell me."

Tom rubbed his jaw, his eyes darting away, then back to hers, sharp with something like fear. "Wasn't just a fall," he said, his voice dropping to a whisper. "I was there, helping the search after. Found a shoe, kid's size, caught in the rocks, blood on it. Police said it was nothing, accident, but I heard the kids talking before they shut up—Noah and Jake, arguing, loud, then quiet. Next thing, Jake's gone."

Lena's breath caught, the shadow sharpening, and she stepped closer, her voice trembling with the thrill. "Arguing about what? Did Noah push him?"

Tom shook his head, his hands clenching. "Don't know," he said, his tone tight. "But he was different after, quiet, closed off. His folks, Ellie and Daniel, they kept him close, said he was shook up. I think he did it, Lena, and they covered it. You gotta stop, though. He's not safe."

The pieces snapped into place, Noah's note a confession now, not just guilt, and she felt the pull of the past tighten, the edge of truth a blade she couldn't drop. "I can't," she said, her voice firm, resolute. "Thanks, Tom." She turned, unlocking the door, stepping back into the fog, the note burning in her pocket, the trail leading her to Ravenswood, to Noah, to a truth she didn't know would end her.

CHAPTER THIRTY-NINE

L ena sat at her kitchen table, the flat above the bakery bathed in the dim, cold light of late November 2024, the fog outside her window a thick shroud that pressed against the glass. The rusted metal box from Ravenswood sat in front of her, its lid open, Noah's confession note—Jake—July 23, 2023. I didn't mean it. I'm sorry—crumpled beside it, its words a quiet storm in her mind. Her notebook lay open, its pages a dense web of her months-long chase, and her latest entry stared up at her, scrawled after Tom's revelation hours ago: November 23—Tom saw blood, heard argument. Noah pushed Jake? Covered up. The pieces had aligned, and now the final thread was pulling her toward a truth she couldn't turn away from.

She leaned back, her chair creaking, her hands trembling slightly as she rubbed her eyes, the exhaustion of sleepless nights settling into her bones. Tom's words looped in her head—*a shoe, blood on it, Noah and Jake arguing*—a chilling echo of the note, the rumors, the whispers she'd collected. Noah Carter had been on that ridge, had fought with Jake, had pushed him, maybe, and the village had buried it, his parents shielding him, the police calling it an accident. She'd seen his crack at the pub, felt his guilt in the note, heard Sarah's fear, and now Tom's story sharpened it all into a shadow she could almost touch.

She stood, pacing to the window, the fog blurring her reflection into a ghost, her breath fogging the glass. Her coat hung by the door, the note still in its pocket, a weight she carried like a talisman, and she thought of Noah's face, his guarded eyes, his warning: *Leave it alone.* She hadn't, couldn't, and now she was too close, the final thread pulling her toward Ravenswood, toward him. She'd go back tonight, she decided, her pulse quickening with the thrill of it, the need to confront him, to pull the truth free before it slipped away. She didn't know what she'd say, not yet, but she'd make him talk, make him face what he'd done.

The pub was closed, her shift tomorrow, but she couldn't wait. She grabbed her phone, ignoring Claire's unanswered texts, and scrolled to a draft she'd started weeks ago, a message to Noah she'd never sent: *We need to talk. I know about the ridge.* She hesitated, her thumb hovering, then deleted it, her breath shallow. No warning, no chance for him to run. She'd find him at Ravenswood, where he'd buried the note, where the shadow of his past lingered, and she'd pull it out of him, face to face.

A knock on the door jolted her, soft but insistent, and

she crossed to the stairwell, her heart thudding as she opened it. Mrs. Hargrove stood there, her scarf loose, her eyes wide with something like panic, the fog curling around her like a shroud. "Lena," she said, her voice trembling, low. "I saw you come back earlier. You've got to stop."

Lena stepped back, gesturing her in, her tone steady despite the knot in her chest. "Come in," she said, closing the door. "What's wrong?"

Mrs. Hargrove stayed by the stairs, her hands twisting together, her voice a whisper. "You're asking too much," she said, her eyes darting to the table, the box, the note. "I heard from Tom, he's scared, says you're onto Noah. It's not safe, Lena. Whatever happened up there, it's done."

Lena's stomach tightened, the final thread pulling harder, and she stepped closer, her voice firm, unyielding. "It's not done," she said, her eyes locking onto hers. "Jake didn't just fall, did he? Noah did something, and you all let it go. I found his note, Mrs. Hargrove. He wrote it down."

The older woman's face paled, her breath catching, and she shook her head, her voice breaking. "You don't understand," she said, stepping back. "He's not... he's not right, Lena. I saw him after, the way he changed, closed off. You're pushing him, and he'll push back. Please, stop."

Lena felt the chill deepen, the shadow sharpening, but she couldn't stop, not now. "I can't," she said, her voice resolute, the pull of the past a force she couldn't resist. "He needs to answer for it."

Mrs. Hargrove turned, her hands trembling as she

opened the door, her voice a whisper lost in the fog. "You're making a mistake," she said, and slipped out, the door clicking shut behind her.

Lena stood still, the silence heavy, the note burning in her pocket, and felt the pieces align, the final thread pulling her toward Ravenswood, toward Noah, toward a confrontation she didn't know would end her. She grabbed her coat, her resolve steeling, and stepped into the fog, the village fading behind her, the shadow waiting ahead.

CHAPTER FORTY

Lena stood at the edge of Ravenswood, the fog thick and cold around her, the estate's crumbling walls looming like ghosts in the late November night of 2024. The village was a distant blur behind her, its lights swallowed by the mist, and the forest stretched dark and silent, the damp earth soft under her boots. She'd walked here straight from her flat, the note in her coat pocket—Jake—July 23, 2023. I didn't mean it. I'm sorry—a weight pulling her forward, her resolve a fire that burned through the chill. She'd seen Noah leave the pub earlier, his hoodie low, his steps quick toward the woods, and she knew this was it, the final thread, the confrontation she couldn't avoid.

Her breath fogged in the air, her heart pounding as she stepped into the clearing, the ruins stark against the fog, their broken stones jagged in the moonlight. She'd been here last night, digging up his confession, and now she felt the pull of the past sharper than ever, the shadow of Jake's death aligning with Noah's guilt, a truth she'd chased for months.

She scanned the trees, her eyes straining through the mist, and saw him—a dark figure near the side door, his back to her, his hands in his pockets, still as the night itself.

"Noah," she called, her voice steady, cutting through the silence, and he turned, slow and deliberate, his face shadowed under the hood, his eyes glinting in the faint light. She stepped closer, her boots crunching leaves, her hands steady despite the tremor in her chest. "We need to talk."

He didn't move, his gaze locking onto hers, cold and unreadable, and she felt the crack she'd seen at the pub widen, the shadow beneath it spilling out. "You shouldn't be here," he said, his voice low, rough, a warning she'd heard before but couldn't heed.

"I know about Jake," she said, her tone firm, unyielding, pulling the note from her pocket and holding it up, its edges trembling in her grip. "I found this. You were on the ridge, you did something to him. Tell me what happened."

Noah's jaw tightened, his hands clenching in his pockets, and he stepped forward, his voice dropping to a whisper. "You don't know what you're doing," he said, his eyes sharp, cutting. "Put that away. Go home."

She shook her head, stepping closer, the fog curling around them, the air thick with the weight of his words. "I'm not going anywhere," she said, her voice rising, fierce. "Jake didn't fall, did he? You pushed him, Noah. You wrote it down —'I didn't mean it.' What didn't you mean? Tell me, or I take this to the police."

His face shifted, a flicker of something—fear, anger,

guilt—breaking through the calm, and he moved faster, closing the gap, his hand grabbing her wrist, tight and cold. "You're wrong," he said, his voice a growl, his breath fogging between them. "You don't understand. Let it go."

She pulled free, her wrist stinging, and stepped back, her heart slamming against her ribs, the note still in her hand. "I understand enough," she said, her voice trembling but resolute. "You killed him, and they covered it up—your parents, the village. I've got proof, Noah. It's over."

He froze, his eyes wide, the crack splitting open, and she saw it, the shadow in him, the weight of 2023 crashing through. "You're gonna ruin everything," he said, his voice breaking, raw, and he lunged forward, his hands reaching for the note, his breath ragged.

She stumbled back, the fog swallowing her steps, and turned to run, her boots slipping on the wet leaves, the note clutched tight. She heard him behind her, his footsteps heavy, his voice a desperate shout—"Lena, stop!"—but she didn't, her legs pumping, the ruins fading into the mist. She'd get to the village, to Tom, to someone, and end this, the truth too big to hold alone.

A shadow moved ahead, tall and quick, cutting through the fog, and she stopped, her breath catching, her eyes straining to see. Not Noah—someone else, a figure she hadn't heard, hadn't sensed, until now. "Who's there?" she called, her voice sharp, trembling, and the shadow stepped closer, silent, deliberate, a glint of metal flashing in the moonlight.

She turned, Noah's footsteps closing in, and saw him

emerge from the fog, his face pale, his eyes wide with something like panic. "Lena, wait—" he started, but the shadow moved faster, a blur of motion, and she felt it—a sharp, searing pain in her side, the knife slicing through her coat, her scream cutting the night as she fell, the note slipping from her hand into the leaves.

She hit the ground, the fog swirling around her, her vision blurring as the shadow loomed, tall and faceless, and Noah's voice roared, distant, frantic—"No!"—before fading into the dark. The pain burned, her breath shallow, and she clawed at the dirt, the truth slipping away, the shadow falling over her as her chase ended, the final thread snapping in a night she couldn't survive.

PART 5: JULIA REYNOLDS

CHAPTER

FORTY-ONE

J ulia Reynolds sat at her desk in the small office above the
village post shop, the late morning light of March 9, 2025,
filtering through the blinds, casting thin stripes across
the cluttered stacks of legal files. The air smelled of ink and old
paper, a faint hum of traffic drifting up from the street below,
and she leaned back in her chair, her dark hair pulled tight in
a bun, her fingers tapping a restless rhythm against a coffee
mug gone cold. She'd been up since dawn, her phone buzzing
with Ellie's frantic call hours ago—Noah's at the station, Hollis
has him, they found Lena's phone—and now the weight of it
sat heavy in her chest, a case she couldn't dodge, a friend she
couldn't abandon.

She'd known Ellie Carter for years, since university,
their friendship forged over late-night study sessions and
shared bottles of cheap wine. Ellie was the steady one, the
psychologist who saw through people's masks, and Julia was

the sharp edge, the lawyer who cut through the bullshit. But now, with Lena Moreau's murder tearing through the village, Ellie's family was cracking, and Julia felt the pull, the call to action she couldn't ignore. She'd been at the Carters' house yesterday, seen the fear in Ellie's eyes, the strain in Daniel's voice, the cold defiance in Noah's, and she knew this wasn't just a client—it was personal.

Her phone buzzed again, Ellie's name flashing, and she picked it up, her voice calm, professional, a shield she'd honed over years in court. "Ellie," she said, leaning forward, her pen poised over a notepad. "What's happening?"

"They're keeping him," Ellie said, her voice trembling, raw with exhaustion. "Hollis says Noah admitted he was at Ravenswood, saw Lena die, but he won't say who did it. They've got his prints, texts, everything. Julia, I don't know what to do."

Julia's stomach tightened, her mind racing, and she scribbled a quick note—*Noah at scene, witness, no ID*—her hand steady despite the jolt. "Slow down," she said, her tone firm, grounding. "He's not charged yet, right? Just held?"

"Yeah," Ellie said, her breath hitching. "Voluntary, Hollis says, but he's pushing. Daniel's there now, trying to talk to him, but Noah's... he's shutting us out. I'm scared, Julia. What if he's lying?"

Julia paused, her pen stilling, and thought of Noah, sixteen, quiet, his eyes sharp but closed off, a kid she'd watched grow up, now tangled in a murder she couldn't unsee. "We'll figure it out," she said, her voice softening, resolute. "I'm coming over. Don't say anything to Hollis without me there, okay?"

"Okay," Ellie said, her voice small, fragile, and the line went dead, leaving Julia in the quiet of her office, the weight of it settling deeper. She stood, grabbing her coat from the rack, her movements quick, deliberate, the lawyer's calm locking into place. She'd seen the news this morning—Lena Moreau, stabbed at Ravenswood, body found Saturday, the village buzzing with shock and whispers—and now Noah was in it, Ellie's son, a boy she'd bounced on her knee, caught in a web she didn't fully understand.

She stepped outside, the March air cold and sharp, the village square bustling with early shoppers, their voices a low hum beneath the overcast sky. She walked toward the Carters' house, her boots clicking on the pavement, her mind piecing it together—Ellie's call days ago about texts, a scarf, a key, then Noah's receipt, the notebook, the silk strip. She'd told them to go to the police, to get ahead of it, but now it was spiraling, and she felt the pull, the need to protect Ellie, to cut through the chaos and find the truth.

The house came into view, its stone walls pale in the gray light, Ellie's car parked crooked in the drive, a sign of her haste. Julia knocked, the sound sharp, and Ellie opened the door, her face pale, her eyes red-rimmed, her sweater slipping off one shoulder. "Julia," she said, stepping back, her voice breaking. "Thank God you're here."

Julia stepped inside, the hall warm but heavy with tension, the faint scent of coffee lingering from the kitchen.

"Where's Daniel?" she asked, shedding her coat, her tone steady, professional.

"Still at the station," Ellie said, sinking onto the couch, her hands twisting in her lap. "He's trying to get Noah to talk, but he won't. Hollis called me an hour ago, said they've got more—texts from Lena's phone, to Noah, to me. I don't know what's happening, Julia."

Julia sat beside her, her notepad out, her voice calm, cutting through the panic. "Tell me everything," she said, her eyes locking onto Ellie's. "Start with the texts. What did they say?"

Ellie took a shaky breath, her voice trembling as she spoke. "One to me, Friday night—'You were right.' Then to Noah, same time—'Meet me at R.E.' Hollis says it's his number, but he swears he didn't send them. He admitted he was there, saw her die, but he says it was someone else, a shadow. He won't say who."

Julia's pen scratched fast, her mind racing—*Texts from Noah's number, shadow killer, Ravenswood*—and she looked up, her voice firm. "He's a witness, not a suspect yet," she said, her tone resolute. "But if he's lying, or hiding something, we need to know. What about this Jake thing? Mrs. Hargrove mentioned it yesterday, said Lena was asking."

Ellie's face crumpled, her hands clenching. "She found a note," she said, her voice breaking. "Noah's, about Jake, 2023. He was on the ridge when a boy fell, died. He wrote he didn't mean it. I don't know what it means, Julia, but Lena did, and now she's dead."

Julia's chest tightened, the pieces shifting, a shadow deepening, and she stood, her resolve steeling. "I'm going to the station," she said, her voice steady, a lawyer's edge. "We'll get Noah out, figure this out. Stay here, Ellie. I've got this."

She left, stepping back into the cold, the village a blur around her, the call to action pulling her toward the station, toward Noah, toward a truth she didn't yet see, a shadow waiting to fall.

CHAPTER FORTY-TWO

J ulia stood outside the police station, the March wind cutting through her coat, the gray brick building looming squat and stern under the overcast sky of March 9, 2025. The village buzzed faintly behind her, a hum of midday life, but here the air was still, heavy with the weight of what waited inside—Noah Carter, sixteen, held for questioning in Lena Moreau's murder, a boy she'd known since he was a toddler, now a wall of silence she had to breach. She adjusted her bag, her lawyer's calm locking into place, and stepped through the door, the fluorescent lights buzzing overhead, the air sharp with disinfectant and tension.

The lobby was small, a row of plastic chairs empty except for Daniel, who sat hunched, his hands clasped tight, his face drawn with exhaustion. He looked up as she approached, his eyes red-rimmed, a flicker of relief breaking through the strain. "Julia," he said, standing, his voice rough, worn. "You're here."

"Ellie called," she said, her tone steady, professional, though her chest tightened at his desperation. "Where's Noah?"

"Still with Hollis," Daniel said, running a hand through his hair, his breath shaky. "They've had him in there an hour. He admitted he saw Lena die, but he won't say who did it. Keeps saying it was a shadow, nothing else. I tried talking to him, but he's... he's shut me out."

Julia nodded, her mind racing, and set her bag down, pulling out her notepad. "I'll get him out," she said, her voice firm, resolute. "He's not charged yet, just a witness. Stay here, Daniel. I've got this."

He sank back into the chair, his hands clenching, and she turned, approaching the desk where a young officer sat, his face blank but curious. "Julia Reynolds," she said, her tone crisp, authoritative. "Legal counsel for Noah Carter. I need to see him, now."

The officer nodded, disappearing through a door, and minutes later Hollis emerged, his coat off, his notebook in hand, his eyes steady and unreadable. "Ms. Reynolds," he said, his voice calm, a faint edge beneath it. "Good timing. We're keeping him for now, voluntary, but he's not talking much. You're welcome to try."

"Take me to him," she said, her gaze locking onto his, unflinching, and he led her down a narrow hall, the walls a dull gray, the air colder here, heavier. He opened a door to an interrogation room, the same stark space she'd seen in a dozen cases, and there sat Noah, slouched in a chair, his hoodie pulled low, his hands resting on the table, still smudged with ink.

"Counsel's here," Hollis said, stepping back, his voice neutral. "I'll give you ten minutes." He left, the door clicking shut, and Julia sat across from Noah, her notepad open, her pen poised, her eyes studying him—his sharp jaw, his guarded eyes, the boy she'd known now a stranger behind a wall of silence.

"Noah," she said, her voice soft but firm, cutting through the quiet. "It's me. You don't have to talk to Hollis, but you need to talk to me. What happened at Ravenswood?"

He didn't look up, his fingers tapping a slow rhythm against the table, his voice low, flat. "I told them," he said, his tone cold, rehearsed. "I was there, saw her die. Someone else did it, a shadow. That's it."

Julia leaned forward, her hands flat on the table, her voice steady, probing. "That's not it," she said, her eyes locking onto his. "They've got your prints on a knife, texts from your number to Lena, to your mom. You're tied to this, Noah, and you're not helping yourself. Who was the shadow? Give me something."

His tapping stopped, his hands clenching, and he looked up, his eyes sharp, a crack flickering in the calm. "I didn't send those texts," he said, his voice rougher now, edged. "I don't know who it was. I saw it happen, that's all. Let it go."

She didn't flinch, her voice dropping, a lawyer's edge cutting deeper. "I can't let it go," she said, her tone firm, unyielding. "Your mom's falling apart, your dad's out there breaking, and you're sitting here with half a story. Lena had a note, Noah—Jake, 2023, 'I didn't mean it.' What did you do?"

His face shifted, a shadow passing through, and he leaned back, his hands dropping to his lap, his voice cold again, a wall snapping back into place. "You don't get it," he said, his eyes narrowing. "It's not about Jake. It's done. I didn't kill her."

Julia's chest tightened, the pieces shifting—Jake, the ridge, Lena's death, Noah's silence—and she felt the psychological weight of it, a boy hiding something dark, a truth she couldn't reach. "Then who did?" she asked, her voice low, steady. "If you saw it, tell me. Hollis isn't stopping, and neither am I."

He stared at her, the crack closing, the silence a wall she couldn't breach, and shook his head, his voice barely a whisper. "I don't know," he said, his eyes dropping, the lie a shield she could feel. "Leave it alone."

The door opened, Hollis stepping in, his notebook closed, his voice cutting through. "Time's up," he said, his eyes flicking between them. "We're holding him a bit longer. Results on the texts are coming in."

Julia stood, her hands clenching her notepad, her resolve steeling despite the wall of silence. "He's done talking," she said, her tone crisp, protective. "Anything else, you go through me."

She left the room, Noah's eyes burning into her back, and found Daniel in the lobby, his face a mask of dread. "He's not saying much," she said, her voice low, steady. "But he's scared, Daniel. There's more here, and I'll find it."

She stepped outside, the wind sharp against her skin, the village a blur around her, the wall of silence echoing in her mind, a shadow she couldn't see pulling the strings.

CHAPTER FORTY-THREE

Julia sat on the Carters' living room couch, the late afternoon light of March 9, 2025, slanting through the windows, casting long shadows across the hardwood floor. The room smelled faintly of coffee and the lavender lotion Ellie always wore, a comforting scent now undercut by the tension thick in the air. Ellie sat across from her, perched on the edge of an armchair, her hands twisted in her lap, her face pale and drawn, her eyes flickering with a mix of fear and exhaustion. Julia's notepad rested on her knee, her pen poised, her lawyer's calm a thin shield against the storm she felt brewing.

She'd left the station an hour ago, Noah's wall of silence echoing in her mind—*I saw it happen, a shadow, that's all*—and now she was here, digging for the buried truth she knew Ellie held, a truth tied to Jake, to 2023, to the shadow that killed Lena Moreau. "Ellie," she said, her voice steady, soft but

194

firm, cutting through the quiet. "We need to talk about the ridge. Noah's note, what Lena found. You've got to tell me everything."

Ellie's breath hitched, her hands clenching, and she looked away, her eyes settling on a framed photo on the mantel—Noah at ten, gap-toothed and grinning, a boy she didn't recognize in the teenager Julia had faced today. "I don't know everything," she said, her voice trembling, low. "It was two years ago, Julia. He was fourteen, on a youth group hike. A boy, Jake, fell. They never found him. Noah came back... different, quiet, but we thought it was shock."

Julia nodded, her pen scratching across the page—*Ridge, 2023, Jake fell, Noah changed*—her mind piecing it together, the weight of it settling deeper. "Different how?" she asked, her tone probing, gentle but insistent. "Lena's note said 'I didn't mean it.' What didn't he mean?"

Ellie's face crumpled, her hands pressing to her mouth, a sob breaking through, and she shook her head, her voice raw. "I don't know," she said, her eyes meeting Julia's, wide and wet. "He wouldn't talk about it, not to me, not to Daniel. We took him to a counselor once, but he shut down, said it was an accident, nothing more. We believed him, Julia. We had to."

Julia's chest tightened, the psychological depth of it hitting her—Noah, a boy hiding a secret, his parents shielding him, maybe themselves, from a truth too dark to face. "But Lena didn't," she said, her voice firm, cutting. "She dug it up, found his note, tied it to Jake. Hollis has him now, Ellie, with prints, texts, a witness account. He saw her die, and he's not saying who. What happened up there?"

Ellie stood, pacing to the window, her arms wrapped tight around herself, her voice trembling as she spoke. "I don't know," she said again, her back to Julia, her reflection faint in the glass. "He came home that day, soaked, pale, wouldn't look at us. Daniel asked, I asked, but he just said Jake slipped, fell, end of story. The police searched, found nothing, called it an accident. We didn't push, didn't want to break him more."

Julia's pen paused, her eyes narrowing, the buried truth sharpening in her mind. "He wrote 'I didn't mean it,'" she said, standing, her voice low, steady. "That's not slipping, Ellie. That's guilt. Did he push him? Did you know?"

Ellie turned, her face flushed, her voice rising, sharp with desperation. "No!" she said, her hands clenching at her sides. "He's not a killer, Julia. He's my son. He was scared, upset, but he didn't do it. Lena got it wrong, twisted it. She pushed him, and now she's dead, and he's caught in it."

Julia stepped closer, her notepad forgotten, her voice dropping, a lawyer's edge cutting through. "Then why's he lying?" she asked, her eyes locking onto Ellie's. "He saw Lena die, Ellie. A shadow, he says, but he won't name it. He's hiding something, and it's not just Jake. What aren't you telling me?"

Ellie's breath caught, her eyes darting away, and she sank back into the chair, her hands trembling in her lap. "I don't know," she whispered, her voice breaking, a confession of its own. "I've been getting texts, Julia. Before Lena died, after. 'You were right,' 'They'll find out.' I thought it was her, but now... I don't know who it is."

Julia's stomach dropped, the shadow deepening, and she sat, her voice steady despite the jolt. "Show me," she said, her tone firm, urgent. "Now."

Ellie pulled her phone from her pocket, her fingers shaking as she unlocked it, scrolling to the messages— unknown number, stark and cold: *March 6, 9:52 p.m.—You were right. March 8, 11:47 p.m.—They'll find out.* Julia's pen scratched fast—*Texts to Ellie, same as Noah's*—her mind racing, the buried truth pulling her deeper into a mystery she couldn't unsee.

"Someone knows," she said, her voice low, resolute. "And they're tying it to Noah, to you. I'm getting him out, Ellie, but we need answers. This isn't just about Lena anymore."

Ellie nodded, her tears falling, and Julia stood, her resolve steeling, the wall of silence cracking but not breaking, a shadow she'd chase to protect her friend, a truth she'd uncover no matter the cost.

CHAPTER FORTY-FOUR

Julia stood in the police station lobby, the late afternoon light of March 9, 2025, fading into a dull gray through the narrow windows, the air sharp with the scent of stale coffee and tension. The hum of voices filtered from the back, a low murmur against the buzz of fluorescent lights overhead, and she adjusted her bag, her lawyer's calm a thin veneer over the unease coiling in her chest. She'd left Ellie an hour ago, the texts—You were right, They'll find out—burning in her mind, a shadow tying Noah to Lena's death, to Jake's, to something darker she couldn't yet see. Now she was here, to pull Noah out, to protect him, but the line between friend and counsel was blurring, and she felt it slipping.

Daniel sat beside her, his hands clasped tight, his face a mask of exhaustion, his eyes flicking to the hall where Noah was still held. "He's been in there too long," he said, his voice rough, worn thin. "Hollis keeps pushing, Julia. What if he breaks?"

"He won't," she said, her tone steady, resolute, though her stomach tightened at the thought. "He's a witness, not a suspect yet. I'll get him out, Daniel. Trust me."

He nodded, his jaw clenching, and she stood as Hollis emerged, his coat on now, his notebook tucked under his arm, his eyes steady but sharp, cutting through her calm. "Ms. Reynolds," he said, his voice calm, a faint edge beneath it. "Back already. Got the text results. You'll want to see this."

"Show me," she said, her voice firm, unflinching, and followed him to his office, a cramped space with a desk piled high with files, a single bulb casting harsh light across the room. Daniel trailed behind, his presence a quiet weight, and Hollis pulled a printout from a folder, sliding it across the desk —text logs, stark and black: *March 6, 9:52 p.m.—To Lena: Meet me at R.E. To Ellie: You were right.*

Julia's eyes scanned the page, her pen poised, her mind racing—*Noah's number, confirmed*—and she looked up, her voice steady despite the jolt. "He says he didn't send these," she said, her tone crisp, protective. "You've got proof it's his phone?"

Hollis leaned back, his hands folding, his gaze locking onto hers. "SIM's his," he said, his voice even, cutting. "Pulled the records. Sent from his device, same tower ping as the pub receipt, 9:47. He's lying, Julia. He lured her there, saw her die, won't name the killer. Why?"

Her chest tightened, the line blurring, and she glanced at Daniel, his face paling, his hands clenching the chair. "He's scared," she said, her voice firm, a lawyer's shield. "He's sixteen, Hollis. A witness, not a murderer. You've got no charge, no grounds to hold him. Let him go."

Hollis's eyes narrowed, his pen tapping the desk, a slow, deliberate rhythm. "He's a witness with a knife print," he said, his tone steady, probing. "Partial match, close enough to question. And this Jake thing—Lena's note, 2023, 'I didn't mean it.' He's got history, Julia. What's he hiding?"

Julia's stomach dropped, the buried truth sharpening, and she leaned forward, her voice low, cutting. "You've got speculation," she said, her eyes locking onto his. "No full print, no murder weapon in hand, texts he denies sending. He saw it, that's all. Release him, or I'll file for coercion. Now."

Hollis held her gaze, the quiet stretching, then nodded, his voice calm but edged. "Fine," he said, standing, his chair scraping back. "He's yours, for now. But we're not done. Those texts, the print—they're piling up."

She followed him back to the interrogation room, Daniel close behind, and the door opened to Noah, slouched in the same chair, his hoodie low, his eyes fixed on the table, his hands still smudged with ink. "Noah," she said, her voice soft, firm, cutting through the silence. "You're coming home. Let's go."

He looked up, his eyes sharp, guarded, a crack flickering in the calm, and stood, slow and deliberate, his voice low, flat. "Thanks," he said, his tone cold, a wall she couldn't breach.

They left the station, the wind sharp against her skin, Daniel's arm around Noah's shoulders, a protective grip that felt hollow. Julia walked beside them, her notepad in her bag, her mind racing—*Noah's phone, the texts, Jake's death*—the line blurring further, suspicion coiling tighter. "Noah," she said, her voice low, steady, as they reached the car. "You need to talk to me. The truth, all of it. What happened with Jake?"

He stopped, his eyes meeting hers, cold and unreadable, and shook his head, his voice a whisper. "It's nothing," he said, the lie a shield she could feel. "Let it go."

Daniel's face tightened, his voice rough. "Noah, please," he said, his hand squeezing his shoulder. "We're trying to help you."

Noah pulled free, climbing into the car, his silence a wall she couldn't break, and Julia stood there, the wind tugging at her coat, the shadow deepening, the buried truth pulling her closer to a line she couldn't unblur.

CHAPTER FORTY-FIVE

J ulia sat at the Carters' kitchen table, the evening shadows of March 9, 2025, stretching long and dark across the tile floor, the faint hum of the fridge a steady pulse in the quiet. The air smelled of burnt toast and the coffee Ellie had brewed, its bitterness sharp against the tension coiling in the room. Ellie stood by the sink, her hands gripping a mug, her face pale and hollow, her eyes darting to the stairs where Noah had retreated after the station, his silence a wall that lingered between them. Julia's notepad lay open, her pen resting beside it, her lawyer's calm fraying under the weight of what she'd seen in Noah's eyes—cold, guarded, a shadow she couldn't shake.

She'd brought him home an hour ago, Daniel's relief a fragile thing as he'd followed Noah upstairs, his voice low, pleading, unanswered. Now it was just her and Ellie, the house settling into an uneasy hush, and Julia felt the echoes of the past resounding, the texts, the note, Jake's death pulling her deeper into a mystery she couldn't unsee. "Ellie," she said, her voice steady, soft but firm, cutting through the stillness. "We need to go back to the ridge, 2023. Noah's not talking, but you know more. What changed him?"

Ellie's mug trembled, coffee sloshing slightly, and she set it down, her hands clenching the counter, her voice low, trembling. "I told you," she said, her eyes fixed on the sink, avoiding Julia's gaze. "He came back quiet, shaken. We thought it was the accident, losing Jake. He wouldn't say more, Julia. We didn't push."

Julia leaned forward, her hands flat on the table, her voice steady, probing. "You didn't push," she said, her tone cutting gently, insistent. "But he wrote 'I didn't mean it.' Lena found that, tied it to Jake, and now she's dead. Hollis has texts from his phone, Ellie—'Meet me at R.E.' He's hiding something, and it's not just grief. What did you see in him after?"

Ellie turned, her face crumpling, her hands twisting together, and she sank into a chair, her voice breaking as she spoke. "He stopped sleeping," she said, her eyes meeting Julia's, wet and wide. "For weeks, he'd sit up all night, staring at nothing. I'd find him in his room, hands shaking, eyes red, but he wouldn't talk. Daniel thought it was shock, trauma, but... there was something else, Julia. He'd flinch when we touched him, like he was scared of us."

Julia's chest tightened, the echoes resounding, and she scribbled a note—*Post-2023, sleepless, flinching*—her mind racing, the psychological weight of it hitting her. "Scared of you?" she asked, her voice low, steady despite the jolt. "Or scared of what he'd done? Ellie, did he ever say anything, anything at all, about Jake?"

Ellie's breath hitched, her hands pressing to her face, and she shook her head, her voice a whisper. "Once," she said, her eyes darting away, then back, sharp with fear. "Months later, he was half-asleep, mumbling. I heard him say, 'I didn't want him to go.' I asked him the next day, but he shut down, said it was a dream. I let it go, Julia. I had to."

Julia's pen paused, her stomach dropping, the buried truth sharpening—*I didn't want him to go*—a confession echoing the note, a crack in Noah's silence she couldn't ignore. "That's not a dream," she said, her voice firm, cutting. "That's guilt, Ellie. He was there, he did something to Jake, and it's following him. Lena saw it, and now she's dead. Who's the shadow, Ellie? What's he protecting?"

Ellie's face flushed, her voice rising, raw with desperation. "He's not protecting anyone!" she said, her hands slamming the table, the mug rattling. "He's my son, Julia, not a killer. He saw Lena die, he said it was someone else. He's scared, not guilty!"

Julia stood, her hands clenching her notepad, her voice low, steady, a lawyer's edge breaking through. "Then why's he lying?" she asked, her eyes locking onto Ellie's. "The texts came from his phone, Ellie. 'Meet me at R.E.' He lured her there, or someone did, using him. He's in this, and you're blind to it. Tell me what you're hiding, or I can't help him."

Ellie's breath caught, her eyes wide, and she sank back,

her voice trembling, a whisper lost in the quiet. "I'm not hiding anything," she said, her hands shaking. "I don't know who it is, Julia. The texts, the shadow—I don't know. But he's my boy, and he's breaking."

Julia's chest tightened, the line blurring further, suspicion coiling around her loyalty, and she sat, her voice softening, resolute. "He's breaking because he's carrying something," she said, her eyes steady. "Jake's death, Lena's, it's connected. I'm getting to the bottom of it, Ellie, for you, for him. But I need the truth."

Ellie nodded, her tears falling, and Julia felt the echoes resound, the shadow deepening, a truth she'd chase through the cracks, no matter the cost.

CHAPTER FORTY-SIX

Julia sat at a table in the village library, the late evening stillness of March 9, 2025, wrapping around her, the air thick with the musty scent of old books and polished wood. The high windows let in only a faint glow from the streetlights, the fog outside a gray veil that muffled the world, and she adjusted her glasses, her fingers brushing the edge of a microfiche reader, its screen casting a blue light across her face. Her notepad lay open beside her, its pages filled with the day's notes—Noah's silence, Ellie's texts, the mumbled I didn't want him to go—and now she was here, chasing the ghost of the ridge, the 2023 accident that haunted the Carters' lives.

She'd left Ellie's house an hour ago, the echoes of their conversation—*He's breaking, He's not a killer*—ringing in her ears, a desperate plea she couldn't fully trust. Noah was at the heart of this, his confession note to Jake, his presence at Lena's death, the texts from his phone, and Julia felt the psychological weight of it, a boy hiding a truth she had to uncover. Mrs. Hargrove had let her in after hours, her scarf loose, her eyes sharp with reluctant curiosity, and now Julia was alone, the library a quiet tomb where the past waited to be exhumed.

She scrolled through the microfiche, the headlines flickering past—village events, weather updates—until she hit July 2023, her breath catching as she found it again: *Teen Missing After Ridge Fall. Search Called Off.* She'd seen it before, with Ellie, but now she read closer, the sparse words sharpening in her mind: *July 23, youth group hike, treacherous terrain, no body recovered.* She flipped to her notepad, scribbling—*Date matches note*—and scrolled further, her pulse quickening as she landed on a follow-up, dated August 5: *Local Youth Group Mourns Loss.* The article was brief, but a line stood out: *Survivors shaken, one boy treated for minor injuries.*

Julia's stomach tightened, the ghost of the ridge whispering, and she leaned back, her pen tapping the table, her mind racing. One boy injured—Noah? She thought of Ellie's words—*soaked, pale, hands shaking*—and the note: *I didn't mean it.* A fall, a push, an injury, a secret buried under the village's silence. She needed more, needed proof, and she stood, crossing to the counter where Mrs. Hargrove sat, sorting books, her hands slow, deliberate.

"Mrs. Hargrove," Julia said, her voice steady, soft but firm, cutting through the quiet. "You remember the ridge accident, 2023? I need anything you've got—records, names, anything."

The older woman looked up, her eyes narrowing, her scarf slipping slightly, and she set the books down, her voice low, cautious. "You're digging deep," she said, her tone sharp with something like warning. "It was a sad thing, Julia. Why stir it up now?"

Julia leaned in, her hands flat on the counter, her voice steady, probing. "Because it's not done," she said, her eyes locking onto hers. "Lena Moreau tied it to Noah Carter, found a note he wrote—'I didn't mean it.' He was there, saw her die, and he's not talking. What do you know?"

Mrs. Hargrove's face paled, her hands trembling as she adjusted her scarf, her voice dropping to a whisper. "I told Lena," she said, her eyes darting to the door, then back. "Jake Ellis, that was the boy. Nice kid, loud, always laughing. They said he fell, but... I heard things, after. Kids talking, before they stopped—one said Noah and Jake were fighting, up top, then he was gone."

Julia's chest tightened, the name *Jake Ellis* cutting through, and she scribbled it down, her voice low, urgent. "Fighting about what?" she asked, her pen pressing hard against the page. "Did Noah push him?"

Mrs. Hargrove shook her head, her voice trembling, a whisper lost in the quiet. "Don't know," she said, her eyes wide, fearful. "No proof, just talk. Noah came back hurt, a cut on his hand, said he'd slipped too, but... he changed, Julia. Closed off, cold. Lena saw it, kept asking, and now she's gone."

Julia's stomach dropped, the ghost of the ridge sharpening, a shadow she could feel—Noah injured, fighting, Jake gone, a secret echoing into Lena's death. "Who else knew?" she asked, her voice firm, cutting. "Ellie, Daniel—did they cover it?"

Mrs. Hargrove stepped back, her hands clenching, her voice breaking. "They protected him," she said, almost inaudible. "Said he was shaken, needed time. I don't know more, Julia. Leave it be, please."

Julia nodded, her resolve steeling, and turned back to the microfiche, the echoes resounding, the buried truth pulling her deeper. She sat, her hands steady despite the tremor in her chest, and felt the line blur further, suspicion coiling around her loyalty, a ghost she'd chase to protect Ellie, to save Noah, to uncover a shadow she couldn't yet name.

CHAPTER FORTY-SEVEN

Julia stood in the Carters' living room, the late evening shadows of March 9, 2025, pooling dark and heavy across the hardwood floor, the faint glow of a single lamp casting a warm circle that didn't touch the chill in the air. The house was quiet, the hum of the village outside muffled by the thick walls, and she adjusted her glasses, her notepad clutched tight, her lawyer's calm a fraying thread against the tension coiling in her chest. Daniel sat on the couch, his face drawn, his hands clasped between his knees, while Ellie hovered by the window, her arms wrapped tight around herself, her eyes red and distant. Noah was upstairs, his door shut since they'd returned from the station, his silence a fracture widening between them all.

She'd come straight from the library, Mrs. Hargrove's words—*Noah and Jake fighting, a cut on his hand, he changed*—ringing in her ears, a ghost of the ridge sharpening the shadow she'd been chasing. "Daniel," she said, her voice steady, soft but firm, cutting through the quiet. "We need to talk about 2023, the ridge. I've got more now, and it's not adding up. Noah was hurt up there, wasn't he?"

Daniel's head snapped up, his eyes narrowing, his voice rough with exhaustion. "What're you getting at, Julia?" he asked, his hands clenching, a flicker of defensiveness breaking through. "You've been at him all day. He's home, let it rest."

Julia stepped closer, her notepad open, her voice steady, probing. "I can't," she said, her eyes locking onto his. "Lena tied him to Jake Ellis, a boy who fell, died, on that hike. Noah wrote 'I didn't mean it.' Mrs. Hargrove heard kids say they fought, said he came back with a cut on his hand. He didn't just see it, Daniel. What happened?"

Ellie's breath hitched, a sharp sound in the silence, and she turned, her face pale, her voice trembling. "A cut?" she said, her eyes darting to Daniel, wide with fear. "You never told me that."

Daniel's jaw tightened, his hands unclenching, and he rubbed his face, his voice low, strained. "It was nothing," he said, his eyes flicking away, then back to Julia. "He scraped his hand, said he slipped trying to help Jake. He was shaken, Ellie, you saw him. We took him to the clinic, got it cleaned, that's it. He didn't fight anyone."

Julia's chest tightened, the fracture widening, and she sat across from him, her pen scratching fast—*Cut on hand, clinic, denied fight*—her mind racing, the psychological weight of it hitting her. "He didn't slip," she said, her voice firm, cutting. "He wrote 'I didn't mean it,' Daniel. Ellie heard him say 'I didn't want him to go.' Kids saw them arguing, then Jake's gone. He's hiding something, and you covered it."

Daniel stood, his hands clenching at his sides, his voice rising, rough with anger. "Covered what?" he snapped, his eyes sharp, cutting. "He's not a killer, Julia. He was fourteen, scared, a kid on a hike that went wrong. The police ruled it an accident, no body, no proof. You're twisting it, like Lena did."

Ellie moved closer, her hands trembling, her voice breaking as she spoke. "Stop it," she said, her eyes flicking between them, wet and desperate. "Both of you. He's not lying, Julia. He saw Lena die, said it was someone else. Why won't you believe him?"

Julia's stomach dropped, the line blurring further, and she stood, her voice low, steady despite the strain. "Because he's not telling us everything," she said, her eyes locking onto Ellie's, then Daniel's. "The texts came from his phone—'Meet me at R.E.' He lured her, or someone used him. He's got a cut from the ridge, a note confessing guilt, and now he's silent about a shadow. What aren't you seeing?"

Daniel's face flushed, his voice rough, a growl breaking through. "I see my son breaking," he said, stepping closer, his hands shaking. "He's scared, Julia, not guilty. You're supposed to help us, not tear us apart."

Julia held his gaze, her resolve steeling, her voice softening, resolute. "I'm trying to help," she said, her eyes steady. "But I can't if you're blind. He was hurt, fighting, and Jake died. Lena found it, pushed him, and she's dead.

Someone's tying it together, texting you both. Who's the shadow, Daniel? Who's he protecting?"

Ellie's sob broke the quiet, her hands pressing to her face, and Daniel sank back onto the couch, his head in his hands, his voice a whisper. "I don't know," he said, his breath ragged. "He wouldn't say. We thought he'd heal, move past it. We didn't know about the note."

Julia's chest tightened, the fracture widening, suspicion coiling around her loyalty, and she sat, her voice low, firm. "He hasn't moved past it," she said, her eyes flicking between them. "It's here, in this house, in him. I'll find out, for you, for Noah. But we're running out of time."

The stairs creaked, a soft sound in the silence, and they turned, Noah's figure a shadow at the top, his eyes sharp, watching, the fracture widening further, a ghost she couldn't unsee.

CHAPTER FORTY-EIGHT

J ulia stood in the Carters' living room, the late evening stillness of March 9, 2025, broken only by the faint creak of the stairs as Noah descended, his figure a dark silhouette against the dim hall light. The air was thick with the scent of burnt toast and unspoken tension, the lamp's glow casting jagged shadows across the walls, and she felt her pulse quicken, her lawyer's calm a thin shield against the fracture widening in the room. Daniel sat frozen on the couch, his hands still in his hair, while Ellie turned from the window, her face pale, her eyes wide with a mix of fear and hope as Noah stepped into the light, his hoodie low, his hands shoved deep in his pockets.

"Noah," Julia said, her voice steady, soft but firm, cutting through the quiet, her notepad clutched tight in her hand. "We need to talk. Now."

He stopped at the edge of the room, his eyes sharp, guarded, flicking between her and his parents, his voice low, flat. "I said everything," he said, his tone cold, rehearsed, a wall she'd hit before. "There's nothing else."

Julia stepped closer, her glasses glinting in the light, her voice steady, probing. "There's plenty," she said, her eyes locking onto his. "I know about the ridge, Jake Ellis, 2023. You were hurt, a cut on your hand. You fought with him, wrote 'I didn't mean it.' Lena found it, pushed you, and now she's dead. You saw it, Noah. Who was the shadow?"

His jaw tightened, his hands clenching in his pockets, and he looked away, his eyes settling on the floor, a crack flickering in the calm. "I told Hollis," he said, his voice rougher now, edged. "I didn't kill her. It was someone else. That's it."

Ellie moved forward, her hands trembling, her voice breaking as she spoke. "Noah, please," she said, her eyes wet, pleading. "Tell her. We're trying to help you. What happened with Jake?"

He flinched, a small, sharp motion, and Julia saw it, the mask slipping, a shadow passing through his eyes as he turned to his mom, his voice low, a whisper cutting through. "You don't want to know," he said, his tone cold, final, a fracture she could feel.

Daniel stood, his face flushing, his voice rough with desperation. "Don't do this, Noah," he said, stepping closer, his hands outstretched. "We're your family. Whatever it is, we'll fix it. Just talk."

Noah's eyes snapped to his dad, sharp and cold, and

he stepped back, his voice rising, raw with something Julia couldn't name. "You can't fix it," he said, his hands pulling free, trembling now, the mask slipping further. "Jake's gone, Lena's gone, and you keep pushing. Let it go."

Julia's chest tightened, the psychological weight of it hitting her, and she set her notepad down, her voice low, steady, a lawyer's edge cutting deeper. "We can't," she said, her eyes locking onto his, unflinching. "The texts came from your phone, Noah—'Meet me at R.E.' You were hurt on the ridge, fighting Jake, and he died. You saw Lena stabbed, and you're protecting someone. Who?"

His breath hitched, his hands clenching into fists, and he stared at her, the crack widening, the shadow spilling out. "I'm not protecting anyone," he said, his voice breaking, a tremor running through it. "I didn't send those texts. I didn't mean for Jake to... I didn't want it."

Ellie's sob broke the quiet, her hands pressing to her mouth, and Daniel reached for him, his voice rough, pleading. "Didn't want what, Noah?" he asked, his hand hovering, then dropping. "What did you do?"

Noah's eyes widened, his face paling, and he stepped back, his voice a whisper, raw and jagged. "I pushed him," he said, the words spilling out, a confession cracking the mask wide open. "We were fighting, he wouldn't stop, and I pushed him. He fell, I tried to grab him, cut my hand, but he was gone. I didn't mean it."

The room froze, the air sucked out, and Julia felt the fracture widen, the ghost of the ridge roaring to life, a truth she'd chased now staring back at her. Ellie sank to the floor, her sobs muffled, and Daniel stood still, his face a mask of shock, his voice a whisper. "Oh God, Noah."

Julia's stomach dropped, the line blurring completely, and she stepped forward, her voice steady despite the tremor in her chest. "And Lena?" she asked, her eyes locking onto his, cutting. "You saw her die. Who was it?"

Noah's eyes darted away, the mask slipping back, cold and tight, and he shook his head, his voice low, a shield snapping into place. "I don't know," he said, the lie a wall she couldn't breach. "A shadow, tall, fast. That's all."

He turned, heading for the stairs, his steps heavy, and Julia called after him, her voice firm, resolute. "This isn't over, Noah," she said, her eyes burning into his back. "I'll find out."

He didn't stop, the door slamming shut upstairs, and Julia stood there, the fracture wide open, the mask slipped, a shadow she couldn't name pulling her deeper into a truth she wouldn't let go.

CHAPTER FORTY-NINE

Julia sat on the edge of the Carters' couch, the late night stillness of March 9, 2025, settling heavy in the living room, the lamp's faint glow casting a dim circle that barely touched the shadows clinging to the walls. The air was thick with the scent of cold coffee and the raw tension left by Noah's confession—I pushed him, he fell—a truth that echoed in the silence, a fracture that had split the family wide open. Ellie knelt on the floor, her face buried in her hands, her sobs muffled but sharp, while Daniel stood by the mantel, his shoulders slumped, his eyes fixed on the stairs where Noah had fled, his door slamming shut like a final wall.

Julia's notepad rested on her lap, her pen still, her lawyer's calm a fragile shield against the weight of knowing what Noah had done. Jake Ellis, a boy lost on the ridge in 2023, pushed by a fourteen-year-old Noah in a fight gone wrong, a secret buried until Lena pulled it free, and now tied to her death at Ravenswood. She felt the psychological strain of it, a boy she'd known unraveling into a stranger, and the shadow he wouldn't name looming larger, a mystery she couldn't let go.

"Ellie," she said, her voice steady, soft but firm, cutting through the quiet, her eyes flicking to her friend's crumpled form. "Daniel. We can't stop here. Noah pushed Jake, admitted it. But Lena—he saw her die, won't say who. We need to figure this out, now."

Ellie's head lifted, her face streaked with tears, her voice trembling, raw with despair. "He's not a killer, Julia," she said, her hands clenching, her eyes wide and pleading. "He didn't mean it, he said so. Jake was an accident, a fight. He's scared, that's why he won't talk."

Daniel turned, his face pale, his voice rough, strained with a mix of anger and grief. "He's our son," he said, his hands shoving into his pockets, his eyes sharp, cutting. "He was a kid, fourteen, panicked. We didn't know, Julia. He didn't tell us. How do we fix this?"

Julia stood, her notepad in hand, her voice steady, probing despite the tremor in her chest. "You fix it by facing it," she said, her eyes locking onto Daniel's, then Ellie's. "He's not just scared, he's hiding something. The texts came from his phone—'Meet me at R.E.' He lured Lena there, or someone did, using him. He saw the shadow kill her, and he's protecting it. Why?"

Ellie's breath hitched, her hands trembling as she stood, her voice rising, desperate. "He's not protecting anyone," she said, her eyes darting to the stairs, then back, wet and fierce.

"He said he didn't know who it was, Julia. He's telling the truth, I know him. He's breaking, not lying."

Julia's stomach tightened, the weight of knowing pressing harder, and she stepped closer, her voice low, steady, a lawyer's edge cutting through. "Then why won't he name it?" she asked, her eyes unflinching. "He's got guilt from Jake, a cut on his hand, a note confessing it. Lena found it, pushed him, and she's dead. The shadow's real, Ellie, and he knows more. We need to go to Ravenswood, see where it happened."

Daniel's face flushed, his voice rough, a growl breaking through. "Ravenswood?" he said, stepping forward, his hands clenching. "You want to drag us there, dig it up more? He's been through enough, Julia. Hollis is already on him, let it go."

Julia held his gaze, her resolve steeling, her voice softening, resolute. "I can't," she said, her eyes steady. "Hollis has prints, texts, a witness account. Noah's tied to two deaths now—Jake's an accident, maybe, but Lena's murder isn't. Someone's out there, texting you both, pulling strings. I'm not letting him take the fall for it."

Ellie's sob broke again, her hands pressing to her face, and she sank back to the floor, her voice a whisper. "What if it's my fault?" she said, her eyes lifting, haunted. "I saw her die, Julia, at Ravenswood. I don't remember how I got there, but I was there. What if he's protecting me?"

Daniel's head snapped to her, his voice sharp, stunned. "Ellie, no," he said, crossing to her, his hands gripping her shoulders. "You didn't do this. You couldn't."

Julia's chest tightened, the fracture widening further,

and she knelt beside Ellie, her voice low, urgent. "You saw her die," she said, her eyes locking onto hers. "And Noah did too. The shadow, Ellie—who was it? Think."

Ellie shook her head, her tears falling, her voice trembling. "I don't know," she said, her hands clenching Daniel's arms. "It's a blur, a shape, tall, fast. I blacked out, woke up here. I thought it was a dream, but it wasn't."

Julia stood, her mind racing—*Ellie and Noah at Ravenswood, same shadow*—the weight of knowing pulling her deeper, suspicion coiling around her loyalty. "I'm going there," she said, her voice firm, resolute. "Tonight. We need answers, and it starts where Lena died."

Daniel's face hardened, his voice rough, pleading. "Julia, stop," he said, standing, his hands outstretched. "You're tearing us apart."

She turned, her eyes steady, the fracture wide open. "I'm saving you," she said, her voice low, cutting. "Stay with him, or come with me. But I'm finding the shadow."

She grabbed her coat, stepping into the night, the fog thick around her, the weight of knowing a burden she'd carry to Ravenswood, to the truth she couldn't unsee.

CHAPTER FIFTY

J ulia stood at the edge of Ravenswood, the night fog of March 9, 2025, thick and cold around her, the estate's crumbling walls rising like jagged teeth from the earth. The village was a faint blur behind her, its lights swallowed by the mist, and the forest stretched dark and silent, the damp leaves crunching under her boots. She'd left the Carters' house minutes ago, Ellie's confession—I saw her die—and Noah's—I pushed him—ringing in her ears, a weight of knowing pulling her here, to the place where Lena Moreau met her end. Her flashlight cut a narrow beam through the fog, her breath fogging in the air, her lawyer's calm a thin shield against the tension coiling in her chest.

She stepped into the clearing, the ruins stark against the night, their broken stones glinting faintly in the moonlight. This was where it happened, where Noah had watched, where Ellie had blacked out, where a shadow had struck, and Julia felt the psychological strain of it, a family fracturing under secrets she couldn't unsee. Her notepad was in her bag, her pen tucked into her coat, but she didn't need them now—her eyes scanned the ground, the trees, searching for the shadow's trace, a clue to break the silence Noah wouldn't.

The wind whispered through the branches, a low moan that sent a shiver down her spine, and she moved toward the side door, the spot Noah had described, where Lena's body had been found. The earth was soft, trampled by police boots days ago, but she knelt, her flashlight sweeping the leaves, her hands brushing the dirt. She thought of Noah's cut hand, Jake's fall, the texts from his phone—*Meet me at R.E.*—and Ellie's blurred memory, a puzzle with a piece missing, a shadow she had to find.

Her light caught something, a glint in the leaves, and she reached down, her fingers closing around a small, cold object—a key, old and rusted, its teeth worn but sharp. Her stomach tightened, the echo of Ellie's key from months ago flashing in her mind, and she turned it over, her breath catching as she saw a faint scratch on the barrel, an initial carved crudely: *J.* Jake? Her pulse quickened, the shadow's trace sharpening, a link between the ridge and Ravenswood she couldn't ignore.

She stood, pocketing the key, and swept her light wider, her eyes straining through the fog. Footprints, faint but there, pressed into the mud near the door—two sets, one small, Noah's size, and another larger, deeper, fresh enough to stand out. Her chest tightened, the weight of knowing hitting her —someone else had been here, recent, after the police, after Lena's death. The shadow, tall and fast, Noah's words, Ellie's blur, and now this, a trace she could feel.

Her phone buzzed in her pocket, a sharp jolt in the silence, and she pulled it out, Ellie's name flashing on the screen. She answered, her voice steady despite the tremor in her hands. "Ellie," she said, her eyes still on the footprints, the fog curling around her. "What's wrong?"

"He's gone," Ellie said, her voice trembling, raw with panic. "Noah, he's not in his room. The window's open, Julia, he's gone. Daniel's looking, but I don't know where he went."

Julia's stomach dropped, the shadow's trace burning in her mind, and she turned, her light sweeping the trees, her voice firm, urgent. "Stay there," she said, her eyes darting through the fog. "Lock the doors. I'm at Ravenswood, I found something—a key, footprints. He might be coming here."

Ellie's breath hitched, a sob breaking through. "Oh God," she said, her voice shaking. "What if he's running? What if he's... Julia, please, find him."

"I will," Julia said, her resolve steeling, her voice steady despite the chill. "I'm on it." She hung up, her hand clenching the key, her light cutting through the mist, the footprints a trail she couldn't follow in the dark. Noah was out there, running from his confession, from the shadow, and she felt the fracture widen, the line blur completely, suspicion and loyalty warring in her chest.

She stepped back, her boots sinking into the mud, and heard it—a rustle in the trees, faint but sharp, a snap of a twig breaking the silence. She turned, her light sweeping, her voice low, cutting. "Noah?" she called, her heart pounding, the fog swallowing her words. "If it's you, come out. We can fix this."

The rustle stopped, the night still again, and she waited, her breath shallow, the shadow's trace a weight she couldn't shake. No answer, just the wind, but she knew—someone was there, watching, a ghost or a killer, and she stood alone, the key in her hand, the truth pulling her deeper into a darkness she couldn't escape.

PART 6: DETECTIVE MARK HOLLIS

CHAPTER FIFTY-ONE

Mark Hollis sat at his desk in the police station, the late night quiet of March 9, 2025, broken only by the faint hum of the heater and the occasional creak of the old building settling. The fluorescent lights buzzed overhead, casting a harsh glow across the cluttered space—files stacked high, a coffee mug stained with rings, a board on the wall pinned with photos of Lena Moreau's crime scene at Ravenswood. He leaned back in his chair, his coat draped over the armrest, his tie loosened, his eyes steady but tired, fixed on the notepad in front of him, its pages filled with the day's notes—Noah's confession, Julia's push, a shadow he couldn't pin down.

He'd let the Carter kid go hours ago, Julia's lawyer voice sharp in his ears—*No charge, no grounds*—but the pieces were shifting, a puzzle he'd been working since Lena's body turned up Saturday, stabbed and cold in the ruins. Noah had cracked under pressure, admitted to pushing Jake Ellis off the ridge in 2023, a fight turned fatal, a secret Lena had dug up and died for. But the shadow, the tall, fast figure Noah swore killed her, stayed a ghost, a name he wouldn't give, and Hollis felt the psychological weight of it, a case slipping through his fingers, a truth he had to chase.

His phone buzzed on the desk, a sharp jolt in the silence, and he picked it up, Julia Reynolds' name flashing on the screen. He answered, his voice calm, steady, a detective's edge honed over years. "Hollis," he said, his pen poised, his eyes narrowing. "What've you got, Julia?"

"Noah's gone," she said, her voice firm but tight, cutting through the line. "Window's open, he ran. I'm at Ravenswood, found something—a key, rusted, scratched with a 'J.' Footprints too, fresh, two sets. One's his size, the other's bigger. Someone's been here, Hollis."

Hollis's stomach tightened, the pieces shifting, and he scribbled fast—*Key with J, fresh prints, Noah fled*—his mind racing, the shadow sharpening in his thoughts. "Stay there," he said, his tone steady, commanding. "Don't touch anything else. I'm coming."

He hung up, grabbing his coat, his boots heavy on the tile as he headed out, the station a blur behind him. The night air hit him hard, cold and damp, the fog thick around the village, swallowing the streetlights into faint halos. He climbed into his car, the engine rumbling to life, and drove toward Ravenswood, his hands steady on the wheel, his mind piecing it together—Noah's partial print on the knife, the texts from his phone, Ellie's matching messages, now a key and footprints. The kid was running, scared or guilty, and the shadow was close, a trace he could feel.

He reached the estate, the ruins looming through the fog, and parked, his flashlight cutting a beam as he stepped into the clearing. Julia stood near the side door, her coat dark against the mist, her glasses glinting as she turned, her voice low, urgent. "Over here," she said, pointing to the ground, her hand steady despite the tension in her face. "The key's in my pocket, footprints are there."

Hollis knelt, his light sweeping the mud—two sets, clear in the damp earth, one small, one larger, deeper, fresh enough to hold shape. He nodded, his voice calm, cutting. "Noah's," he said, tracing the smaller print, then the bigger. "And someone else. Recent, after we cleared it Saturday."

Julia pulled the key from her pocket, holding it out, her voice firm, probing. "This was in the leaves," she said, her eyes locking onto his. "Scratched with a 'J.' Jake Ellis, maybe? Noah pushed him, Hollis, confessed it. Lena tied it to him, now this. What's it mean?"

Hollis took the key, turning it in his fingers, the rust flaking slightly, the *J* a crude mark that cut through him. "Means it's connected," he said, his tone steady, his mind racing. "Jake's death, Lena's, same thread. Noah's running from it, or to it. The shadow's here, Julia, and he's leaving traces."

She stepped closer, her voice low, steady despite the strain. "He saw it," she said, her eyes sharp, cutting. "Said it was tall, fast, wouldn't name it. Ellie saw it too, same night, blacked out. Someone's pulling strings, Hollis. Who?"

Hollis stood, pocketing the key, his light sweeping the

trees, his voice calm, resolute. "Don't know yet," he said, his eyes narrowing. "But the texts, the prints, now this—they're closing in. Noah's the key, Julia. We find him, we find the shadow."

A rustle broke the silence, faint but sharp, and he turned, his light cutting through the fog, his hand resting on his holster, his voice low, commanding. "Who's there?" he called, his breath fogging, the night still again.

Julia tensed beside him, her voice a whisper. "Noah?" she said, her eyes straining through the mist, but no answer came, just the wind, a shadow's trace lingering in the dark, pulling them deeper into a mystery he wouldn't let slip.

CHAPTER FIFTY-TWO

Mark Hollis stood in the Ravenswood clearing, the fog thick and cold around him, the night of March 9, 2025, pressing heavy against his skin. The estate's crumbling walls loomed through the mist, their jagged edges catching the faint moonlight, and he swept his flashlight across the trees, its beam cutting a narrow path through the dark. Julia Reynolds stood beside him, her breath fogging in the air, her glasses glinting as she peered into the shadows, her voice still echoing from moments ago—Noah's gone, he might be here—a lead that tightened the hunt he'd been on since Lena's body turned up.

He'd heard the rustle minutes ago, a snap in the fog that had stilled the night, and now he moved forward, his boots sinking into the damp earth, his hand resting lightly on his holster. The footprints he'd seen—small, Noah's size, and larger, fresh—burned in his mind, a shadow's trace he couldn't ignore, and the key Julia had found, scratched with a *J*, sat heavy in his pocket, a link between Jake Ellis's death in 2023 and Lena's murder here. He felt the psychological weight of it, a case shifting under his feet, a boy running from a confession, a killer he had to name.

"Spread out," he said, his voice calm, steady, cutting through the silence, his eyes flicking to Julia. "Stay close, but check the trees. If he's here, we'll find him."

Julia nodded, her flashlight sweeping right, her voice low, tense. "He's scared, Hollis," she said, her steps careful, deliberate. "He ran after admitting he pushed Jake. What if he's not just hiding?"

Hollis's jaw tightened, his light tracing the ground, his voice steady, probing. "Then he's running to something," he said, his eyes narrowing. "Or someone. The texts came from his phone, Julia. He's tied to this, scared or not."

She didn't respond, her beam cutting through the fog, and he moved left, his steps slow, methodical, his ears straining for sound—a crunch, a breath, anything. The clearing stretched wide, the ruins a dark bulk ahead, and he thought of Noah's words at the station—*A shadow, tall, fast, I don't know*—a half-truth he'd seen through, a crack in the kid's calm that didn't add up. Jake's fall, Lena's stab wound, the Carters' silence, it all circled back here, to Ravenswood, and the hunt was narrowing.

His light caught something—a glint in the leaves near the side door, a small, dark shape half-buried in the mud. He knelt, his fingers brushing the earth, and pulled it free —a phone, cracked but intact, its screen dark. His stomach tightened, the pieces shifting, and he turned it over, the case scratched, a faint sticker peeling: *L.M.* Lena Moreau. He stood, his voice low, urgent, cutting through the fog. "Julia, over here."

She crossed to him, her light joining his, her breath catching as she saw it. "That's hers," she said, her voice trembling, sharp with recognition. "Lena's. Hollis, it's been here since Friday?"

He nodded, pocketing it, his mind racing—*Lena's phone, missed by the sweep*—his voice calm, steady despite the jolt. "Could be," he said, his eyes sweeping the trees. "Or someone brought it back. The footprints, fresh, bigger than Noah's. The shadow's been here, after us."

Julia's face paled, her voice low, cutting. "Noah ran here," she said, her eyes darting through the mist. "He knew where it was, Hollis. What if he's meeting them?"

Hollis's chest tightened, the hunt narrowing, and he turned, his light cutting deeper into the woods, his voice firm, commanding. "Noah!" he called, his breath fogging, the name echoing in the dark. "If you're out there, come out. We've got your phone, your prints. It's over."

The fog swallowed his words, the silence stretching, and he waited, his hand on his holster, his eyes straining for movement. A rustle came again, sharper now, from the trees to his right, and he moved, his boots heavy on the leaves, Julia close behind, her voice a whisper. "Hollis, careful," she said, her light trembling slightly, her breath shallow.

He stopped at the tree line, his beam catching a shape —small, hunched, a hoodie low—and his voice cut through, steady, sharp. "Noah, stop," he said, his hand raised, his light steady. "It's me. Come out."

The figure froze, then turned, Noah's face pale in the beam, his eyes wide, sharp with fear, his hands trembling at his sides. "I didn't do it," he said, his voice rough, breaking, a crack in the calm Hollis knew too well. "I didn't kill her, I swear."

Hollis stepped closer, his voice calm, cutting. "Then who did?" he asked, his eyes locking onto Noah's, unflinching. "You ran here, kid. You knew about the phone. Talk."

Noah's breath hitched, his eyes darting to Julia, then back, his voice a whisper, raw with something Hollis couldn't name. "I don't know," he said, the lie a shield he clung to. "I came to find it, to stop it. The shadow's out there, not me."

Hollis's jaw tightened, the pieces shifting, the hunt narrowing, a shadow he could feel but couldn't see, pulling him deeper into a truth he wouldn't let slip.

CHAPTER FIFTY-THREE

Mark Hollis stood in the Ravenswood clearing, the fog thick and cold around him, the night of March 9, 2025, pressing heavy against the trees, their skeletal branches clawing at the mist. His flashlight beam pinned Noah Carter in place, the boy's pale face stark in the light, his hoodie low, his eyes wide with fear, his hands trembling at his sides. Julia Reynolds stood a step behind, her breath fogging in the air, her glasses glinting as she watched, her voice silent but her presence a steady weight. Hollis felt the hunt narrow, the pieces shifting—Lena's phone in his pocket, the key with J, the footprints—and now Noah, caught running, a boy on the edge of truth he couldn't outrun.

Hollis stepped closer, his boots crunching leaves, his voice calm, steady, cutting through the silence. "You're done running, Noah," he said, his eyes locking onto the boy's, unflinching. "You came here, knew where her phone was. Tell me what happened, all of it. Who's the shadow?"

Noah's breath hitched, his hands clenching into fists, his eyes darting to Julia, then back, his voice rough, breaking. "I told you," he said, his tone sharp, a crack in the calm Hollis knew too well. "I didn't kill her. I saw it, that's all. I came to find the phone, to stop it."

Hollis's jaw tightened, his light steady, his voice low, probing. "Stop what?" he asked, his eyes narrowing, cutting deeper. "You pushed Jake Ellis, 2023, confessed it. Lena found out, came here, and died. Texts from your phone lured her —'Meet me at R.E.' You ran tonight, straight to this spot. You're not just a witness, Noah. Who's out there?"

Noah's face paled further, his eyes flickering, a shadow passing through, and he stepped back, his voice trembling, raw with something Hollis couldn't name. "I don't know," he said, his hands shaking, the lie a shield he clung to. "I didn't send those texts. I came because... I thought it'd be here, proof it wasn't me."

Julia moved forward, her voice soft, urgent, cutting through the fog. "Noah, please," she said, her eyes sharp, pleading. "You're scared, I see it. You pushed Jake, didn't mean it, but Lena—someone killed her. You saw them. Tell us, we can protect you."

Noah's eyes snapped to her, wide and wet, and he shook his head, his voice breaking, a whisper lost in the mist. "You can't," he said, his hands clenching tighter, the mask slipping. "It's too late. They know I saw, they'll come for me."

Hollis's chest tightened, the edge of truth sharpening,

and he stepped closer, his voice steady, commanding. "Who's they?" he asked, his light unwavering, his hand resting on his holster. "You're not running again, Noah. The phone, the key with Jake's initial, the prints—someone's been here, after Lena, after us. Give me a name, or I take you in, right now."

Noah's breath caught, his eyes darting to the trees, then back, his voice a jagged whisper, raw with fear. "I didn't see a face," he said, his hands trembling, the crack widening. "Tall, fast, dark coat. They moved like they knew the place, like they'd been here before. I ran, hid, that's all. I didn't want this."

Hollis's stomach dropped, the pieces shifting—a dark coat, familiar ground, a shadow tied to Ravenswood—and he thought of Ellie's blur, her blackout, the texts matching Noah's. He leaned in, his voice low, cutting. "Before," he said, his eyes locking onto Noah's, unflinching. "You mean the ridge? Jake? Someone from back then?"

Noah's face froze, his breath shallow, and he shook his head, his voice a whisper, a shield snapping back. "I don't know," he said, his eyes dropping, the lie a wall Hollis could feel. "I didn't see."

Julia's voice cut through, sharp, desperate. "Noah, stop it," she said, stepping closer, her light trembling slightly. "You're protecting someone, or scared of them. Hollis has the phone, the key. It's over. Tell us."

Noah's eyes lifted, sharp and cold, and he stepped back, his voice low, breaking. "It's not over," he said, his hands unclenching, trembling in the light. "They're still out there. I came to end it, but I can't."

A rustle broke the silence, faint but sharp, from the trees behind, and Hollis turned, his light sweeping, his hand tightening on his holster, his voice firm, commanding. "Who's there?" he called, his breath fogging, the night still again. "Show yourself."

The fog swallowed his words, the rustle fading, and he turned back, Noah's eyes wide, his face pale, his voice a whisper. "They're here," he said, his hands shaking, the edge of truth a blade cutting through. "They've always been here."

Hollis's pulse quickened, the hunt narrowing, the shadow's trace a weight he couldn't shake, pulling him deeper into a truth he wouldn't let slip.

CHAPTER FIFTY-FOUR

Mark Hollis sat across from Noah Carter in the police station's interrogation room, the early morning stillness of March 10, 2025, settling heavy in the air, the fluorescent lights buzzing overhead. The gray walls were scratched and bare, the table between them cold and scuffed, and he leaned back in his chair, his coat off, his notepad open, his eyes steady on the boy slouched before him. Noah's hoodie was low, his hands clasped tight, his face pale and drawn, his eyes darting to the door where Julia Reynolds waited outside, her silhouette faint through the glass. Hollis felt the hunt narrow, the threads tightening—Lena's phone, the key with J, Noah's flight to Ravenswood—a shadow he could sense but couldn't name.

He'd brought the kid back an hour ago, the fog still clinging to his boots from the woods, Noah's whispered *They're here* echoing in his ears, a crack in the boy's silence that sharpened the chase. "Noah," he said, his voice calm, steady, cutting through the quiet, his pen poised over the page. "You ran to Ravenswood, found Lena's phone, said 'They've always been here.' Who's they? Stop lying, kid. The threads are tightening."

Noah's hands twitched, his eyes flicking up, sharp and guarded, his voice low, rough. "I told you," he said, his tone flat, a shield Hollis knew too well. "I don't know. I saw the shadow, that's it. I went to find the phone, to prove it wasn't me."

Hollis's jaw tightened, his light steady on the boy's face, his voice low, probing. "Prove it how?" he asked, his eyes narrowing, cutting deeper. "You pushed Jake Ellis, 2023, confessed it. Lena tied it to you, died for it. Texts from your phone lured her—'Meet me at R.E.' You ran tonight, straight there, said they're close. Who's been here, Noah? Give me something."

Noah's breath hitched, his hands unclenching, trembling slightly, and he looked away, his voice breaking, a whisper raw with fear. "I didn't send those texts," he said, his eyes darting to the table, then back, the crack widening. "I don't know who it is. Tall, dark coat, fast. They knew Ravenswood, like it was theirs. I ran because... they're after me now."

Hollis's chest tightened, the threads tightening, and he leaned forward, his voice steady, commanding. "After you why?" he asked, his pen scratching fast—*Dark coat, knows Ravenswood*—his mind racing. "You saw them kill Lena, didn't name them. Jake's death, your guilt—they're tied to it, aren't they? Someone from back then?"

Noah's face froze, his eyes wide, and he shook his head, his voice trembling, a shield fraying at the edges. "I don't know," he said, his hands clenching again, the lie a wall Hollis could feel. "I didn't see a face, just... them. They've been watching, always. I thought I could stop it."

The door opened, Julia stepping in, her face tight, her voice soft but sharp, cutting through the tension. "Hollis, enough," she said, her eyes flicking to Noah, then back, steady with resolve. "He's scared, look at him. He's not lying about the shadow. Let me talk to him."

Hollis held her gaze, the quiet stretching, then nodded, his voice calm, resolute. "Five minutes," he said, standing, his notepad closing with a snap. "But he's not leaving, Julia. The phone, the key, his prints—he's in this, deep."

He stepped out, the door clicking shut, and leaned against the wall, his mind piecing it together—Ellie's blackout, Noah's flight, the shadow's familiarity with Ravenswood. He pulled the key from his pocket, turning it in his fingers, the *J* a crude mark that cut through him, and thought of the ridge, Jake's fall, a fight Noah couldn't undo. The threads were tightening, a shadow from 2023 weaving into Lena's death, and he felt the psychological strain of it, a case he couldn't let slip.

His phone buzzed, a text from the tech lab flashing on the screen: *Lena's phone data—new message, sent post-mortem, March 7, 1:03 a.m.: "He'll pay." From Noah's number.* Hollis's stomach dropped, the pieces shifting, and he turned back to the room, his voice low, cutting through the glass. "Julia, out here. Now."

She emerged, her face paling as he showed her the screen, his voice steady, sharp. "Sent after she died," he said, his eyes locking onto hers, unflinching. "From his phone. He's lying, or someone's using him. The shadow's close, Julia, and it's not done."

A faint noise echoed down the hall, a soft thud from outside, and Hollis turned, his hand on his holster, his voice low, commanding. "Stay here," he said, his eyes sweeping the shadows, the threads tightening, a hunt he wouldn't let end.

CHAPTER FIFTY-FIVE

Mark Hollis stepped into the station's back lot, the early morning fog of March 10, 2025, thick and cold around him, the gray brick building a solid bulk against the mist. The air was sharp with the scent of damp asphalt and exhaust, the village silent beyond the faint hum of a distant car, and he swept his flashlight across the ground, its beam cutting through the dark. The thud he'd heard minutes ago—a soft, deliberate sound from outside— echoed in his ears, a shadow's breath he could feel, tightening the threads of a case that wouldn't let go. His hand rested on his holster, his boots steady on the pavement, his eyes straining for movement in the haze.

Inside, Noah sat with Julia, the boy's whispered *They're here* still ringing, the post-mortem text—*He'll pay*—from his phone burning in Hollis's pocket, a chilling jolt that shifted the pieces. He'd left them in the interrogation room, Julia's face pale with the weight of it, and now he was here, chasing a sound, a trace, a shadow that had been too close since Lena's death at Ravenswood. He felt the psychological strain of it, a hunt narrowing to a razor's edge, a killer watching from the dark.

He moved along the wall, his light sweeping the ground —wet from the fog, scuffed by boots—and stopped at the corner, his beam catching a glint in the gravel. He knelt, his fingers brushing the stones, and pulled it free—a cigarette butt, fresh, the tip still warm, a faint wisp of smoke curling into the mist. His stomach tightened, the shadow's breath sharpening, and he stood, his light tracing the lot, his voice low, cutting through the silence. "You're out here," he said, his breath fogging, his eyes narrowing. "I know it. Show yourself."

The fog swallowed his words, the stillness stretching, and he waited, his hand tightening on his holster, his ears straining for sound—a step, a breath, anything. The butt was new, dropped within the hour, a trace too close to the station, to Noah, to the threads he'd been pulling—Jake's fall, Lena's stab wound, the Carters' secrets. He thought of Noah's fear, *They've always been here*, and Ellie's blackout, a dark coat moving fast, a shadow tied to Ravenswood, now here.

A rustle came from the alley beyond the lot, faint but sharp, and he turned, his light cutting through the mist, his voice firm, commanding. "Police," he called, his boots crunching gravel as he moved, his pulse steady but quick. "Step out, hands up. Now."

The rustle stopped, the alley dark and still, and he advanced, his beam sweeping the shadows—a dumpster, a stack of crates, the glint of wet pavement—but no figure, no face, just the fog curling around him. He reached the crates, his light catching a mark in the dirt—a boot print, large, deep, fresh enough to hold shape, matching the bigger set from Ravenswood. His chest tightened, the shadow's breath a weight he could feel, and he knelt, his fingers tracing the edge, his mind racing—*Same size, same tread, too close.*

His radio crackled at his hip, a sharp jolt in the quiet, and he grabbed it, his voice low, steady. "Hollis," he said, his eyes still on the print, his light unwavering.

"Sir, it's Davies," came the voice, young, tense, cutting through the static. "Got a call from the Carters' house. Ellie says someone's outside, watching. Daniel's with her, they're locked in. You want backup?"

Hollis's stomach dropped, the threads tightening, and he stood, his voice firm, urgent. "Send a unit," he said, his eyes sweeping the alley, the fog thick around him. "Now. I'm heading there after I check in. Keep it quiet, no sirens."

He clipped the radio back, his light cutting through the mist, his hand on his holster as he turned back to the station. The cigarette butt, the boot print, the shadow's breath —it was here, then gone, now at the Carters', a thread weaving through Noah, through Ellie, through Ravenswood. He felt the psychological weight of it, a killer circling, a truth he couldn't let slip, and he moved fast, his boots heavy on the pavement, his mind piecing it together—*Tall, fast, dark coat, always here.*

He reached the door, stepping inside, the warmth hitting him hard, and found Julia in the hall, her face tight, her voice low, urgent. "What was it?" she asked, her eyes locking onto his, sharp with fear. "You heard something, Hollis."

"Cigarette butt, fresh," he said, his voice calm, cutting, his hand pulling it from his pocket, holding it up. "Boot print, matches Ravenswood. Someone's been here, Julia, minutes ago. Ellie just called—someone's at the house."

Her breath caught, her hands clenching, her voice trembling but firm. "Noah," she said, her eyes darting to the interrogation room, then back. "He said they're here. Hollis, what if they're after him?"

Hollis's jaw tightened, the shadow's breath a weight he couldn't shake, and he nodded, his voice steady, resolute. "Then we're close," he said, his eyes sharp, cutting. "Stay with him. I'm going to the house. The hunt's not over."

He turned, stepping back into the fog, the threads tightening, a shadow he could feel breathing down his neck, pulling him deeper into a truth he wouldn't let go.

CHAPTER FIFTY-SIX

Mark Hollis pulled up to the Carters' house, the early morning fog of March 10, 2025, thick and gray around him, the stone walls of the home a pale blur in the mist. The village was silent, the streetlights faint halos against the dark, and he cut the engine, his flashlight in hand, his boots heavy on the pavement as he stepped out. The cigarette butt and boot print from the station lot burned in his mind, the shadow's breath a weight he couldn't shake, and now Ellie's call—Someone's outside, watching—tightened the circle, pulling him back to the family at the heart of it all.

He approached the front door, his light sweeping the yard—wet grass, a tipped lawn chair, no tracks yet—and knocked, the sound sharp in the quiet. The door opened fast, Ellie's face pale in the frame, her eyes wide and red, her hands trembling as she clutched a sweater tight around her. "Hollis," she said, her voice trembling, raw with fear, stepping back to let him in. "Thank God. They're out there, I saw them."

He stepped inside, the hall warm but heavy with

tension, the faint scent of coffee lingering, and saw Daniel behind her, his face drawn, his hands clenched at his sides. "Where?" Hollis asked, his voice calm, steady, cutting through the panic, his eyes locking onto Ellie's. "Show me."

She pointed to the living room window, her voice shaking, urgent. "There," she said, crossing to it, her hands brushing the curtains. "A shape, tall, in a dark coat, just standing by the trees. I saw them when I went to check Noah's room, after he ran."

Hollis moved to the window, his light cutting through the glass, sweeping the yard beyond—the trees a dark line, the fog curling low, no figure now, just shadows. He turned, his voice low, probing. "When?" he asked, his eyes flicking between them, his pen poised over his notepad. "Exact time, Ellie."

"Ten minutes ago," she said, her hands twisting together, her eyes darting to Daniel, then back. "Maybe 2:30? I called right after. Daniel looked, but they were gone."

Daniel nodded, his voice rough, strained. "Nothing out there now," he said, stepping closer, his eyes sharp with exhaustion. "I checked the doors, locked everything. What's this mean, Hollis? Noah's at the station, right?"

Hollis's chest tightened, the circle closing, and he set his flashlight down, his voice steady, cutting. "He was," he said, his eyes locking onto Daniel's, then Ellie's. "Ran from his room, went to Ravenswood. Found Lena's phone there, said the shadow's after him. I brought him back, then found a cigarette butt, fresh, and a boot print outside the station. Now here.

Someone's circling you."

Ellie's breath caught, her hands pressing to her mouth, her voice trembling, a whisper breaking through. "Oh God," she said, her eyes wide, wet with fear. "They know he talked, don't they? About Jake, about Lena. Hollis, who is it?"

Hollis's jaw tightened, the threads tightening, and he stepped closer, his voice low, steady despite the jolt. "That's what I'm asking," he said, his eyes sharp, cutting. "Noah said tall, fast, dark coat, knows Ravenswood. You saw it too, Ellie, that night—same description. The texts, 'You were right,' 'He'll pay,' from his phone, after Lena died. Who's been here, always?"

Daniel's face flushed, his voice rough, rising with desperation. "We don't know!" he said, his hands clenching, his eyes darting to the window, then back. "He's scared, Hollis, not lying. He pushed Jake, didn't mean it, but Lena—he didn't kill her. Someone's framing him, using us."

Hollis's stomach dropped, the shadow's breath sharpening, and he pulled the cigarette butt from his pocket, holding it up, his voice calm, probing. "This was outside the station," he said, his eyes locking onto theirs, unflinching. "Minutes ago, while Noah was inside. Boot print matches Ravenswood. They're not framing him, Daniel—they're watching him, you, this house. Why?"

Ellie sank onto the couch, her face crumpling, her voice trembling, raw with guilt. "Because of me," she said, her hands shaking, her eyes lifting to Hollis's, haunted. "I was there, saw her die, didn't stop it. What if they think I know? What if they're after us all?"

Daniel knelt beside her, his voice rough, pleading. "Ellie, no," he said, his hands gripping hers, his eyes sharp with fear. "You didn't do anything. You blacked out, you said so. Hollis, tell her—she's not part of this."

Hollis stood still, his mind racing—*Ellie at Ravenswood, Noah's flight, the shadow's traces*—the circle closing, suspicion coiling around the family. "I don't know what she's part of," he said, his voice steady, cutting. "But you're all in it. The shadow's been here, at Ravenswood, the station, now your yard. They know this place, your lives. I need names, Daniel— friends, enemies, anyone from 2023."

Ellie's sob broke the quiet, her voice a whisper. "There's no one," she said, her hands clenching Daniel's, her eyes wet. "Just us, Hollis. Just us."

Hollis's chest tightened, the shadow's breath a weight he couldn't shake, the circle closing tighter, a truth he'd chase through the fog, no matter the cost.

CHAPTER FIFTY-SEVEN

Mark Hollis stood in the Carters' backyard, the early morning fog of March 10, 2025, thick and cold around him, the trees at the property's edge a dark wall against the mist. The house loomed behind him, its stone walls pale in the dim light, and he swept his flashlight across the wet grass, its beam cutting through the haze. Ellie and Daniel waited inside, their voices—They're out there, Just us— still echoing in his ears, a desperate denial that clashed with the shadow's breath he'd felt at the station, at Ravenswood, now here. His boots sank into the soft earth, his hand steady on his holster, his eyes straining for the mark of the watcher he knew was close.

He'd stepped out minutes ago, leaving them in the living room, Ellie's fear and Daniel's strain a weight he couldn't ignore. The cigarette butt, the boot print, the figure Ellie saw —tall, in a dark coat—tightened the circle, and he felt the psychological intensity of it, a hunt closing in on a shadow that knew this family too well. He moved toward the trees, his light tracing the ground—matted grass, a snapped twig—and stopped, his beam catching a glint in the mud near the fence, a small, dark shape half-buried.

He knelt, his fingers brushing the earth, and pulled it free—a pocketknife, old and rusted, its blade scratched but sharp, a faint *J.E.* carved into the handle. His stomach tightened, the mark of the watcher sharpening—Jake Ellis, the boy Noah pushed in 2023, a thread from the ridge now here, outside their home. He stood, pocketing it beside the key with *J*, his mind racing—*Lena's death, Noah's flight, the shadow's traces*—a circle closing tighter than ever.

He swept his light wider, his eyes catching a boot print in the soft soil, large, deep, matching the ones from Ravenswood, the station lot, fresh enough to hold shape. His chest tightened, the shadow's breath a weight he could feel, and he turned back to the house, his voice low, cutting through the fog. "You're still here," he said, his breath fogging, his eyes narrowing. "I'll find you."

He stepped inside, the warmth hitting him hard, and found Ellie and Daniel in the kitchen, her hands trembling around a mug, his clenched on the counter. "Hollis," Daniel said, his voice rough, rising as he saw him, his eyes sharp with exhaustion. "Anything?"

Hollis set the knife on the table, its rusted blade glinting in the light, his voice calm, steady, cutting through the tension. "This," he said, his eyes locking onto theirs, unflinching. "In your yard, near the trees. Initials *J.E.*—Jake Ellis. Boot print matches Ravenswood, the station. They were here, minutes ago, watching."

Ellie's mug slipped, coffee splashing across the table, her voice trembling, a whisper breaking through. "Jake's?" she said, her hands shaking, her eyes wide with fear. "Oh God, Hollis, how? Noah said he pushed him, but this—someone's doing this to us."

Daniel's face paled, his voice rough, strained with desperation. "It's not possible," he said, stepping closer, his hands clenching, his eyes darting to the knife, then back. "Jake's dead, Hollis. Noah saw him fall, the police searched. Who's got his knife?"

Hollis's jaw tightened, the threads tightening, and he leaned forward, his voice low, probing. "Someone who knows," he said, his eyes sharp, cutting. "Noah confessed, ran to Ravenswood, said the shadow's after him. Ellie, you saw it too —tall, dark coat, fast. The key with *J*, now this knife, here. They're tied to Jake, to you, to this house. Who's been close, all this time?"

Ellie sank into a chair, her face crumpling, her voice trembling, raw with guilt. "I don't know," she said, her hands pressing to her face, her eyes wet. "I saw her die, Hollis, didn't stop it. What if it's my fault? What if they think I saw them?"

Daniel knelt beside her, his voice rough, pleading. "Stop it, Ellie," he said, his hands gripping hers, his eyes sharp with fear. "You didn't do anything. Hollis, she's not part of this—she blacked out, woke up here. Tell her."

Hollis stood still, his mind racing—*Jake's knife, the shadow's prints, Ellie's blackout*—the circle closing, suspicion coiling tighter. "I don't know what she saw," he said, his voice steady, cutting. "But the shadow does. They've been at Ravenswood, the station, now your yard, leaving marks —Jake's key, his knife. They know this family, your secrets. Noah's scared, running, hiding something. Who's left from 2023?"

Daniel's face hardened, his voice rough, rising with defiance. "No one," he said, standing, his hands clenching. "The group split after, kids moved away, parents grieved. It's just us, Hollis. You're chasing ghosts."

Hollis's chest tightened, the mark of the watcher a weight he couldn't shake, and he stepped closer, his voice low, resolute. "Not ghosts," he said, his eyes sharp, cutting. "Someone real, breathing, watching. I'll find them, Daniel, with or without you."

He turned, stepping back into the fog, the knife in his pocket, the circle closing, a shadow he'd chase through the dark, no matter the cost.

CHAPTER FIFTY-EIGHT

Mark Hollis sat at his desk in the police station, the early morning quiet of March 10, 2025, broken only by the faint buzz of the fluorescent lights and the steady drip of coffee from the machine in the corner. The room was stark, files stacked high, the board on the wall pinned with photos—Lena's crime scene, Noah's prints, now Jake's knife—and he leaned forward, his coat off, his eyes steady on the rusted blade resting beside his notepad, its J.E. carving glinting in the harsh light. The fog outside pressed against the windows, a gray shroud that mirrored the weight in his chest, a shadow's breath he'd felt at the Carters' house, now tightening the circle around a truth he couldn't let slip.

He'd left Ellie and Daniel an hour ago, their denials —*Just us, No one*—ringing hollow against the knife, the boot print, the watcher in their yard. Noah was still in the interrogation room, Julia with him, the boy's whispered

They're here a crack Hollis had widened at Ravenswood, and now Jake's knife sharpened it further, the past bleeding through into Lena's death. He felt the psychological strain of it, a case weaving through years, a family fracturing under secrets, a shadow he had to name.

He stood, grabbing the knife, and headed to the interrogation room, his boots heavy on the tile, his mind racing—*Jake's fall, Noah's push, Lena's stab, the shadow's traces.* He opened the door, the air cold and stale, and saw Noah slouched in the chair, his hoodie low, his hands clasped tight, Julia beside him, her face tight with exhaustion, her voice soft as she turned. "Hollis," she said, her eyes sharp, cutting through the tension. "He's not talking. Give him a break."

Hollis set the knife on the table, its blade thudding softly, his voice calm, steady, cutting through the quiet. "No breaks," he said, his eyes locking onto Noah's, unflinching. "Found this in your yard, Noah. Jake Ellis's initials, *J.E.* The shadow dropped it, minutes ago, watching your house. Who are they?"

Noah's eyes widened, his hands trembling, his voice rough, breaking as he stared at the knife, a crack splintering through the calm. "That's his," he said, his breath hitching, his eyes darting to Julia, then back. "Jake's. I saw it on the ridge, he had it. How's it here?"

Hollis's chest tightened, the past bleeding through, and he leaned forward, his voice low, probing. "You tell me," he said, his eyes sharp, cutting deeper. "You pushed him, 2023, confessed it. Lena tied it to you, died at Ravenswood. Now this knife, your yard, fresh boot prints matching the ones there, the station. The shadow's carrying Jake's ghost, Noah. Who's been with you, all this time?"

Noah's face paled, his hands unclenching, shaking in the light, and he shook his head, his voice trembling, raw with fear. "I don't know," he said, his eyes dropping, the lie a shield Hollis could feel. "I didn't see them, just the coat, fast, like I said. They're after me, Hollis, not them."

Julia stood, her voice sharp, urgent, cutting through the tension. "Hollis, stop," she said, her eyes flicking to Noah, then back, steady with resolve. "He's scared, look at him. The knife—it's someone else, not him. He didn't kill Lena."

Hollis's jaw tightened, the threads tightening, and he leaned closer, his voice steady, commanding. "Maybe not," he said, his eyes locking onto Noah's, unflinching. "But he knows more. The texts—'He'll pay'—sent from your phone, after she died. The key with *J*, now this knife, dropped where you live. The shadow's tied to Jake, to you, to your family. Who's left from that hike, Noah? Who's still here?"

Noah's breath caught, his eyes wide, wet, and he stood, his chair scraping back, his voice breaking, a whisper raw with something Hollis couldn't name. "No one," he said, his hands clenching into fists, the crack widening. "They're all gone, moved, dead. I didn't see a face, I swear. They're just... there, always."

Hollis's stomach dropped, the past bleeding through sharper, and he stood, his voice low, cutting. "Always," he said, his eyes narrowing, his hand resting on the knife. "You said that at Ravenswood—'They've always been here.' Your mom saw them too, same night, same description. The shadow's not a ghost, Noah—it's someone you know. Tell me."

Noah's face froze, his breath shallow, and he sank back into the chair, his voice trembling, a shield fraying at the edges. "I can't," he said, his eyes dropping, his hands shaking. "I don't know who. They're watching, waiting. I ran to stop it, but I can't."

Julia's hand gripped his shoulder, her voice soft, pleading. "Noah, please," she said, her eyes flicking to Hollis, then back. "He's right—the knife, the texts, it's too close. Tell us something, anything."

Noah's eyes lifted, sharp and cold, and he shook his head, his voice low, breaking. "There's nothing," he said, his hands unclenching, trembling in the light. "Just them, always them."

Hollis's chest tightened, the mark of the watcher a weight he couldn't shake, the past bleeding through, a shadow he'd chase to the end, no matter the cost.

CHAPTER FIFTY-NINE

Mark Hollis sat at a table in the station's records room, the mid-morning quiet of March 10, 2025, settling around him, the air thick with the musty scent of old files and dust. The fluorescent lights buzzed faintly overhead, casting a harsh glow across the stacks of boxes, and he leaned over a folder labeled Ridge Incident, July 2023, its pages yellowed and worn, his eyes steady on the faded ink. The fog outside pressed against the small window, a gray veil that dulled the village beyond, and he felt the weight of the chase, the shadow's breath tightening the threads—Jake's knife, Noah's confession, Lena's death—a past bleeding through he couldn't ignore.

He'd left Noah and Julia in the interrogation room an hour ago, the boy's trembling *They're always here* a crack Hollis couldn't widen, the knife with *J.E.* now locked in evidence beside the key and Lena's phone. He'd sent a unit to patrol the Carters' house, Ellie and Daniel's fear still sharp in his mind, and now he was here, digging into the ridge, chasing the echoes that aligned with the shadow's traces. He felt the psychological strain of it, a case spanning years, a family fracturing under a truth he had to name.

He flipped through the file, his fingers brushing the pages—police reports, witness statements, a map of the ridge —and stopped at the youth group roster, twelve names scrawled in tight script, Noah Carter's near the top, Jake Ellis's below it. His eyes narrowed, tracing the list, and landed on a note at the bottom, handwritten in blue ink: *Chaperone: Tom Bennett, local volunteer, assisted search.* His stomach tightened, the echoes aligning—Tom, the hardware store owner, a man he'd seen around, gruff and quiet, a name Lena had chased, now here.

He pulled Tom's statement, a single page clipped to the back, his words stark and brief: *Heard the boys arguing, turned back, Jake was gone. Noah said he fell, cut his hand trying to help. No body found, terrain too steep.* Hollis's chest tightened, the past sharpening—Tom on the ridge, Noah's cut, Jake's knife now in the Carters' yard, a shadow circling. He thought of Noah's fear, Ellie's blackout, the dark coat moving fast, and felt the threads pull tighter, a connection he couldn't shake.

He stood, grabbing the file, and headed to his desk, his boots heavy on the tile, his mind racing—*Tom knew Jake, knew Noah, knew the family*. He dropped into his chair, pulling his notepad, and scribbled fast—*Tom Bennett, 2023, chaperone, link to Jake*—then reached for his phone, dialing the front desk, his voice calm, steady, cutting through the quiet. "Davies," he said, his eyes on the file, his pen poised. "Get me Tom Bennett's address, hardware store owner. Now."

"On it, sir," Davies said, his voice young, tense, cutting through the line. "He's on Mill Street, lives above the shop. You want him brought in?"

Hollis's jaw tightened, the echoes aligning sharper, and he leaned back, his voice firm, resolute. "Not yet," he said, his eyes narrowing. "I'll go to him. Keep it quiet, but put a car near his place, watch him. He moves, you call me."

He hung up, his hand resting on the file, his mind piecing it together—*Tom at the ridge, Jake's knife, the shadow's traces.* He thought of the cigarette butt at the station, the boot prints matching Ravenswood, the Carters' yard, and felt the psychological weight of it, a man tied to 2023 now circling the present, a shadow he could feel breathing. He stood, grabbing his coat, and stepped into the hall, his voice low, cutting through the stillness. "Julia," he called, his eyes sharp, his boots echoing. "Need you."

She emerged from the interrogation room, her face pale, her voice soft but steady. "What's happening?" she asked, her eyes locking onto his, sharp with exhaustion. "Noah's breaking, Hollis. He's terrified."

Hollis held up the file, his voice calm, cutting. "Tom Bennett," he said, his eyes unflinching. "Chaperoned the ridge hike, 2023. Heard Noah and Jake fight, saw the fall. Jake's knife was in their yard tonight, fresh prints. He's been close, Julia, always. I'm going to him."

Her breath caught, her hands clenching, her voice

trembling but firm. "Tom?" she said, her eyes wide, cutting through the tension. "He warned Lena to stop, weeks ago. Said it was dangerous. Hollis, what if he's the shadow?"

Hollis's chest tightened, the circle closing, the echoes aligning, and he nodded, his voice steady, resolute. "That's what I'm finding out," he said, his eyes sharp, cutting. "Stay with Noah. The past's bleeding through, and I'm ending it."

He turned, stepping into the fog, the file in his hand, the shadow's breath a weight he'd chase to the truth, no matter the cost.

CHAPTER SIXTY

Mark Hollis stood outside Tom Bennett's hardware store on Mill Street, the mid-morning fog of March 10, 2025, thick and cold around him, the shop's faded sign swaying faintly in the mist. The village was quiet, its streets hushed under the gray shroud, and he adjusted his coat, his flashlight clipped to his belt, his hand resting on his holster as he peered through the darkened windows. The echoes of the ridge—Tom's name on the 2023 roster, Jake's knife in the Carters' yard, the shadow's boot prints—aligned in his mind, a past bleeding through that tightened the circle around a truth he couldn't let slip. He felt the psychological weight of it, a hunt reaching its edge, a shadow he'd chase to its voice.

He knocked, the sound sharp against the glass, and waited, his eyes sweeping the street—a patrol car idled two blocks down, Davies's eyes on him, a silent backup he'd ordered. The door creaked open, Tom's figure filling the frame, his face weathered and hard, his gray hair tousled, his eyes narrowing as they met Hollis's. "Detective," he said, his voice gruff, rough with sleep or something darker, stepping back to let him in. "Early for a visit. What's this about?"

Hollis stepped inside, the air sharp with the scent of metal and wood, the shop dim, shelves stacked with tools casting jagged shadows in the faint light. "Tom," he said, his voice calm, steady, cutting through the quiet, his eyes locking onto the man's, unflinching. "We need to talk. The ridge, 2023, Jake Ellis. You were there, heard the fight, saw Noah push him. Now his knife's in their yard, fresh prints matching Ravenswood. Where've you been?"

Tom's jaw tightened, his hands shoving into his pockets, his voice low, rough. "What're you saying, Hollis?" he asked, his eyes darting to the door, then back, a flicker of something—fear, defiance—breaking through. "I told the police back then—Jake fell, Noah was shook up, cut his hand. I searched, found nothing. That's it."

Hollis pulled the knife from his pocket, setting it on the counter, its *J.E.* glinting in the dim light, his voice steady, probing. "This," he said, his eyes sharp, cutting deeper. "Jake's, dropped outside the Carters' house, an hour ago. Boot prints match the ones at Ravenswood, the station. Lena tied Noah to Jake, died for it. The shadow's circling, Tom, and you're in the middle. Talk."

Tom's face paled, his hands trembling slightly, and he stepped back, his voice breaking, raw with something Hollis couldn't name. "That's his," he said, his eyes fixed on the knife, his breath hitching. "Jake's. I gave it to him, a gift, before the hike. How's it here?"

Hollis's chest tightened, the shadow speaking, and he leaned forward, his voice low, commanding. "You tell me," he said, his eyes narrowing, cutting through the haze. "You warned Lena to stop digging, weeks ago. Said it was dangerous. Noah confessed he pushed Jake, ran to Ravenswood, said the shadow's after him. Texts from his phone, post-mortem —'He'll pay.' You've been close, Tom, always. Where were you last night?"

Tom's hands clenched, his eyes wide, wet, and he shook his head, his voice trembling, a crack splintering through the calm. "I didn't kill her," he said, his breath shallow, his eyes darting to the knife, then back. "I told Lena to stop, yeah, because I knew—knew Noah did it, saw it on the ridge. He pushed Jake, I heard the yell, turned back, he was gone. I kept quiet, for them, for Ellie, Daniel. But I didn't kill her, Hollis."

Hollis's stomach dropped, the past bleeding through sharper, and he stepped closer, his voice steady, cutting. "Then who did?" he asked, his eyes locking onto Tom's, unflinching. "You saw the push, kept it buried. The shadow's tall, fast, dark coat—matches what Noah saw, Ellie too, at Ravenswood. They've got Jake's knife, been at the station, their yard. You're tied to it, Tom. Who's out there?"

Tom's face froze, his breath ragged, and he sank onto a stool, his voice trembling, a whisper raw with fear. "I don't know," he said, his hands shaking, the shield fraying. "After the ridge, I saw someone, later—tall, dark coat, watching the house, weeks after Jake. Thought it was grief, a parent, didn't tell. Then Lena started asking, I warned her, stayed away. Last night, I was home, alone."

Hollis's chest tightened, the shadow speaking louder, and he pulled the cigarette butt from his pocket, holding it up, his voice low, cutting. "This," he said, his eyes sharp, unflinching. "Dropped outside the station, an hour ago, while Noah was inside. You smoke, Tom?"

Tom's eyes widened, his hands trembling, and he shook his head, his voice breaking, desperate. "Not anymore," he said, his eyes darting to the butt, then back. "Quit years ago, before the ridge. Hollis, I swear, it's not me."

A creak broke the silence, faint but sharp, from the back of the shop, and Hollis turned, his hand on his holster, his voice firm, commanding. "Who's there?" he called, his eyes sweeping the shadows, the air thick with tension. "Come out, now."

Tom stood, his face paling, his voice trembling, a whisper cutting through. "No one's here," he said, his eyes wide, fearful. "Just us, Hollis. It's old wood, creaks all the time."

Hollis's pulse quickened, the shadow's breath a weight he couldn't shake, the echoes aligning, a truth breaking through the dark, pulling him deeper into a hunt he wouldn't let end.

PART 7: ELLIE CARTER

CHAPTER SIXTY-ONE

Ellie Carter sat at her kitchen table, the mid-morning light of March 10, 2025, weak and gray through the fog pressing against the windows, casting a dim pallor over the room. The air was thick with the scent of spilled coffee and the faint tang of fear, the mug she'd dropped hours ago still shattered on the floor, its dark stain a jagged scar across the tile. Her hands trembled in her lap, her sweater slipping off one shoulder, her eyes fixed on the back door where Hollis had left, his words—Jake's knife, in your yard—ringing in her ears, a weight of silence she couldn't shake. Daniel stood by the sink, his face drawn, his hands clenched on the counter, the quiet between them heavy with the fracture of their son's confession.

Noah was at the station, taken by Hollis after running to Ravenswood, his voice—*I pushed him*—a blade that cut through her, a truth she'd buried under years of hope, now bleeding into the present. She'd seen the shadow last night, tall and still in a dark coat, watching from the trees, and now Jake's knife, a ghost from 2023, lay in Hollis's hands, a mark of the watcher she couldn't unsee. She felt the psychological strain of it, a mother losing her boy to a past she didn't know, a shadow she'd glimpsed at Ravenswood closing in.

"Daniel," she said, her voice trembling, soft but sharp, cutting through the silence, her eyes lifting to his back, his stillness a wall she couldn't breach. "He's gone again, isn't he? Noah. He ran, and now this knife—Jake's. What are we doing?"

Daniel turned, his face pale, his voice rough with exhaustion, his eyes sharp with a mix of fear and defiance. "He's with Hollis," he said, his hands unclenching, trembling slightly. "Safe, for now. Ellie, we didn't know—he didn't tell us about Jake, not really. He's scared, not a killer."

Ellie's breath hitched, her hands clenching, her voice breaking, raw with despair. "Scared of what?" she asked, her eyes wet, pleading. "He pushed him, Daniel, said it last night. I heard him mumble it once, years ago—'I didn't want him to go'—and I let it go. Now Lena's dead, and this shadow's here, with Jake's knife. What didn't we see?"

Daniel crossed to her, his hands gripping the table, his voice low, strained. "We saw a boy," he said, his eyes locking onto hers, steady but fraying. "Shaken, quiet, hurt. We thought it was the accident, Ellie, not this. Hollis is chasing something —someone—else. Noah didn't kill her, he saw it."

Ellie stood, her chair scraping back, her voice rising, trembling with a weight she couldn't hold. "I saw it too," she said, her hands shaking, her eyes darting to the window, then back. "At Ravenswood, that night. Tall, fast, a dark coat—I blacked out, woke up here, thought it was a nightmare. But it's real, Daniel, and it's here, watching us. Why?"

Daniel's face crumpled, his hands reaching for hers, his voice rough, pleading. "I don't know," he said, his grip tight, his eyes wide with fear. "Maybe they think you saw them, know them. But you didn't, Ellie—you didn't do anything. We've got to trust Hollis, let him find it."

Ellie pulled free, her hands trembling, her voice trembling, a whisper raw with guilt. "Trust him?" she said, her eyes wet, cutting through the quiet. "Noah's breaking, Daniel. He ran to stop it, he said, but he won't tell us who. The texts —'You were right'—to me, 'He'll pay'—from his phone. What if it's my fault? What if I brought this here?"

Daniel's breath caught, his voice sharp, desperate. "Stop it," he said, stepping closer, his hands outstretched, his eyes sharp with pain. "You didn't bring anything. You were there, saw her die, but you didn't do it, Ellie. We're in this together, always have been."

Ellie's sob broke the silence, her hands pressing to her face, her voice trembling, a weight of silence spilling out. "Then why's it here?" she asked, her eyes lifting, haunted. "Jake's knife, in our yard. The shadow, always close. Noah knows, Daniel—he knows who it is, and he's silent. Why won't he tell us?"

Daniel sank into a chair, his head in his hands, his voice a whisper, raw with despair. "Because he's scared," he said, his breath ragged, his eyes lifting to hers. "Scared of them, of us, of what it means. Ellie, we've got to get him back, make him talk."

Ellie stood still, the fog pressing closer, the weight of silence a burden she couldn't shed, a shadow's breath she felt in her bones, pulling her deeper into a truth she couldn't face alone.

CHAPTER SIXTY-TWO

Ellie Carter stood at the kitchen window, the mid-morning fog of March 10, 2025, pressing thick and gray against the glass, blurring the trees where the shadow had stood hours ago. The room was cold, the shattered mug still scattered across the tile, the air heavy with the weight of silence she'd carried since Noah's confession—I pushed him—cut through her last night. Her hands gripped the sink's edge, her sweater hanging loose, her eyes tracing the faint outline of the yard, searching for the dark coat she'd seen, a ghost from Ravenswood now haunting her home. Daniel sat at the table behind her, his head in his hands, his breath ragged, the fracture between them a chasm she couldn't bridge.

She'd barely slept, the image of Jake's knife—*J.E.* scratched into its handle—burning in her mind, Hollis's steady voice—*They're watching*—a hammer striking her resolve. Noah was at the station, held by Hollis, his silence a wall she'd failed to break, and she felt the psychological strain of it, a mother losing her son to a secret she couldn't reach, a shadow she'd glimpsed closing in. "Daniel," she said, her voice trembling, sharp with a resolve she hadn't felt in days, turning to face him. "We can't wait for Hollis. Noah's hiding something, and it's here, in this house. We've got to find it."

Daniel's head lifted, his face pale, his eyes red-rimmed, his voice rough with exhaustion. "Find what, Ellie?" he asked, his hands unclenching, trembling slightly. "He's scared, breaking. Hollis has him, the knife, everything. What's left to do?"

Ellie stepped closer, her hands clenching, her voice breaking, raw with desperation. "The truth," she said, her eyes locking onto his, wet but fierce. "He ran to Ravenswood, said he wanted to stop it, wouldn't say who. The shadow's been here, Daniel—Jake's knife, in our yard. He knows who it is, and he's protecting them, or scared of them. We've got to look—his room, his things, something."

Daniel stood, his chair scraping back, his voice low, strained with doubt. "You want to dig through his life?" he asked, his eyes sharp, cutting through the tension. "He's our son, Ellie, not a suspect. Hollis is chasing this shadow, let him. We'll get Noah back, talk to him."

Ellie's breath hitched, her hands trembling, her voice rising, a resolve steeling through her fear. "Talk?" she said, her eyes darting to the stairs, then back, sharp with pain. "He won't talk, Daniel—he's silent, like after the ridge. I let it go then, thought it was grief, but it's more. I saw Lena die, felt that shadow, and now it's here, with Jake's knife. We're running out of time."

Daniel's face crumpled, his hands reaching for her, his voice rough, pleading. "Ellie, stop," he said, his grip tight, his eyes wide with fear. "You're tearing us apart. What if there's nothing? What if he's just scared, like he said?"

Ellie pulled free, her hands shaking, her voice trembling, a whisper cutting through the quiet. "Then why's it here?" she asked, her eyes lifting, haunted. "The shadow knows us, Daniel—knows Noah, knows me. I can't sit here, waiting for Hollis. I'm going up."

She turned, her boots heavy on the stairs, Daniel's voice a faint protest behind her—"Ellie, wait"—but she didn't stop, the weight of silence driving her to Noah's room. The door was ajar, the window still open from his escape, the fog curling in, and she stepped inside, her breath shallow, her eyes scanning the mess—clothes strewn, books toppled, a desk cluttered with papers. She moved to it, her hands trembling as she sifted through—school notes, receipts, nothing—until her fingers brushed a small, folded paper tucked under a textbook, its edges worn, yellowed.

She unfolded it, her heart pounding, and saw Noah's handwriting, faint but stark: *July 25, 2023—He wouldn't stop. I didn't mean it. T saw.* Her stomach dropped, the past bleeding through, a truth she couldn't unsee—*T saw*—Tom Bennett, the chaperone, a name Hollis had tied to the ridge, now here, in Noah's hand. She felt the breaking point, the shadow's breath a weight she couldn't shed, a secret her son had carried, pulling her deeper into a truth she had to face.

CHAPTER SIXTY-THREE

Ellie Carter stood in Noah's bedroom, the mid-morning fog of March 10, 2025, seeping through the open window, curling cold and damp around her feet. The room was a mess of shadows, clothes strewn across the floor, books toppled on the desk, and she clutched the folded note in her trembling hand, its words burning in her mind: July 25, 2023—He wouldn't stop. I didn't mean it. T saw. The faint hum of the village drifted in, muted by the mist, but the silence in the house pressed heavier, a weight she couldn't shake. Her sweater hung loose, her breath shallow, her eyes fixed on the paper, a confession from her son that cracked the world she'd known.

She turned, her boots thudding softly on the hardwood, and descended the stairs, the note a blade in her grip, her heart pounding with a resolve she couldn't quiet. Daniel was still in the kitchen, slumped at the table, his hands cradling his head, the shattered mug a dark stain at his feet. She stopped in the doorway, her voice trembling but firm, cutting through the stillness. "Daniel, look at this."

He lifted his head, his face pale and drawn, his eyes red with exhaustion, and frowned as she stepped closer, holding out the note. "What is it?" he asked, his voice rough, strained with a fatigue she felt too, his hands unclenching as he took it, his gaze dropping to the words.

Ellie watched him read, her hands twisting together, her voice breaking as she spoke. "It's Noah's. From after the ridge. 'He wouldn't stop. I didn't mean it. T saw.' Tom saw, Daniel. He saw Noah push Jake, and we didn't know. What else didn't we know?"

Daniel's breath caught, his fingers tightening on the paper, his voice low, trembling with disbelief. "Tom?" he said, his eyes lifting to hers, sharp with a mix of fear and confusion. "He was there, yeah, chaperoned the hike, but he never said anything. Noah wrote this? When?"

Ellie stepped closer, her hands clenching, her voice rising, raw with a desperation she couldn't hold back. "Two days after," she said, her eyes wet, locking onto his. "July 25, 2023. He hid it, Daniel, under a book, all this time. Tom saw, and Noah knew he saw. Now Jake's knife is in our yard, the shadow's here, and Noah's silent. Why didn't he tell us?"

Daniel stood, the note crumpling slightly in his grip, his voice rough, pleading as he moved toward her. "He was scared, Ellie," he said, his hands reaching for hers, his eyes wide with pain. "He was fourteen, a kid, panicked. Tom didn't say anything because there was nothing—no body, no proof. It was an accident, he told us that."

Ellie pulled back, her hands shaking, her voice trembling with a crack that deepened between them. "An accident Tom saw," she said, her eyes darting to the window, then back, sharp with fear. "Noah wrote 'I didn't mean it,' Daniel. He pushed him, and Tom knew, kept quiet. Now Lena's dead, and the shadow's leaving Jake's things—his knife, here. Tom warned her to stop, weeks ago. What if he's part of this?"

Daniel's face flushed, his voice rising, strained with a defiance she hadn't heard in days. "Tom?" he said, stepping closer, his hands clenching at his sides. "He's a friend, Ellie, not a killer. He helped us after, checked on Noah, brought food. You're reaching, tearing us apart over this."

Ellie's sob broke the quiet, her hands pressing to her face, her voice trembling, a weight spilling out. "I'm not reaching," she said, her eyes lifting, haunted and fierce. "I saw Lena die, Daniel, felt that shadow—tall, fast, dark coat. Noah saw it too, said it's after him. The texts—'You were right,' to me, 'He'll pay,' from his phone. It's here, in our lives, and Noah's hiding it. Tom saw, and he's tied to it."

Daniel sank back into the chair, his hands dropping the note to the table, his voice a whisper, raw with despair. "Then what do we do?" he asked, his breath ragged, his eyes lifting to hers. "Hollis has him, digging into Tom now, probably. We can't fix this, Ellie. Noah's breaking, and we're losing him."

Ellie stood still, her hands trembling, her voice steadying with a resolve she hadn't felt before, cutting through the crack. "We go to him," she said, her eyes sharp, locking onto his. "To the station, now. He's got to tell us—about Tom, about the shadow. I can't wait anymore, Daniel. The crack's too deep."

Daniel nodded, his face crumpling, his voice soft, broken. "Okay," he said, standing, his hands shaking as he grabbed his coat. "But if he won't talk, Ellie—what then?"

Ellie turned to the door, the fog pressing closer, the weight of silence a burden she'd carry to her son, a shadow's truth she'd force into the light, no matter the cost.

CHAPTER SIXTY-FOUR

Ellie Carter sat in the passenger seat of their car, the midday fog of March 10, 2025, thick and gray around them, blurring the village streets as Daniel drove toward the police station. The air inside was cold, the heater humming faintly, and she clutched Noah's note in her hand, its crumpled edges digging into her palm, the words replaying in her mind: July 25, 2023. He wouldn't stop. I didn't mean it. T saw. Her sweater hung loose, her breath fogging the window, her eyes fixed on the road, a resolve burning through the fear that had gripped her since the shadow appeared in their yard. Daniel's hands were tight on the wheel, his face pale, his silence a heavy weight between them, broken only by the soft creak of leather as he shifted.

They'd left the house minutes ago, the kitchen still a mess of spilled coffee and shattered glass, her decision to confront Noah a force she couldn't stop. Jake's knife, found by Hollis in their yard, lingered in her thoughts, a ghost from 2023 tied to Tom Bennett, a man who'd seen her son push a boy to his death and kept quiet. She felt the psychological strain of it, a mother facing a truth she'd buried, a shadow she'd glimpsed at Ravenswood now closing in, and she knew the silence had to shatter, no matter the cost.

"Ellie," Daniel said, his voice rough, low, cutting through the quiet as he pulled into the station lot, his eyes flicking to her, sharp with exhaustion. "What if he won't talk? Hollis has him, pushing him. What do we say?"

Ellie turned, her hands trembling, her voice steady despite the tremor in her chest, cutting back with a fierce edge. "We make him," she said, her eyes locking onto his, wet but resolute. "He's our son, Daniel. He wrote this, hid it—Tom saw him push Jake. The shadow's here, leaving Jake's things, and Noah knows who it is. We can't wait anymore."

Daniel parked, his hands dropping from the wheel, his voice breaking, raw with doubt. "He's scared," he said, his eyes dropping to the note in her hand, then lifting, pained. "You saw him last night, Ellie—breaking, not lying. What if he can't face it?"

Ellie's breath hitched, her hands clenching the note, her voice trembling, a crack deepening as she spoke. "Then we face it for him," she said, her eyes sharp, cutting through the fog. "I saw Lena die, Daniel, felt that shadow. Noah saw it too, and he's silent. Tom knew, and now this. We're losing him to it."

She opened the door, stepping out, her boots crunching gravel, and Daniel followed, his coat pulled tight, his steps heavy behind her. The station loomed ahead, its brick walls stark in the mist, and she pushed through the doors, the air inside sharp with disinfectant and tension. Hollis met them in the lobby, his face drawn, his voice calm, steady as he nodded. "Ellie, Daniel," he said, his eyes flicking to her hand, the note visible. "He's in there. Julia's with him. What've you got?"

Ellie held up the note, her voice trembling but firm, cutting through the quiet. "This," she said, her eyes locking onto his, sharp with desperation. "Noah wrote it, after the ridge. 'T saw'—Tom saw him push Jake. The knife in our yard, Hollis—he knows who's doing this. Let me see him."

Hollis's jaw tightened, his eyes narrowing, and he took the note, his voice low, probing. "Tom," he said, his fingers tracing the words, his gaze lifting. "I just came from him. He admits he saw, kept quiet. Says he didn't kill Lena. You're sure Noah knows more?"

Ellie nodded, her hands shaking, her voice breaking, raw with a mother's plea. "He ran to stop it," she said, her eyes wet, cutting deeper. "He's hiding it, Hollis—for me, for us, I don't know. Let me talk to him."

Hollis stepped aside, leading them to the interrogation room, the door clicking open, and Ellie saw Noah slouched in the chair, his hoodie low, his hands clasped tight, Julia beside him, her face tight with strain. "Noah," Ellie said, her voice trembling, sharp, shattering the silence as she crossed to him, her hands gripping his shoulders. "Look at me. I found this —Tom saw you push Jake. The shadow's here, with his knife. Who is it?"

Noah's eyes lifted, wide and wet, his voice rough, breaking as he stared at her, a crack splintering through the wall. "Mom," he said, his breath hitching, his hands trembling in hers. "I didn't want this. T saw, yeah, but it's not him. It's... I saw them, after, at the ridge, watching. They're back."

Ellie's chest tightened, the silence shattering, her voice low, urgent, cutting through the fog. "Who, Noah?" she asked, her eyes locking onto his, fierce with love and fear. "Tell me. Now."

Noah's face froze, his breath shallow, his voice a whisper, raw with terror. "Jake's brother," he said, his hands shaking, the truth spilling out. "Ryan. He was there, after. He knows."

The room stilled, the crack deep, the shadow's name a weight Ellie felt in her bones, pulling her deeper into a truth she couldn't unhear.

CHAPTER SIXTY-FIVE

Ellie Carter stood frozen in the police station's interrogation room, the midday stillness of March 10, 2025, heavy and cold around her, the fluorescent lights buzzing faintly overhead. The gray walls pressed in, the air sharp with the scent of stale coffee and tension, and she gripped Noah's shoulders, her hands trembling, her breath caught in her throat. His words—Jake's brother, Ryan. He knows—echoed in her mind, a ghost taking shape from the fog of 2023, a shadow she'd felt at Ravenswood now named. Daniel stood beside her, his face pale, his hands clenched at his sides, while Hollis loomed near the door, his notepad open, his eyes sharp with a detective's focus. Julia sat at the table, her face tight, her voice silent but her presence a steady anchor.

Ellie's sweater hung loose, her eyes locked onto Noah's, wide and wet with fear, and she felt the psychological weight of it, a mother staring into a truth her son had buried, a shadow she couldn't unsee. "Ryan," she said, her voice trembling, low but cutting through the quiet, her hands tightening on him. "Jake's brother. You saw him, after the ridge? Noah, what does he know?"

Noah's breath hitched, his hands shaking in his lap, his voice rough, breaking as he stared at her, a crack spilling open. "Everything," he said, his eyes darting to Hollis, then back, raw with terror. "He was there, later, after the search. I went back, alone, to look for Jake's knife, thought I could hide it. Ryan was watching, tall, in a dark coat. He didn't say anything, just stared, then left. I thought he'd forgotten."

Ellie's chest tightened, the ghost taking shape, and she stepped back, her hands falling, her voice trembling with a desperate edge. "Forgotten?" she asked, her eyes flicking to Daniel, then Hollis, sharp with fear. "He's here, Noah—with Jake's knife, in our yard. The shadow, tall and fast, at Ravenswood. He knows you pushed him, doesn't he? Why didn't you tell us?"

Daniel moved closer, his voice rough, strained with disbelief, cutting through the tension. "Ryan Ellis?" he said, his hands unclenching, trembling slightly. "He was a kid too, Ellie—older, sure, but he moved away after, with their mom. Noah, you're sure it was him?"

Noah nodded, his face paling, his voice breaking, a whisper raw with guilt. "I saw him again," he said, his eyes dropping, his hands clenching the table. "Last year, at the shop with Tom. He looked at me, same stare, didn't speak. I thought he'd let it go, but then Lena started asking, and he was back."

Hollis stepped forward, his pen scratching fast, his voice calm, steady, cutting deeper. "Back how?" he asked, his eyes locking onto Noah's, probing with a detective's edge. "You saw him before Lena died? Where?"

Noah's breath caught, his eyes lifting, wet and wide, his voice trembling, a shield fraying. "Outside the pub," he said, his hands shaking, the truth spilling out. "Weeks ago, late, in the fog. He was across the street, watching me. I ran home, didn't tell. Then the texts started, from my phone—I didn't send them, Hollis, I swear."

Ellie's stomach dropped, the ghost taking shape sharper, and she turned to Hollis, her voice trembling, urgent, cutting through the fog. "Ryan," she said, her eyes locking onto his, fierce with a mother's dread. "He's the shadow, isn't he? He saw Noah push Jake, waited, came back for Lena, for us. Where is he?"

Hollis's jaw tightened, his eyes narrowing, his voice low, resolute. "I don't know yet," he said, his hand resting on the notepad, his gaze flicking to Noah, then back. "But he's close —Ravenswood, your yard, the station. The knife, the key, the texts—he's leaving marks, tying it to Jake. I'll find him, Ellie."

Daniel's face flushed, his voice rising, raw with desperation, cutting through the room. "Find him how?" he asked, stepping closer, his hands clenching again. "He's a ghost, Hollis—moved away, no trace. Noah's here, breaking, and you're chasing shadows. What if he's gone?"

Ellie's sob broke the quiet, her hands pressing to her face, her voice trembling, a weight shattering through. "He's not gone," she said, her eyes lifting, haunted and fierce. "I felt him, Daniel—at Ravenswood, last night. He's here, for Noah, for me. We didn't see, all this time, and now he's taking it all."

Noah stood, his chair scraping back, his voice breaking, a whisper cutting through the tension. "I didn't want this," he said, his hands trembling, his eyes wet with guilt. "I pushed Jake, yeah, but Ryan—he's doing this, Mom. He knows, and he won't stop."

Ellie reached for him, her hands shaking, her voice steadying with a resolve she hadn't felt before, cutting through the crack. "Then we stop him," she said, her eyes sharp, locking onto Hollis, then Noah. "Tell us everything, Noah—every time you saw him. Hollis, find him, now. The ghost has a name."

Hollis nodded, his face hardening, his voice calm, cutting. "I will," he said, his eyes steady, a detective's promise. "Stay here, all of you. The silence is done."

Ellie held Noah close, the ghost taking shape, a shadow's breath she'd face to save her son, pulling her deeper into a truth she couldn't escape.

CHAPTER SIXTY-SIX

Ellie Carter sat beside Noah in the police station's interrogation room, the late afternoon light of March 10, 2025, filtering weakly through the fogged window, casting a dim glow across the scuffed table. The room was cold, the air stale with the scent of old coffee and metal, and she held her son's hand, his fingers trembling in hers, his hoodie pulled low over his pale face. The walls seemed to close in, the fluorescent lights flickering overhead, and she felt the weight of his confession—Jake's brother, Ryan—settling into her bones, a vendetta unfolding she couldn't outrun. Daniel paced near the door, his coat unbuttoned, his breath uneven, while Hollis stood by the table, his notepad open, his eyes sharp with a detective's focus. Julia leaned against the wall, her face drawn, her silence a steady presence amid the tension.

Ellie's sweater hung loose, her other hand resting on the table, her voice trembling but firm as she spoke, cutting through the quiet. "Ryan Ellis," she said, her eyes lifting to Hollis, locking onto his with a mother's fierce resolve. "Jake's brother. Noah saw him after the ridge, then last year, before Lena died. He's the shadow, Hollis. What does he want?"

Noah's grip tightened, his breath hitching, his voice rough, breaking as he stared at the table, a crack spilling wider. "Me," he said, his eyes wet, his words raw with guilt. "He knows I pushed Jake, saw it somehow. He's been waiting, Mom. The texts, the knife—he wants me to pay."

Ellie's chest tightened, the ghost taking shape sharper, and she turned to him, her voice low, urgent, cutting through the fog of fear. "Waiting how?" she asked, her hand squeezing his, her eyes searching his face, desperate for more. "You saw him at the shop with Tom, then outside the pub. Why now, Noah? Why Lena?"

Noah's eyes lifted, wide and haunted, his voice trembling, a whisper cutting through the stillness. "She found out," he said, his hands shaking, his gaze darting to Hollis, then back. "Lena asked about the ridge, kept pushing me, Tom, everyone. Ryan must've heard, followed her. I saw him that night, at Ravenswood, before she died. He didn't see me, but I ran, hid. Then the texts started."

Daniel stopped pacing, his face flushing, his voice rough with disbelief, cutting through the tension. "He followed her?" he said, stepping closer, his hands clenching at his sides. "Noah, you're saying Ryan killed Lena because she knew? Why not come for you then, after the ridge? Why wait?"

Hollis set his pen down, his voice calm, steady, cutting deeper as he leaned forward, his eyes locking onto Noah's. "Revenge," he said, his words measured, his gaze unflinching.

"Ryan saw you push Jake, waited, planned. Lena stirred it up, gave him a reason to move. The knife in your yard, the key, the texts—he's tying it to Jake, making you feel it. Where's he been, Noah? Any hint?"

Noah's breath caught, his hands unclenching, trembling on the table, his voice breaking, raw with terror. "I don't know," he said, his eyes dropping, then lifting to Ellie, wet and wide. "After the shop, he was gone. Then the pub, weeks ago, just watching. I thought he'd moved away, forgotten, but he's here, Hollis. He's always been here."

Ellie's stomach dropped, the vendetta unfolding clearer, and she turned to Hollis, her voice trembling, sharp with a desperate edge. "Always here," she said, her eyes locking onto his, fierce with dread. "I saw him too, at Ravenswood—tall, fast, dark coat. He stabbed her, and I blacked out, woke up home. He's after Noah, Hollis, but why me? What did I do?"

Hollis's jaw tightened, his eyes narrowing, his voice low, probing as he flipped a page in his notepad. "Maybe nothing," he said, his hand resting on the table, his gaze steady. "Or maybe he thinks you saw him, know him. You were there, Ellie —same night, same shadow. He's leaving marks—Jake's things —near you, your house. It's personal, not just Noah."

Daniel's voice rose, strained with desperation, cutting through the room. "Personal?" he said, stepping closer, his hands shaking as he faced Hollis. "He's a kid, Hollis—Ryan was, what, seventeen then? He moved away with their mom, grieving. Why come back now, for this? It doesn't make sense."

Ellie's sob broke the quiet, her hands pressing to her

face, her voice trembling, a weight shattering through. "It does," she said, her eyes lifting, haunted and resolute. "Jake was his brother, Daniel. Noah took him, and Ryan waited, watched us—our lives, our home. Lena brought it back, and now he's here, undoing us. Hollis, you've got to find him."

Hollis stood, his face hardening, his voice calm, cutting through the tension. "I'm trying," he said, his eyes sharp, locking onto hers. "Tom saw the push, kept quiet—Ryan must've too, from a distance. The cigarette butt, the prints, the knife—he's circling, close. I've got units out, checking his old haunts. Noah, anything else—places, words, anything?"

Noah's breath steadied, his eyes wet, his voice low, breaking as he spoke. "The ridge," he said, his hands clenching again, his gaze distant. "He said something, that day I went back—'You'll fall too.' I ran, thought it was nothing, but it's him."

Ellie's chest tightened, the vendetta unfolding fully, a ghost's voice from the past, and she stood, her hands shaking, her voice firm, cutting through the crack. "He's not taking you," she said, her eyes locking onto Noah's, fierce with a mother's love. "Hollis, find him. End this."

Hollis nodded, his resolve steeling, his voice steady, a promise in the quiet. "I will," he said, his eyes sharp, cutting through the fog. "Stay here, locked down. The ghost's real, and I'm close."

Ellie held Noah close, the vendetta unfolding, a shadow's breath she'd fight to her last, pulling her deeper into a truth she'd shield her son from, no matter the cost.

CHAPTER SIXTY-SEVEN

Ellie Carter sat on a hard plastic chair in the police station's waiting area, the late afternoon shadows of March 10, 2025, stretching long and dark across the tiled floor. The fog outside pressed thick against the windows, muting the village beyond into a gray haze, and the air inside was cold, heavy with the scent of disinfectant and the faint hum of a flickering light overhead. Noah slumped beside her, his hoodie pulled low, his hands clasped tight in his lap, his breath shallow and uneven. Daniel stood near the desk, his coat rumpled, his hands shoved deep into his pockets, his eyes darting to the hall where Hollis had disappeared minutes ago, chasing Ryan Ellis, the ghost who'd taken shape in their lives.

Ellie's sweater clung damply to her shoulders, her fingers twisting together, her voice silent but her mind racing with Noah's words—*You'll fall too*—a threat from Ryan that echoed from the ridge to Ravenswood, now tightening like a noose around her family. She felt the psychological weight of it, a mother trapped in a station's cold walls, her son's guilt a blade she couldn't pull free, a shadow's vendetta closing in. Julia had stepped out to call Claire, leaving them alone, and the quiet stretched taut, broken only by the soft creak of Noah's chair as he shifted.

"Noah," Ellie said, her voice trembling, low but firm, cutting through the stillness as she turned to him, her eyes locking onto his shadowed face. "You're sure it was Ryan, at the ridge, after? He said that—'You'll fall too'? Tell me again, everything."

Noah's breath caught, his hands unclenching, trembling slightly, his voice rough, breaking as he spoke. "Yeah," he said, his eyes lifting, wet and wide, meeting hers with a haunted glint. "I went back, Mom, two days after. Thought I could find Jake's knife, hide it. Ryan was there, by the rocks, tall, dark coat. He looked at me, said it—'You'll fall too'— then walked away. I ran, didn't tell anyone."

Ellie's chest tightened, the noose tightening, and she leaned closer, her voice steady despite the tremor in her hands, cutting deeper. "And you saw him again," she said, her eyes searching his, fierce with a mother's dread. "Last year, at Tom's shop, then outside the pub. He's been watching us, Noah—all this time. Why didn't you say?"

Noah's face paled, his hands clenching again, his voice breaking, raw with guilt. "I was scared," he said, his eyes dropping, his breath ragged. "Thought he'd forgotten, moved away. Then Lena started asking, and he was back. I didn't want you to know, Mom—what I did, what he might do."

Daniel turned, his face flushing, his voice rough with strain, cutting through the tension. "Scared?" he said, stepping closer, his hands pulling free from his pockets, trembling slightly. "Noah, you let this build—Ryan, out there, because of Jake. We could've helped, told someone. Now Lena's dead, and he's at our house."

Ellie's breath hitched, her hands reaching for Noah, her voice trembling, sharp with desperation. "He's right," she said, her eyes locking onto her son's, wet but resolute. "I saw him too, Noah—at Ravenswood, killing her. I blacked out, woke up home, thought it was a dream. But it's real, and he's here, leaving Jake's knife. We're trapped because of this silence."

The door swung open, Hollis stepping in, his coat damp with fog, his face hard, his voice calm, cutting through the quiet. "He's closer," he said, his eyes flicking to Ellie, then Noah, steady with a detective's edge. "Found a car, abandoned, half a mile out—registered to Ryan Ellis's mother, reported stolen last year. Fresh tracks near it, big boots, heading this way."

Ellie's stomach dropped, the noose tightening sharper, and she stood, her hands shaking, her voice breaking, urgent as she faced him. "This way?" she asked, her eyes wide, cutting through the fog of fear. "He's coming here, Hollis? For Noah, for us? What do we do?"

Hollis's jaw tightened, his hand resting on his holster, his voice low, resolute. "Lock it down," he said, his eyes sharp, locking onto hers. "Units are out, sweeping the area. He's bold —left the car, the knife, the key. Wants you to know he's near.

Noah, anything else—where he'd go, what he'd want?"

Noah's breath steadied, his eyes lifting, wet with terror, his voice trembling, a whisper cutting through the crack. "The ridge," he said, his hands unclenching, shaking on his lap. "He said I'd fall. Maybe he's waiting there, or here, to finish it. He hates me, Hollis—hates us."

Daniel's voice rose, raw with desperation, cutting through the room. "Finish it?" he said, stepping closer, his hands clenching again. "He's a kid, Hollis—grieving, sure, but this? Stalking us, killing Lena? We need to get out, hide, not sit here."

Ellie's sob broke the quiet, her hands pressing to her face, her voice trembling, a weight shattering through. "No," she said, her eyes lifting, fierce and haunted. "He's not just a kid, Daniel—he's a ghost, carrying Jake. I felt him, saw him. He's here, and running won't stop him. Hollis, keep us safe, find him."

Hollis nodded, his face hardening, his voice steady, cutting through the tension. "You're safe here," he said, his eyes sharp, a promise in the quiet. "Doors locked, officers posted. I'm heading out—ridge, streets, wherever he's lurking. The noose is tight, Ellie. He's slipping."

Ellie pulled Noah close, the vendetta unfolding, the noose tightening, a shadow's breath she'd face to her last, pulling her deeper into a truth she'd fight to end.

CHAPTER SIXTY-EIGHT

Ellie Carter stood by the station's locked front door, the evening gloom of March 10, 2025, pressing thick and dark against the glass, the fog outside a heavy shroud that swallowed the village beyond. The waiting area was cold, the air sharp with the scent of old linoleum and tension, and she wrapped her arms around herself, her sweater damp from nervous sweat, her eyes darting to the shadows beyond the window. Noah sat slumped in a chair behind her, his hoodie low, his hands trembling in his lap, his breath shallow and ragged. Daniel paced the small space, his coat unbuttoned, his face pale, his voice silent but his footsteps a restless thud against the tile. The fluorescent lights buzzed overhead, casting a harsh glow that deepened the lines of exhaustion on their faces.

Hollis had left an hour ago, his promise—*You're safe here* —ringing hollow in Ellie's ears as the minutes stretched into a taut, endless wait. Ryan Ellis, Jake's brother, was out there, his car found abandoned, his tracks leading closer, his vendetta a noose tightening around them. She felt the psychological strain of it, a mother trapped in a locked room, her son's guilt a weight she couldn't lift, a shadow's breath she couldn't escape. The station was quiet, two officers posted at the back, their radios crackling faintly down the hall, but the stillness felt like a lie, a calm before a storm she knew was coming.

"Ellie," Daniel said, his voice rough, low, cutting through the quiet as he stopped pacing, his eyes flicking to her, sharp with strain. "You need to sit. Hollis is out there, handling it. We're locked in, safe. He'll find him."

Ellie turned, her hands clenching, her voice trembling but firm, cutting back with a desperate edge. "Safe?" she asked, her eyes locking onto his, wet with fear. "Ryan's been watching us, Daniel—years, not days. Noah saw him, I saw him, and now he's here, leaving Jake's knife, his threats. Hollis doesn't know where he is."

Noah's breath hitched, his hands unclenching, shaking slightly, his voice breaking as he spoke, raw with guilt. "He's right, Mom," he said, his eyes lifting, wide and haunted, meeting hers. "I brought this. Ryan wants me, not you. I should've told you, after the ridge, after the pub. I thought he'd go away."

Ellie's chest tightened, the edge of the abyss looming, and she crossed to him, her voice steady despite the tremor in her hands, cutting through the fog of despair. "You didn't bring this," she said, her hands gripping his shoulders, her eyes fierce with love. "He chose this, Noah—hate, revenge, whatever it is. We're here, together. He's not taking you."

A sharp thud broke the silence, a heavy bang against the glass door, and Ellie spun, her heart slamming against her ribs, her voice trembling, sharp with terror. "What was that?" she asked, her eyes darting to the window, the fog swirling outside, a dark shape flickering in the mist.

Daniel moved fast, his hands pulling her back, his voice rough, urgent, cutting through the tension. "Stay there," he said, stepping closer, his eyes narrowing as he peered out, his breath fogging the glass. "It's nothing, Ellie—probably a branch, the wind."

The thud came again, louder, deliberate, and the glass rattled, a faint crack splintering across its surface. Ellie's stomach dropped, her hands shaking, her voice breaking, a whisper cutting through the quiet. "That's not the wind," she said, her eyes wide, locking onto Daniel's, then Noah's. "He's here."

Noah stood, his chair scraping back, his voice trembling, raw with panic. "Ryan," he said, his hands clenching into fists, his eyes darting to the door. "He's out there, Mom. He said I'd fall—he's doing it now."

Footsteps echoed down the hall, the two officers rushing in, their radios crackling, their voices sharp, cutting through the chaos. "Front door," one said, his hand on his holster, his eyes flicking to the glass, the crack widening. "Something hit it, hard. Stay back."

Ellie pulled Noah close, her arms wrapping around him,

her voice trembling, fierce with a mother's resolve. "No," she said, her eyes locking onto the officer's, cutting through the fog of fear. "He's here, Ryan Ellis—tall, dark coat. He's after my son. Do something."

The second officer moved to the door, his flashlight sweeping the fog, his voice steady, cutting through the tension. "Nothing out there," he said, his hand resting on the lock, his eyes narrowing. "Fog's thick, but I'll check. Stay put."

A third thud struck, the glass shattering inward, shards raining across the tile, and a dark shape loomed in the mist, tall and fast, a coat flapping as it vanished into the fog. Ellie's scream broke the quiet, her hands shielding Noah, her voice trembling, a weight crashing through. "He's here!" she said, her eyes wide, cutting through the chaos. "Hollis was wrong— we're not safe!"

The officers drew their guns, one shouting into his radio, his voice sharp, urgent. "Breach, front door—suspect on foot, heading west. Backup, now!" The other pulled them back, his hand firm, his voice steady, cutting through the panic. "Behind me, all of you. Move!"

Ellie held Noah tight, Daniel's arm around them, the edge of the abyss yawning wide, a shadow's breath shattering their fragile hold, pulling her deeper into a fight she couldn't lose.

CHAPTER SIXTY-NINE

Ellie Carter crouched behind the station's front desk, the evening chill of March 10, 2025, seeping through the shattered glass door, the fog outside swirling thick and dark across the tile. The waiting area was a chaos of shadows, shards glinting under the flickering fluorescent lights, and she held Noah tight against her, his hoodie damp with sweat, his breath ragged in her ear. Daniel knelt beside them, his arm shielding her, his face pale, his eyes darting to the broken window where Ryan Ellis had vanished moments ago. The air was sharp with the scent of glass dust and fear, the officers' shouts echoing down the hall, their radios crackling with urgent calls for backup.

Ellie's sweater clung to her skin, her hands trembling as she gripped Noah, her voice trembling but firm, cutting through the quiet panic. "Stay down," she said, her eyes locking onto his, wide and wet with terror. "He's out there,

Noah, but Hollis will find him. We're not losing you."

Noah's breath hitched, his hands clenching her arm, his voice rough, breaking as he whispered, raw with guilt. "He wants me, Mom," he said, his eyes darting to the door, then back, haunted by the shadow's threat. "Ryan—he said I'd fall. He's not stopping."

Daniel's hand tightened on her shoulder, his voice low, strained with desperation, cutting through the tension. "He's gone, Ellie," he said, his eyes flicking to the fog, his breath fogging in the cold. "The officers saw him run west. Hollis is out there, with units. We need to hold on, stay here."

Ellie's chest tightened, the chase beginning, and she shook her head, her voice trembling, sharp with a mother's resolve. "Hold on?" she asked, her eyes lifting to his, fierce with dread. "He broke the door, Daniel—came for us. Hollis didn't stop him last time, at Ravenswood. What if he's circling back?"

The officer at the back door returned, his gun holstered, his voice steady, cutting through the chaos. "West perimeter's clear," he said, his eyes sweeping the room, his hand resting on his radio. "Partner's with backup, sweeping the ridge—Hollis thinks he's heading there. Stay here, locked in. We've got this."

Ellie stood, pulling Noah up, her hands shaking, her voice breaking, urgent as she faced him. "The ridge," she said, her eyes wide, locking onto the officer's, cutting through the fog of fear. "That's where it started—Jake fell there, Ryan said Noah would too. He's drawing us out, isn't he?"

The officer's jaw tightened, his eyes narrowing, his voice calm, probing as he nodded. "Could be," he said, his hand adjusting his radio, his gaze steady. "Hollis is on it—called in more units, heading that way. He's bold, this guy, but we're closing in. Sit tight."

Daniel's face flushed, his voice rising, raw with panic, cutting through the room. "Sit tight?" he said, stepping closer, his hands clenching at his sides. "He's out there, breaking in, and you're telling us to wait? We're targets, officer—not safe here, not anywhere."

Ellie's breath caught, her hands gripping Noah tighter, her voice trembling, a weight shattering through. "He's right," she said, her eyes lifting, fierce and haunted. "I saw him kill Lena, felt him at our house. He's not running—he's hunting. Hollis needs us, Noah's voice, to end this."

Noah's eyes widened, his voice breaking, a whisper cutting through the crack. "I can't," he said, his hands trembling, his gaze dropping to the floor. "He'll kill me, Mom— said I'd fall. I saw him, I know him, but I can't face him."

Ellie knelt, her hands cupping his face, her voice steadying with a resolve she hadn't felt before, cutting through the abyss. "You won't," she said, her eyes sharp, locking onto his, fierce with love. "You're mine, Noah, and I'm here. Tell the officer—everything, every place Ryan's been. We're ending this chase."

The officer nodded, his radio crackling, his voice firm, cutting through the tension. "Talk, kid," he said, his eyes steady, a promise in the quiet. "Ridge, pub, shop—anywhere else? Hollis is close, but we need more."

Noah's breath steadied, his eyes wet, his voice

trembling, raw with a final push. "The old barn," he said, his hands unclenching, shaking as he spoke. "Edge of town, near the ridge road. Saw him there, last month, just standing. It's his place, maybe."

Ellie's chest tightened, the chase beginning fully, a shadow's lair in reach, and she stood, her voice firm, cutting through the fog. "Tell Hollis," she said, her eyes locking onto the officer's, fierce with a mother's stand. "The barn, now. He's there, waiting."

The officer keyed his radio, his voice sharp, urgent. "Hollis, suspect possible at old barn, ridge road—witness tip. Move in." Ellie held Noah close, Daniel's arm around them, the edge of the abyss sharp and near, a chase she'd see through, pulling her deeper into a truth she'd fight to end.

CHAPTER SEVENTY

Ellie Carter clung to Noah in the backseat of Hollis's patrol car, the night fog of March 10, 2025, thick and black around them, the headlights cutting a narrow path through the mist as they sped toward the old barn on the ridge road. The air was cold, the engine's rumble a low growl beneath her pounding heart, and she held her son tight, his hoodie damp against her arm, his breath shallow and trembling. Daniel sat beside her, his hands gripping the seat, his face pale in the dim glow of the dashboard, his eyes fixed on Hollis ahead, steering with a detective's steady focus. The officer from the station followed in a second car, his lights a faint blur behind, and the radio crackled with static, a tense lifeline to the units closing in.

Ellie's sweater hung loose, her voice silent but her mind screaming with Noah's tip—*The old barn, edge of town*—a shadow's lair where Ryan Ellis waited, his vendetta a noose that had tightened since the ridge in 2023. She felt the psychological abyss of it, a mother racing toward a truth she couldn't outrun, her son's guilt a chain she'd break at any cost. Hollis had insisted they come—*He knows your voice, Ellie, might draw him out*—and now the barn loomed ahead, its sagging roof a dark silhouette against the fog, a ghost from the past she'd face.

Hollis slowed, cutting the lights, his voice calm, steady, cutting through the quiet as he turned to them. "Stay here," he said, his eyes locking onto Ellie's, sharp with resolve. "Doors locked, windows up. I'm going in, with backup. If it's Ryan, we'll get him."

Ellie's breath hitched, her hands tightening on Noah, her voice trembling but firm, cutting back with a desperate edge. "He's there," she said, her eyes flicking to the barn, then back, fierce with dread. "I feel it, Hollis—he's waiting, for Noah, for me. Don't let him slip away again."

Noah's voice broke, rough with panic, cutting through the tension as he leaned forward, his hands shaking. "He'll kill you," he said, his eyes wide, wet with terror, locking onto Hollis. "He said I'd fall, like Jake. He's fast, Hollis—don't go alone."

Daniel's hand gripped her arm, his voice low, strained with fear, cutting through the fog. "Listen to him," he said, his eyes darting to the barn, his breath ragged. "He broke the station door, came for us. Hollis, wait for more—don't risk it."

Hollis's jaw tightened, his hand resting on his holster, his voice steady, resolute. "Backup's here," he said, his eyes sharp, cutting through the doubt. "Two units, armed. I've got this. Stay put, all of you."

He stepped out, the door clicking shut, and Ellie watched him move, a shadow in the fog, joining the officer from the second car, their flashlights sweeping the barn's edge. Her chest tightened, the chase ending, and she pulled Noah closer, her voice trembling, a whisper cutting through the quiet. "He's wrong," she said, her eyes locked on the barn, fierce with a mother's instinct. "Ryan's not slipping—he's waiting."

A sharp crack split the night, a gunshot echoing from the barn, and Ellie's scream broke the silence, her hands shielding Noah, her voice trembling, raw with terror. "Hollis!" she said, her eyes wide, cutting through the fog as Daniel lunged for the door, his hands fumbling the lock.

The radio crackled, Hollis's voice sharp, urgent, cutting through the chaos. "Shots fired—suspect inside, west wall. Hold position, backup move in!" Another crack followed, then silence, and Ellie's stomach dropped, the edge of the abyss yawning wide.

The barn door burst open, a tall figure staggering out, dark coat flapping, and Hollis shouted, his flashlight pinning the shape, his voice firm, cutting through the mist. "Ryan Ellis, hands up—now!" The officer flanked him, gun drawn, and the figure froze, hands rising slow, a knife glinting in one, blood streaking the blade.

Ellie's breath caught, her hands shaking, her voice breaking as she pressed against the window, cutting through the tension. "That's him," she said, her eyes locking onto the figure, fierce with recognition. "Ryan—I saw him, at Ravenswood."

Ryan's voice rasped, low and jagged, cutting through the night as he turned, his face pale, his eyes sharp with hate. "You took him," he said, his gaze piercing the car, locking onto Noah. "Jake—he fell because of you. I waited, planned, and she knew—Lena. You'll fall too."

Hollis stepped closer, his gun steady, his voice calm, cutting deeper. "Drop it, Ryan," he said, his eyes unflinching, his words a command. "It's over—knife down, hands up. You're done."

Ryan's laugh broke, cold and raw, and he lunged, the knife flashing, but a shot rang out, the officer firing, and Ryan fell, his body crumpling into the fog, the knife skittering across the dirt. Ellie's sob broke the quiet, her hands pressing Noah's face to her chest, her voice trembling, a weight shattering through. "He's down," she said, her eyes wet, cutting through the chaos. "It's him, Noah—he's gone."

Hollis knelt, checking Ryan, his voice steady, cutting through the mist as he radioed, sharp with finality. "Suspect down, wounded, alive. Send medics, secure the scene." He stood, turning to the car, his eyes locking onto Ellie's through the glass, a nod of grim resolve.

Daniel's breath steadied, his voice low, breaking as he gripped her hand, cutting through the fog. "It's over," he said, his eyes wet, his hands trembling. "He's got him, Ellie—Noah's safe."

But Noah pulled free, his voice trembling, raw with a truth spilling out, cutting through the crack. "No," he said, his eyes wide, locking onto the barn, then back, haunted beyond the fall. "It wasn't just Ryan. Jake—he didn't fall alone. Someone else was there, pushed him after me. I saw."

Ellie's stomach dropped, the fall revealed, a twist shattering her world, the shadow's breath a lie she'd believed, pulling her deeper into an abyss she couldn't escape.

CHAPTER SEVENTY-ONE

Ellie Carter sat in the station's waiting area, the night fog of March 10, 2025, thinning outside the shattered front window, the village lights flickering faintly through the mist. The room was cold, the air heavy with the scent of antiseptic and drying blood, and she held Noah close on the plastic chair beside her, his hoodie pulled tight, his breath steadying against her shoulder. Daniel slumped in the seat next to them, his hands resting limp in his lap, his face pale and drawn, his eyes fixed on the floor where glass shards still glinted under the fluorescent lights. The chaos of the barn was over, Ryan Ellis wounded and cuffed, medics hauling him away, but Noah's words—Someone else was there, pushed him after me—hung in the silence, a truth settling like ash over their lives.

Ellie's sweater was damp with sweat and fog, her hands trembling as she smoothed Noah's hair, her voice trembling but soft, cutting through the quiet. "You're safe now," she said, her eyes locking onto his, wet with a mother's fierce love. "Ryan's gone, Noah. Hollis has him. But you need to tell me—everything. Who else was there?"

Noah's breath caught, his hands unclenching, shaking slightly, his voice rough, breaking as he spoke, raw with a guilt he couldn't shed. "I don't know," he said, his eyes lifting, wide and haunted, meeting hers. "It was dark, after I pushed Jake. He was yelling, wouldn't stop, and I shoved him, ran. Then I heard it—a scream, different, longer. I looked back, saw a shape, tall, moving fast, near the edge. They pushed him, Mom, after me. I didn't tell, thought it was my fault."

Ellie's chest tightened, the truth settling deeper, and she pulled him closer, her voice steady despite the tremor in her hands, cutting through the fog of fear. "Not your fault," she said, her eyes sharp, fierce with resolve. "You were a kid, scared. Someone else did this, Noah—finished it. Ryan thought it was you, all this time."

Daniel's head lifted, his voice low, strained with exhaustion, cutting through the tension. "Ryan didn't know?" he asked, his eyes flicking to Noah, then Ellie, sharp with disbelief. "He came back, killed Lena, hunted us—because he missed the real one? Who else was on that ridge?"

Hollis stepped in from the hall, his coat streaked with mud, his face hard, his voice calm, cutting through the quiet as he set his notepad down. "That's what I'm finding out," he said, his eyes locking onto Noah's, steady with a detective's edge. "Ryan's alive, talking—says he saw Noah push Jake, didn't see anyone else. Thought it was all him, waited years, snapped when Lena dug it up. But your story, Noah—another shape, another push. We missed something in '23."

Ellie's breath hitched, her hands gripping Noah, her voice trembling, urgent, cutting deeper. "Missed what?" she asked, her eyes wide, locking onto Hollis, fierce with dread. "Someone else was there, saw it, did it. Ryan's vendetta was wrong, but who's left? Who knew?"

Hollis's jaw tightened, his eyes narrowing, his voice low, probing as he leaned forward. "Tom Bennett," he said, his words measured, cutting through the haze. "Chaperone, saw Noah push, kept quiet. I pressed him—he swears he didn't see another figure, but he was close, could've missed it in the dark. Someone from that hike, maybe—another kid, a parent, someone who stayed silent."

Daniel's face flushed, his voice rising, raw with frustration, cutting through the room. "Silent?" he said, standing, his hands clenching at his sides. "For two years, Hollis? They let Noah carry this, let Ryan hunt us, and now what? Ryan's down, but this other one's out there?"

Ellie's sob broke the quiet, her hands pressing to her face, her voice trembling, a weight settling through. "Out there," she said, her eyes lifting, haunted and resolute. "I felt it, Daniel—at Ravenswood, the shadow wasn't just Ryan. Something else, watching, always watching. Noah saw it too, and we didn't listen."

Noah's voice steadied, his eyes wet, his hands unclenching as he spoke, cutting through the crack. "I thought it was him," he said, his gaze distant, raw with a truth he couldn't unsee. "Ryan, all this time. But that scream—it wasn't just Jake falling. Someone else was there, Mom, and they're still here."

Hollis nodded, his face hardening, his voice steady, cutting through the tension. "We'll dig," he said, his eyes sharp, locking onto Ellie's, a promise in the quiet. "Old reports, witnesses, anyone from that day. Ryan's locked up, but this isn't done. You're safe now—home, guarded, until we know."

Ellie pulled Noah close, Daniel's arm around them, the truth settling like a cold stone, a shadow's breath lingering beyond Ryan, a lie they'd lived with cracking open. She stood, her voice firm, cutting through the fog, fierce with a mother's love. "Find them, Hollis," she said, her eyes locking onto his, resolute. "Whoever they are, they don't get to hide. Not anymore."

The station hummed with officers moving, radios crackling, and Ellie walked out with her family, the fog thinning, the night still, the truth settling heavy, a twist that broke her world and held it together, a shadow she'd chase no more.

EPILOGUE

Ellie Carter stood at the kitchen window of their home, the pale dawn light of April 15, 2025, filtering through the thinning fog, casting soft shadows across the scrubbed tile floor. The village beyond was waking, its rooftops glinting faintly under a sky that promised spring, and she held a mug of coffee, its warmth seeping into her hands, her sweater pulled tight against the lingering chill. The house was quiet, the shattered mug from a month ago replaced, the back door repaired, but the air still carried a weight she couldn't shed, a truth settled deep in her bones since that night at the barn. Noah slept upstairs, his breath even at last, and Daniel moved in the garage, tinkering with something to keep his hands busy, a fragile rhythm they'd rebuilt from the ashes.

She set the mug down, her fingers tracing its rim, her eyes drifting to the yard where Jake's knife had lain, a ghost from 2023 that Ryan Ellis had wielded like a blade through their lives. Hollis had called yesterday, his voice steady over the line, cutting through the quiet of her days—Ryan was locked away, recovering in a prison hospital, his vendetta silenced, but the other shadow, the one Noah saw push Jake after him, remained a whisper in the dark, a name they couldn't find. She felt the psychological depth of it, a mother who'd faced the abyss and pulled her son back, only to learn the fall wasn't hers to fully mend, a lie they'd lived with cracking open into something larger, something still out there.

"Noah's sleeping better," Daniel said, his voice low, rough with the wear of weeks, cutting through her thoughts as he stepped in from the garage, his hands smudged with grease, his eyes lifting to hers, steady but shadowed. "No nightmares last night. First time since."

Ellie nodded, her hands trembling slightly, her voice soft but firm, cutting back with a fragile hope. "Good," she said, her eyes locking onto his, wet with a love that had weathered too much. "He's talking more, too—told me yesterday he wants to see Tom, ask him about that day again. Maybe he'll remember something."

Daniel's breath caught, his hands wiping on a rag, his voice breaking, strained with a father's doubt. "Tom?" he asked, stepping closer, his eyes sharp with unease. "Hollis pressed him, Ellie—swears he didn't see another figure. What if Noah's wrong, chasing ghosts? We've lost enough."

Ellie's chest tightened, the truth settling heavier, and she turned to the window, her voice trembling, cutting through the quiet with a resolve she'd forged in fear. "He's not wrong," she said, her eyes tracing the trees, fierce with a mother's certainty. "I felt it, Daniel—at Ravenswood, that night. Ryan wasn't alone, not in spirit. Someone else was there, on the ridge, and they're still here, watching us live with it."

Daniel sank into a chair, his hands dropping the rag, his voice low, raw with a weariness she shared. "Then what do we do?" he asked, his breath steadying, his eyes lifting to hers, searching. "Hollis is digging—old reports, kids from the hike, parents. But if they're out there, Ellie, how do we heal?"

Ellie's sob caught in her throat, her hands pressing to the counter, her voice breaking, a weight settling through as she spoke. "We don't," she said, her eyes lifting, haunted but resolute. "Not fully. Noah pushed Jake, yes, but someone else finished it, hid it, let Ryan break us. We live with that, Daniel— keep him safe, keep us whole. Hollis will find them, or they'll fade, but we don't let go."

Footsteps creaked on the stairs, Noah stepping in, his hoodie loose, his face pale but calm, his voice trembling, cutting through the crack with a quiet strength. "I heard you," he said, his eyes locking onto hers, wet with a guilt he'd carried too long. "I want to help Hollis, Mom—tell him everything, every shadow I saw. I can't run anymore."

Ellie crossed to him, her arms wrapping around him, her voice steadying with a love she'd never lose, cutting through the fog. "You won't," she said, her eyes sharp, fierce with a promise. "You're mine, Noah, and we're here. The truth's out, whatever it is. We face it together."

Daniel stood, joining them, his arm around them both, his voice soft, breaking with a father's hope. "Together," he said, his breath warm, his eyes wet, a family holding tight. "Whoever's left, they don't get us. Not now."

Ellie held them close, the dawn breaking clearer, the truth settling like a stone in the earth, a shadow's breath fading but never gone, a lie they'd survived that left them scarred and strong. She looked out the window, the fog lifting, the village stirring, and felt the weight of it—a mystery unsolved, a twist that broke her world and remade it, a life she'd guard with every beat of her heart, a perfect lie laid bare.

AFTERWORD

Writing *The Unseen Drop* felt like stepping off a ridge myself —uncertain where the fall would lead, trusting the fog would clear just enough to see the truth. Now that you've reached the end, I hope you felt that same rush: the chill of secrets unraveling, the weight of a mother's fight, and the jolt of a twist that shifts everything. This story began with a boy's guilt and a shadow no one saw, but it grew into something more—a mirror for the unseen burdens we all carry, the lies we cling to, and the strength we find when they crumble.

I didn't set out to tie every thread in a neat bow. The ridge's echo lingers, a second shadow still out there, because life doesn't always hand us clean endings. Ellie, Noah, and Daniel found their footing, but the fog hasn't fully lifted—and maybe that's the point. I wanted you to wonder, to feel the unease of what might still lurk, just as I did while piecing this tale together late at night, the wind howling outside my window like a voice from the story itself.

Thank you for walking this path with me. Your time, your trust, and your willingness to peer into the dark mean more than I can say. If *The Unseen Drop* stayed with you—kept you up, made you question, or stirred something deep—I've done what I set out to do. The shadows may fade, but their whispers don't. I'd love to hear what they said to you, so feel free to reach out. For now, I'll step back into the mist, dreaming up the next drop. Until then, keep watching the edges.

Tilly Presland

ACKNOWLEDGEMENT

No story emerges from the fog alone, and *The Unseen Drop* is no exception. This book owes its life to a constellation of people who guided me through the shadows, held me steady when the ground felt uncertain, and believed in the tale when I doubted it myself. I'm deeply grateful to each of them, and I hope these words do justice to their impact.

First, to my family—my rock and my refuge. You weathered my late-night scribbles, my endless questions about cliffs and guilt, and my quiet days lost in thought. Your patience and love kept me going, and this story's heartbeat belongs to you. To my parents, who taught me to chase the unseen with courage, thank you for lighting the way.

To my writing circle—those brilliant souls who read early drafts and saw the ridge before it took shape—you know who you are. Your sharp eyes, honest feedback, and late-night coffee runs turned a whisper into a roar. Special thanks to my friend Jane, whose knack for spotting twists sharpened this one beyond measure, and to Tom, who reminded me shadows need light to dance.

I'd be remiss not to thank the team who brought this book to the page. My editor, Sarah, wielded her pen like a flashlight, cutting through the haze to make every word sing. My cover designer, Alex, captured the fog and the drop with an artistry I still can't get over. And to the countless others—proofreaders, formatters, cheerleaders—your work is the backbone of this journey.

Finally, to you, my readers. You took a chance on this tale, walked the ridge with Ellie and Noah, and faced the unseen with me. Your trust is the greatest gift, and I hope this story lingers with you as it has with me. Thank you for stepping into the mist.

Tilly Presland

ABOUT THE AUTHOR

Tilly Presland

Tilly Presland is a master of psychological suspense, crafting dark, twist-laden tales that plunge readers into the shadows of the human mind. With The Unseen Drop, she spins a gripping thriller that unearths buried secrets, explores the razor's edge of guilt and survival, and leaves you questioning what lurks just out of sight. Tilly thrives on weaving stories where ordinary lives unravel into extraordinary mysteries, proving that the quietest whispers can hide the loudest truths.

Fueled by a fascination with the complexities of fear, trust, and the unseen forces that shape us, Tilly writes to pull readers into the fog of uncertainty, where every step teeters on the brink of revelation. Her work pulses with the tension of untold stories, drawing inspiration from the fragile threads that bind families and the shadows that threaten to tear them apart.

When she's not plotting her next heart-pounding twist, Tilly loses herself in the stillness of nature, unravels the knots of human connection, and chases the thrill of a good mystery—whether in books, life, or the world around her. A private soul with a restless imagination, she lets her stories speak loudest, inviting readers to find their own courage in the dark.

Tilly hopes The Unseen Drop keeps you up late, turning pages, and peering into the corners of your own shadows. Step into her world—if you dare.

www.ingramcontent.com/pod-product-compliance
Lightning Source LLC
Chambersburg PA
CBHW020934260626
47169CB00006B/1711